Fantastik

—

C. A. McGroarty

Copyright © 2014 C. A. McGroarty
All rights reserved.

ISBN: 0615977537
ISBN 13: 9780615977539

For my father, J. Robert McGroarty

CHAPTER 1

Georgia State Prison

J ake Mott heard the guards' whispers long before the official notice, and when guards whispered, so did inmates. The lifeless, late-night silence of the hundred-foot-long prison hallway sometimes acted like the bullhorn at a Texas rodeo. The prayers, the mutters of hope, the insanity…it didn't matter where in line you fell. The cold walls absorbed nothing, but talked all night.

Funny how a man sees you differently once he knows where you're headed. You can see it in how he looks at you, the things he no longer says, and the distance he keeps.

Just bitterness and envy. People change. All the men on the fourth floor of block E knew where Jake was headed; he was up for parole. But he was numb, and being numb had put him right where he was sitting now, so not much had changed there.

How the hell did I get this far? He had smiled exactly three times in the ten years since he'd come off death row. During the inmate riot of 1979, he'd taken an ice pick to the right kidney that had left him bleeding on the prison floor for two hours before order was restored. He could have sworn the place he was drifting in and out of that day was hell—the real one—and he'd been ready for it. And those ten days in '85 when he'd been in a prison hospital bed with a 103-degree fever while some bug he couldn't pronounce ravaged his insides, again he'd thought it was finally over. Then the last, eight months ago, when he'd stood just a few feet from Lionel Meeks inside the small courtyard and was the only witness to the bolt of lightning that struck old Lionel dead. Everything around him that day had trembled: Lionel's body, the metal picnic tables, and the ground beneath him. But whatever was left of the charge never found its way past Jake's knees. He didn't know Lionel, had never said two words to him, but if he'd seen it coming, he would have pushed Meeks aside. Disappointment wasn't the only aftereffect, either. Lionel's sudden, gruesome death played back in Jake's head that night and many thereafter, adding to the inventory already stored in the dark place of his mind.

He looked over at the spot where Lionel had died and wondered why, but he knew why. They weren't done with him yet. *No more smiles, then. Never again.*

"Hey, pops?"

Two young inmates were sitting on the picnic table across from him. They were just a couple of kids, and like most fresh prisoners, they wore a permanent cocky smile.

"Don't worry." He nodded to Jake's hand as it dangled over the table. "It's gonna be OK."

His buddy chimed in, "Yeah, pops, those trembles you got…they got pills for shit like that now."

Jake's hand was shaking, his long, skin-dried fingers doing an uncontrolled tap dance in midair. He tucked his fingers into his palm and covered up his fist with his other hand.

"Wait a second," the kid said, "aren't you the guy—"

"Don't say it!"

"Don't say what?"

Jake stood up. "Don't say *anything.*" He approached their table, and he thought he saw a flinch of hesitation. At least his size was still intimidating.

"What are you in for?" Jake asked.

"Man, get the fuck out of my face."

Jake grabbed the kid's throat and tilted his chin skyward. "You never killed no one; your eyes say it loud and clear. You tell people otherwise, like your buddy here, but it ain't true."

"Jake!" a guard called out, rifle in hand, as he held the door open. "What the hell you doin'? Come on now, boys, let's wrap it up."

Jake's grip loosened, and his hands fell to his sides. He looked at them both. "I've been in here longer than you've been livin'," he said quietly, "and it don't mean nothin'."

---

10 Nebraska Lane, Philadelphia, PA

Charlie! The voice was clear, assertive but peaceful. He could listen to that call forever. *Charlie! Come with me, it's OK.* It was his mother, the one he had known for only a short period of time but could never forget. The days when she was right, when her mind was clear. She was maternal then, always observing him with her beaming smile and a playful stir, sure his little belly was always full. Those were the days when he was still a kid, no more than three feet tall and truly unknowing. Short-lived times for sure, but a lasting memory they made. And then, just like that, his mother is gone from his dream. No more call of his name and no more invitations. Gone just as quick as when he was three feet tall, before he even knew what had happened.

Just as in life, this was a real nightmare, and like many times before, he knew the outcome. Next thing he'd hear would be the pop of a handgun… *bang…bang…bang! Leaving behind nothing but an echo, the way it might sound up close in a canyon—only these surroundings aren't as picturesque. The small, narrow aisle he stands in hints at a convenience store. His stomach tightens, he closes his eyes.*

The cold air from the frosted glass cooler provides a little comfort, but not for long—his body stills, he becomes paralyzed. A distinct odor of blood carries up to his nose. "Please wake up." He hears himself say it. He tries to pry himself from the refrigerator case as if movement will pull him from the dream, but he can't leave yet. Not until the part when he hears the labored breaths of someone dying and the awkward gurgling sound that comes with it. It's a grotesque and violent sound, always coming from someone close by—maybe at his feet—but he can't look down; he won't. "Please…"

Charlie sat upright in bed. There was a time not long ago when he would awake from that dream gasping for air, but on this morning, minus a swift heartbeat and a cold shiver, one might never know just how scared he was.

Any residual echoes were replaced by the cries of his baby boy Billy coming from the kitchen. He glanced at the doorway, half expecting to see Billy's big brother Eddie standing there as he'd been so many mornings before, but thankfully not today. It was one thing to wake up frightened from your dreams, another entirely for your son to see it.

His bones ached. He could feel the bags under his eyes. Ironically, his constant exhaustion did little to help him sleep; unsettling dreams would do that, and they had for many years. His body sank and fell backward onto the bed.

Staring at the ceiling, he kneaded away the sweat on his brow with his thumb and index finger as he considered the dream, which, like many others, had just become a part of who he was.

He peeled himself off the bed and walked into the bathroom. He could stand there for hours, silent, looking into the mirror, having the same thoughts and asking the same questions. *What the hell is wrong with me?* He called the dreams and visions his "fantastic," after a childhood game he'd played with himself about the things happening in his head.

He thought about the insanity test he'd taken in last week's *Inquirer*. It was a series of sixty-eight questions, mostly yes and no, all of which had to be answered in sequential order. It was probably a joke, full of questions like: *Do you count steps? Do you tie your shoelaces over or under? Have you ever eaten dog food?*

But then there were other questions, some of which hit close to home, such as: *Were you someone else in another life? Do you have a history of mental illness in your family?* And the one that had made him put the paper down altogether: *Do you ever hear voices in your head?* His immediate answer had been no, but there'd been a constant knot in his stomach ever since.

He heard another minute strike down on the digital clock, pressing him into action. He splashed some cold water on his face and slicked his hair back, wondering if there would ever come a day when he wouldn't have to shave. It seemed he'd been with Septa a lifetime already, and their no-facial-hair policy was one he abided by.

He opened the medicine cabinet, picked up his prescription bottle, and read its label. An action that always produced the same feelings: an equal mix of guilt and anger.

He grimaced, put the bottle back in its place, and slammed the cabinet door. But another stare into the mirror returned him to the small canister of pills...he popped two and put on his uniform.

His mother now occupied his boyhood room—first door on the right, top of the stairs, and a morning didn't go by that he didn't stop and open that door.

Sometimes it was just to pop his head in and listen for her breathing; other times, he would just stand and stare at her.

He bent down and kissed the frail woman on the forehead. "Good morning, Mom," he whispered. He stroked some strands of silver-black hair off her forehead. "I'd go with you anywhere."

She turned her head toward him. The shades in the room were drawn tight, and for that he was thankful; the darkness hid her confusion, but the silence was gripping. He grabbed the empty juice bottle on her nightstand and left.

His wife, Lisa, stood over a hot frying pan in the kitchen, shoveling eggs from stove to table. The trip was a short one, not even a full turn of her slender body.

"Morning, babe," he said.

Lisa shut off the water. "You're late."

He watched Billy dunk his head into his cereal bowl and slurp it up.

"Billy, get your face out of the bowl," Lisa said. "You're not a dog."

Billy looked up with a big smile and giggled. Drops of milk fell from his chin.

"You're a hell of a crier, boy, you know that?" Charlie said. "What was all the commotion about?"

"He tripped on Bear's leash," Lisa said.

He glanced down at the black puppy they'd given Eddie for his ninth birthday, who was sitting at Lisa's feet and hoping for a morsel of egg to fall from the sky.

"Eddie gone?" Charlie asked.

"Yup, ran out as soon as Billy started crying."

He still had that picture of his oldest son in his head, just standing there watching him wake up in a panic. "Seems awfully nervous anymore, doesn't he?"

Lisa laughed. "Whole house seems awfully nervous anymore. So, do you have time for breakfast or what?"

"You rushing me out the door again?"

Lisa stopped what she was doing in the sink, and her head dropped. "You're barely sleeping again, Charlie. Tossing and turning all night, getting up late. I just don't want to be going backward."

He came up from behind her and wrapped his arms around her waist. "It's gonna get better, and when it does, I'll make it all up to you, I promise."

Lisa turned nose-to-nose with him. "You don't have to make anything up to me, Charlie. I just want you to be well."

It was a simple request for most; if she were a mind reader, though, she would run now. Billy let out something between a cry and a laugh. They both glanced over at him.

Charlie gave her half a smile. "I'll see you tonight."

She nodded and replied, "We'll be here."

CHAPTER 2

The entrance to Septa's bus depot sat fifty yards past the Ben Franklin Bridge on the Delaware River. Charlie drove under the massive blue structure every day without notice, but today something prompted him to stop. He pulled over in its shadow and took a flight of rusty steps to the catwalk above.

The view from the bridge was something to see. The day was crystal clear, the sky blue. He stood on the west end of the bridge about halfway up its arch and felt a rare surge of confidence rush through his body; his struggles felt a world away. He felt safe.

To his right across the water was the Camden County Correctional Facility. From his perch, he could see the orange-suited inmates wandering around in the fenced-in yard, tangles of barbed wire tipping over its edge. They looked like orange ants meandering back and forth, but he studied them anyway.

Hugging the water on the left sat Philadelphia's Old City section, and to the west was the skyline. He didn't know much about skylines and had only seen a few in pictures, but with the sun beaming off Liberty Place and shooting jagged shadows across the steel structure landscape, it was the prettiest he'd ever seen.

He turned back toward the north end of the city and looked down on the bus depot and the fleet of buses lined up end to end in uniform rows.

The longer he studied them, the more he hated their perfect symmetry. How could something as big and unattractive as a fleet of city buses look so peaceful and in balance? Every bumper lined up in order with the next, every rearview mirror set at the exact same angle. He had pulled his own bus into one of those very spots the night before—the keys were still in his pocket—but he couldn't recall doing anything special to maintain such an order.

The sum of the buses' parts: that was it. Together they created balance… tragic how everything always brought him back to his own troubles.

"What am I doing here?" he whispered.

He glanced back to his right from the corner of his eye at the little orange inmates wandering about the concrete yard. *What is it?*

He felt something there, then he saw it in his mind's eye, as clear as the sky above him: a black man, tall, chains around his ankles and wrists, with an eight-man armed escort surrounding him. Charlie could see only his backside, not his face, but that was fine; he'd seen enough.

He took a deep breath; the air was crisp in his lungs, reminding him where he was. His heart slowed. *So much for feeling safe.*

———

The phone rang. Plate and dish towel in one hand, Lisa reached over with her other and grabbed it. "Hello."

"Good morning, is Charlie home?"

She recognized the woman's voice but couldn't place it.

"Who's calling?"

"Mrs. Boone? It's Maureen from Dr. Murphy's office. We met on Charlie's first visit."

The young girl's face popped into her head: sparkly smile, hopeful expression. *What would it be like to be that optimistic again?*

"Yes, I remember. Is something wrong?"

"Well, we did want to call. Charlie's missed his last three appointments with Dr. Murphy, and in all honesty, his prescription should have run out two months ago. We just wanted to make sure everything was OK."

Her head dropped, and she rubbed her forehead to ward off the migraine she felt coming.

"He hasn't seen Murphy in three months?"

There was an awkward silence on the phone. "If there's something you'd like us to do, Mrs. Boone, please let me know."

She was thankful that the girl at the other end couldn't see the tears welling in her eyes. "What?" Lisa asked.

"I'm sorry?" she replied.

"You said, if there's something you can do. Well, what is that? What can you do? I mean who's the fucking doctor here anyway, you or us?"

"I...I...don't know what to say—"

"Exactly! So just shut up!"

She slammed the phone down on its cradle but missed and scraped her knuckles. She watched the phone bob up and down on its cord against the wall while little beads of blood formed on her fingers. She fell back into the kitchen chair. What had happened in seconds had felt like days.

Six months earlier, Charlie had finally agreed to seek professional help, but only after her threat to leave him and take the kids. Hope had filled her that day and a lot of days after, but all that was drained now.

He had lied to her. With the sound of dial tone filling the kitchen air, she buried her face in her hands. "You son of a bitch."

CHAPTER 3

Charlie snuck into the basement through the rusted-out metal doors attached to the back of the house. It had been his favorite entrance as a child and, unfortunately, on some days remained so. What he called the passage to the dark tunnel growing up was now just a way to avoid contact with Lisa and the kids for another hour or so. He loved them more than anything, but there were days when he needed to sit and be alone before playing father and husband for what was left of the day. Shamefully, they were acts he wasn't very good at pulling off anymore...*Lisa sees through everything.*

He pulled the old hollow cinder block from the basement wall and placed it down on the damp floor. The space was dark and cold inside. He couldn't remember how he'd found the hiding spot or just how long he'd been using it, but in it lived the shattered pieces of his childhood.

He pulled out the soft, leather-bound book given to him by his mother when he was eight and opened its cover; fitting the very first entry read "fantastik"; with a *k*. To call this piece of tragic history a diary would be a grievance against anyone who ever kept one. Real diaries made sense, were well organized with entries in sequential order, and kept in nice-smelling wooden drawers. What he had was a scattering of scribbled-down notes, the smallest of details about random events, along with the occasional and alarming sketch or image, its home a dirty, wet tomb.

He hadn't made an entry in years, and though he may have lived it, even now some of those words scribbled in his diary still had the ability to bring him to a quick freeze. *"The crazy lady's back"* or *"Another horrible trip to Trenton."* Trenton. The bane of his existence as a child and no doubt the start of all their troubles. Today, though, he brought out the diary for another reason, and he knew just where to find it. It was middle in, just past the section titled "Dreams," although what he had written down that day was no dream at all.

It was the sketch of a man, a stranger. He was charcoal, colored in by pencil, and he was a big man—unusually big—but the man had no face. *Big, dark, mean looking.* Those were the scribbled words of a young boy. He read the full entry at the bottom of the page.

I was up really early today. I like it early. Mom sleeps in; things are normal when it's quiet in the house. I get to do whatever I want. Mom finally got up and called for me. I went to the steps. Her hair was all messy, and she was wrapped super tight in her robe. I could see the dirt under her fingernails from all the way downstairs. I asked her if she was sick, but she stayed quiet. She looked away from me. She asked me for a glass of water, and I went to get her one. I reached for the biggest glass and turned on the water, and it happened again. Everything slows down, that's when I see the stranger. This time he went by the kitchen window, but he was gone as fast as he came. I don't like him. I don't like the way he walks; it seems as if he's already dead. I dropped the glass and it broke. I hope I never see him again, but I know I will. Mom's sick. She's getting worse, and Pop Grey doesn't help. He just makes things worse every time we go to Trenton, but I can't figure how. I don't like him either.

His mother had been sick for so long now, yet he couldn't bring himself to get her help. Charlie looked back over at the child's sketch on the edge of the page and closed his eyes.

CHAPTER 4

Jake never pulled his focus from the nameplate that hung from the large table before him. It read *Georgia State Board of Pardons and Parole*. He avoided eye contact whenever possible; it was hard to look people in the eye, and today would be no different. Especially today. It had taken him weeks to try to come up with the right words, and even then, he could only scribble down half a line. In the end, he had done what made him feel a little bit better—neatly written their names on a sheet of paper. He could study those names, carefully printed in black ink on a sheet of loose-leaf paper, for hours at a time.

Much had changed since the last time he'd been before the three-member board four years ago. The room was painted a different color, the armored convoy to get there had been a bit smaller, and only one member remained the same.

As in any pack, there was a ringleader. The one in the middle was the member who hadn't changed from four years earlier. He whispered details of Jake's file to the other members and then pulled his glasses off his head.

"Well, Mr. Mott, do you have any remorse for what you've done?"

Jake sat silent for several seconds. "If fearing…" His voice cracked, and he cleared his throat. "If fearing God makes you remorseful, sir, then I got plenty…but I don't think it does."

"Is that a no?"

"All I got is what's in my head. That's where it starts, the thoughts 'bout where I just might end up after I'm dead. It's just about the only thing that consumes me anymore."

"And where will that be?"

"Sir?"

"Where will you end up, Mr. Mott…after you're dead?"

He glanced over to the warden, who'd brought him here both times over the last eight years. For some strange reason, he felt it was more important to the warden that they free his sorry ass than it was even to Jake himself. He wanted to say the right thing; just the look on the warden's face was an appeal to do so, but he didn't know what the right thing was.

"I belong in the ground; that I know. Where I go from there is his will."

He heard a slight exhale coming from Warden Brendan Frank.

The ringleader nodded to the folded-up piece of paper Jake held in his hand. "You have something you want to read?"

Jake unfolded the paper. Here was his time to bare all. For thousands of sleepless nights, this moment had played out in his head. Four years ago he had been a coward; four years ago he had gone back to his cell and wallowed...*what will I do today?*

"We've got a busy day, Mr. Mott. Now do you or don't you have something you want to share with us? Because, frankly, if you have little interest in leaving Georgia State, which I believe you do, then I have very little interest in letting you go."

Silence grabbed hold of him. He saw every name clearly, and they all meant something. He relived it every time. Just the thought of their names was taxing. Seeing them in print made it all the worse. In a dark way, they still existed...they still lived within him.

"Mr. Mott! I'll ask again, what is that you have in your hand?"

Jake heard his question but couldn't answer.

The ringleader stood up. "Guard, bring me that piece of paper...now!"

A young guard came from behind and ripped the paper from Jake's hand. The ringleader studied it for a few seconds. "Who are these people, and why do you have them written down?"

Jake slowly stood up from the table and raised his arms to the ceiling.

"What is this?" the ringleader asked.

Jake remained silent again.

"Mr. Mott, if you have something to say, I suggest you say it...now is your moment. I *demand* you tell me who these people are."

He hadn't shed a tear since Praire, Texas, and though it strained him, he wouldn't do so today either.

Warden Frank stood up from his chair. "If I may say something on Jake's behalf."

"Yes," the ringleader replied, "someone speak!"

"Jake Mott came to Georgia State in 1969. I was the warden then, just as I am now. I've seen many men pass through those doors, and I tell you the man sitting before you today is not the man I took in. Now, he might not admit it; hell, he might not even know it. But I know it...I know prisoners."

Still holding onto the piece of paper, the ringleader sat back down. "While I respect your opinion, Warden Frank, I do not believe you quite understand what you have here." He looked to his counterparts on either side of him, jotted something down on a piece of paper, and closed Jake's file.

CHAPTER 5

"*Fire, Charlie.*"

"*What about it?*" he asked.

"*Watch for it…it'll show you the way.*"

"*What do you mean? Tell me…I'm confused.*"

He didn't know if it was his head talking to him or if someone was there with him. He guessed the former as he sat in a dark space, unable to even see his own hands.

A small circle of light emerged in the distance before him, but it grew at a snail's pace. He could hear two people talking on the other side of it. They were voices he didn't recognize and they spoke from a far away place, but he could hear their words clearly enough.

"*There is one thing I've thought of doing…thought of it quite a bit, actually.*"

"*What's that?*"

"*When I came back to the States, I hooked up with a guy that I ran with for a little while.*"

As if a trapdoor had opened beneath him, Charlie fell from the darkness, the distant conversation he was hearing long gone. He was standing on his grandfather's street in Trenton. He ran up to the porch and busted through the front door, scaling the steps two at a time. He stared down the long hall at the closed door and ran to it.

Slamming into it, he fell back; it was locked. He shot up off the floor and kicked at its base, slammed his fists on its front. A door behind him opened. He turned and saw his grandfather standing in the doorway, laughing.

"Charlie? Charlie?"

He opened his eyes and found Lisa standing above him.

"God, baby, you're soaking wet."

"What? What is it?" he asked.

"You were calling out fire. You were having a nightmare."

He swung his feet onto the floor and sat there silent. She was right. There was no hiding the sweat dripping from his forehead, and it didn't matter that it was only Lisa witnessing it. He wanted to bear what he always considered the stripping of his dignity in private, but it was too late.

"What was it, Charlie?" She was behind him on the bed.

He shook his head. "Sometimes I just wanna get in the car, drive up there, and kill the bastard."

He felt her cold hand rub his bare back. "You don't mean that," she said. "They'd send you away, and you'd never see me or the boys again."

He glanced over his shoulder. "Maybe...it's just that some days I need to know that feeling. Nothing would give me more..." He paused. "I know all the shit in my head would just go away. I'd be clear."

He was half expecting to hear, "That's crazy talk" or "Tell the doctor about it," but it never came. He thanked her for her silence by reaching behind him and grasping her hand. He needed that moment, even if killing his grandfather was a fleeting fantasy. Just playing it out in his head was sometimes therapy enough.

"Any ill words she and I ever had were his fault. It was always the same. She'd be in her room all morning, and as soon as I'd hear her getting ready, I'd pray she'd leave without me."

"She needed help," Lisa said. "Professional help."

"I'd be staring out my window, and I'd hear her come in. I had that picture of her in my mind, and without even turning around, I knew what she looked like. Her hair was curled, and she was in that stupid polka-dot dress and red lipstick."

"How do I look?" She smiled and turned her face slightly to the left.

"I don't wanna go, Momma...please let me stay here, please!"

"Oh Charlie! Stop it! Don't be a baby." She walked over to his drawer and pulled out the first shirt she touched. "You should be happy to be going."

"I'm not! I hate it there. I don't wanna go to Trenton. I don't ever wanna go."

His words weren't out even a full second when he saw that switch go off inside her. She threw his shirt to the ground. "Then get happy! You think I enjoy it? You think I like it? I do it for you; don't you get that?"

She bent down and pointed at him. He could smell the perfume his grandfather had given her the last trip up. "I do it for you! Now put that shirt on and meet me downstairs."

"Charlie, did you hear me?"

Lisa was off the bed now, standing before him.

"What?"

"Dr. Murphy's office called today."

His expression said it all; he'd been waiting for the shoe to drop on this for some time.

"What did you promise me?"

"I don't have the energy for this argument...not tonight."

"Bullshit you don't have the energy, Charlie. You owe me an explanation."

"Why? So we can both yell and scream for an hour and then not talk to each other for the next three days? Is that what you want? Because that's how it always ends."

Her tone was softer. "What was our deal? What was your promise?"

He shook his head. "I can't do this."

"Damn it, Charlie! What about me? This is it for me! I'm at my end. You promised to see this through with Murphy. You made a commitment to make it work this time."

"They don't help me! Making a promise to do something means nothing if it doesn't help."

"Who says it's not working? You never give it a chance because it's in your thick head that you're the only one who can help yourself."

"And I should know. I'm the one dealing with it."

"Oh, bullshit, Charlie! You don't know whether you're coming or going!"

"I've told you before. No doctor is going to help me through this."

"And I told you before that if you don't get help, then I'm leaving!"

He fell silent and then said softly, "I just don't know what I'm supposed to do."

"Take your medicine...that's what you're supposed to do. You got a family to take care of."

"No, that's…that's not it. I mean there's something happening…I just don't know what this is."

"Charlie! Listen to me." She pointed to the wall. "See that woman next door? That's what this is, and I can't go there." She started to break down. "I won't."

"I can't take those drugs, Lisa. When I'm on them, it's not me."

"So then we'll find another drug."

"But I don't want another drug. I don't want any drugs!"

"Then we'll find another doctor."

"I don't *need* another *fucking* doctor!"

"But how can you know that?"

"Because what I have doctors don't cure, that's why. They can't!"

He made an attempt to get off the bed, but she blocked his path with her body. She met another try by even more force. "What are you doing?" He asked.

"Don't do this; don't walk out of here. We need to finish this."

She put up a good fight, but he eventually pushed his way up. He gripped her wrists as they jockeyed for position. "Get out of my way," he said.

"Cut the shit!" Tears were falling down her cheeks. "You haven't slept in weeks! You're up all hours of the night and don't take your medication…for what? Because you're too stubborn. You're too stubborn to know what's good for you, just like your mother."

Now it was she who wanted out, doing her best to wiggle free of his hold. "My wrists…let go."

"I haven't slept in fifteen years," he said. "What's so different about that?"

"Because now it's killing our marriage, and if you can't feel that, then you're ignoring that too."

"You interrogating me doesn't work. I don't wanna talk about it like this."

"But you never want to talk about it. And this is what happens when you stop your medication. You get angry, we fight."

"It's not real…I'm in space when I'm on it," he whispered.

"Oh, Charlie, half the fucking neighborhood's on Prozac."

"Well maybe half the neighborhood needs it, but I don't. I've got enough shit on my mind…I don't need some superdrug clouding my judgment. It's some whacked-out sense of normalcy, and it's all a lie."

"Normalcy! Did you hear yourself, Charlie? You said it yourself. Haven't you ever thought that people take their medication so they can lead normal lives?"

"And haven't you ever thought that people take their medication so they can lie to themselves, lie to their families, to the people around them about what's really going on? I'm done lying, Lisa. I've been lying to myself my whole damn life, and I can't afford to do it anymore."

He took a seat at the end of the bed.

Lisa got down on her knees in front of him. "Charlie, I can't go through what we went through before, I just can't. You've got to start communicating with me, or else this is gonna blow up right in our faces."

"I'm not crazy," he whispered.

She was fighting back the tears. "I know you're not." She clenched his hand. "You've had this your whole life, but no one ever did anything for you. No one gave you a chance, so you think it's normal to ignore it and fight through it, but it's not."

"She did her best. She had nobody; she was just a kid."

"And maybe that's true, but *we* can do better, we *have* to do better because we know better."

The room's silence took over.

She clenched his hand. "Promise me you'll go back to Dr. Murphy."

He shook his head. "I can't. I can't make that promise anymore."

She shoved him away and stood up. "Damn it! This is your family we're talking about! Me, the kids—now you listen to me, Charlie. Either you get help, or you're coming home to an empty house, and I won't be back!"

He wanted to cry but swallowed it. "The day I come home and you're gone is the day I stop fighting."

She was as beaten down as he, no doubt; her head hung low, her shoulders slouched, and she looked much older than her twenty-eight years. Just as he had, she was becoming a shadow of the person she had once been—the physically fit, emotionally strong, confident young girl who deserved so much better than he could give.

A calm came over the room, and she took a seat next to him on the bed. "Where were you?"

He looked over to her.

"All those Saturdays you were supposed to be at the doctor, where were you?"

"Church," Charlie replied softly. "I walked by it one day and realized I'd never been in one." He let out a sarcastic laugh. "Amazing, right? I'd never been in a church until three months ago."

"What did you do there?"

"Ever heard of Proverbs?"

"No," she whispered.

"It's a book in the Old Testament. Its last verse says, 'Give her the reward she has earned and let her works bring her praise at the city gate.' When I read that, I thought of you." He grabbed her hand. "Someday you'll get your reward, babe, because you've earned it. Just marrying me has earned you a thousand."

"I don't want rewards, Charlie. I just want things right." She leaned in close to his face. They were almost nose to nose. "I wanted a family and you gave me one, and I love you for that. All I ask now is that you don't screw it up."

CHAPTER 6

He'd been sitting in the break room of the bus depot for over an hour, unable to pick himself up and go home. Lisa's words from the day before were weighing on him.

Fred Wagner entered the room and fed four coins into the vending machine. A Styrofoam cup dropped into the slot and filled with coffee. "Hey, Charlie, how's it going?"

He answered with as much enthusiasm as he could muster, "Not too bad, Fred...you?"

Fred took a sip of coffee, made a face, and pulled a seat up next to him. "I'm not complaining, but you, on the other hand, don't sound so good."

"Must be the fumes. You know how that is."

"Yeah, you ain't kiddin' about fumes; you should see what I cough up every morning. My oldest kid's in the seventh grade. He came home from school last week and asked me if I was takin' in any carbon monoxide by driving a bus all day. Said his science teacher told him carbon monoxide kills organs—brain cells too."

Fred looked over at the machine. "I swear that machine hasn't put out good coffee in two years." He rubbed the back of his neck. "This job is suckin' the life out of me."

Not exactly the words he needed to hear, but they rang true. Lisa's threat to leave had stayed with him. She'd said it before, but this time, it was different. He felt it. He needed answers and was ready to start looking for them anywhere he could.

"What did you tell your kid?"

"About what?" Fred replied.

"About the carbon monoxide. What did you tell him?"

"I told him to bring home his science teacher for dinner; I'd like to meet her. Maybe she can help me form a lawsuit against the city." Fred laughed. "Nah, I told him what I always do: just keep your eye on the ball. Don't worry about the old man, just keep your eye on the ball. I'm gonna be just fine."

"He a ballplayer?"

Fred nodded. "Pitcher. Not a kid in the league that can hit 'im. Just needs a little work with his swing. Your kids play?"

Eddie and Billy came to mind, their sweet faces and crooked smiles. "No, they're still a little young."

"Hey, how long you been driving, Charlie?"

"Eight years…I think. Why?"

"Your service patch says four years' service on it. I *thought* you'd been around longer than that."

He looked down at the patch sewn on his jacket sleeve. "It does, doesn't it? Guess I haven't gotten around to putting the new ones on."

"Yeah, well, I'd get to it if I were you. There's plenty of turnover in this job, and management looks kindly on those who stick around. Besides, we might not get good coffee, but seniority is one of the few things we do get around here."

Charlie watched Fred return to the vending machine for something else. "Hey, Fred?"

"What?"

"You think carbon monoxide plays with your head?"

"Who knows? I'm sure it ain't good for us. Why? Somethin' wrong with your head?"

If the answer weren't such a tragedy, he may have laughed off Fred's question, but instead he closed his eyes and rubbed his forehead. "Fumes, Fred. Fucking fumes."

He reopened his eyes and caught sight of the letters W-I-L-D in bold, black lettering. They were printed on the newspaper sitting on the table across from him. He could make out only half the headline, but it was enough to get his full and undivided attention. He knew exactly what it read.

"Wildfire," he whispered.

It was the title of a small article on the front page of the *Philadelphia Inquirer*.

CHAPTER 7

It was seven a.m. on Tuesday, October 25, a day Jake had been thinking of for over a quarter century, yet he had never truly believed it would come. He sat in his cell reading the King James Bible. He had picked it up three months earlier upon the long-awaited news of his release from prison. The "Book," as he called it, was one of the few things that had brought a bit of peace to his life. That was what he'd said to Warden Brendan Frank on a few occasions.

The warden had been good to him, a friend of sorts—or at least as much a friend as Jake could ever allow. Jake knew his limits with relationships, and they didn't stretch very far. But there was something different about the warden that allowed him to accept and respect him for the authority figure he was.

In simple terms, the warden neither judged him for his previous misdeeds, nor did he judge him for his newfound fear of God, which was more than Jake could say for himself. Every time he opened his Bible, he felt like the ultimate hypocrite, but at least the Book had the power to make him forget, even if it was short lived.

The memories of his past were as much a prison term as the one he'd just served. If it were possible, he'd rather die by one of his victims' own hands than have to live another day remembering the horrible things he'd done in his youth. At the very least, he had assumed he'd die right where he stood, in his prison cell of the last three decades. Three decades...he'd never thought a second shot at life would come his way.

The thought of living in the outside world made his stomach tense; "terrifying" was putting it mildly. He was a total head case, unsure of what the world had in store for him or what he had in store for the world.

On this day, Jake was reading a passage he'd come to like and hoped it would stay with him for whatever days he had left on this earth. Psalm 59. He whispered its words as he awaited Warden Frank's arrival: "Deliver me from my enemies, O God. Protect me from those that rise up against me. Deliver me from evildoers and save me from bloodthirsty men."

It sounded like something one of his victims may have read in protection from the likes of him. Ironic that today it was he who read it, and he did so sincerely, taking solace in the words and their meaning.

He stood up and stretched his legs, walked over to the mirror just the size of his face, and looked into it. He stared at the handful of scars there. Surely he would be asked about them now. At least in prison, nobody asked you anything. He looked at his hands, the ones that had mended fences and cleaned horse stalls in his childhood. Were they still capable of doing an honest day's work for an honest dollar?

He let go of a deep sigh and chuckled. His somber tone was that of a man walking to the chair, not to freedom.

A buzzer went off behind him, and a guard shouted, "Released!"

He could hear the tight seal being broken on the eight-by-eight-foot solid steel door. A second call from the same guard, "Secure," and Jake heard the door shut once again. This was how he had lived for the last ten years of his life, since he had been downgraded to the minimum-security floor at Georgia State Prison in Reidsville, Georgia.

Warden Brendan Frank, flanked by two armed guards, stopped in front of his cell. "Jake?"

He took fond note of the warden's friendly Southern drawl.

"It's time."

One of the guards opened the cell door, and all three men entered.

Jake grabbed his Bible off the cot, secured it in his hand, and fell in stance for the cuffs to be put on. A guard took a set of cuffs off the back of his belt. Warden Frank spoke as he touched the guard's elbow. "That won't be necessary."

Somewhat embarrassed by the warden's gesture of dignity, Jake looked down at his feet and mumbled a courtesy as he stepped out of his cell. A loud buzzer went off: the guards' call to release. The seal was broken, and a rush of cool air hit Jake's face, then another call from the guard that all was secure. Two signatures later, one his own and the other Warden Frank's, and Jake found himself minutes away from being a free man.

He stood in a holding zone outside of the main prison staring down the colossal-looking doors that led to his freedom. Thirty years ago, he'd walked into a population of animals, a man who had little hope and nothing to lose, not a sliver of fear in his whole body. The irony of it all was that he was more scared now than he'd ever been in his life.

"Jake?" the warden said.

One of the large doors swung open, letting a ray of sunlight into the dreary hall and across his feet.

"Jake?" the warden said louder.

He heard the warden's voice, but the words seemed foreign. What would happen when he walked through those doors? What would happen tomorrow morning when he woke at the time he had always woken in his cell? What would happen next year? He looked toward the warden. "Hmm?"

The warden faintly smiled. "I'll never forget the first day you got here, Jake."

He shifted his eyes away from the door and back to the warden.

"You were angry. One mean-looking, son of a bitch. I've walked a lot of men through those doors, but you stood out, and I was scared to shit. You had the look of death in your eyes, and sure as hell I didn't think you'd last three weeks without killing yourself or somebody else." The warden looked to the ground. "Well, guess what I'm trying to say is you proved me wrong, and I'm glad you did."

Jake looked back at the doors to his freedom. "It's been a long time, Warden."

"Yeah, it has. But don't remember who you were, remember who you are. You came into this jail in shackles with an eight-guard escort, but today you leave on your own accord, and you're a changed man."

"You believe that?" Jake asked.

"What I believe is that it would have been downright wrong to cuff you in that cell today. Now you've served your time, and there's nothing to be ashamed of for that."

But he had plenty to be ashamed of that he'd never been caught for or fessed up to. For a fleeting moment, he thought of confessing to the warden, confessing to every last crime, just fifty yards from freedom.

The warden extended his right hand. "Congratulations, Jake. You take care of yourself, now."

The two men shook hands and exchanged respectful nods.

Jake looked down at the shaft of sunlight across his black cowboy boots and took his first steps toward freedom. It was a sunny October day.

CHAPTER 8

S outhern California was being decimated by wildfires, and Charlie was reading anything he could get his hands on to learn about it.

He'd read every newspaper article he could find only to go back and read
the previous day's as if there were something there, a clue that he was missing.

If he could just make some small connection! If he wrote down every last
crazy dream he had ever had, every vision, every nonsensical thought, what
would it look like? Could he piece any of it together?

Staring down at the biggest piece of paper he could find, Charlie found
himself doing just that. An hour later, every last edge of loose-leaf was full,
leaving only a hollowed-out center staring back up at him.

What are you? Where are you?

Another night of pretending to be asleep, lying perfectly still in hopes Lisa
wouldn't wake at the subtlest movements; if he weren't crazy yet, this would
surely take him there.

He slipped out of bed and tiptoed out of the room. As usual, his mother's
bedroom door was ajar. He entered and took a seat on the rocker, where his
jacket lay over the armrest. With the light of the moon through the window as
his guide, he continued to sew a service badge on his blue winter Septa coat.

He moved the needle in and out of his coat lining careful not to prick himself…it was his first sew job. "Oww!" A small bubble of blood rose on the tip
of his index finger. He rubbed it away, but as quickly as it was gone, it appeared
again. He felt a slight throbbing at the tip of his finger. How could something
so small be so painful?

The heat was so dense he could see it rising off the cracked ground beneath him. It was sweltering; dust swirled all around him, making it difficult to see, and stuck to the sweat on his face.

Thirst! That was the first thing he was sure of: unconscionable thirst.

A drop of sweat fell from his forehead, then another. He couldn't take it anymore. He wanted to bring his hand up and rub his eyes—maybe he could rub the stinging out of them, rub some of the dirt out too, but his hand never got there.

What was that ahead? A pair of boots. The heels of the boots were all he could see. They were walking away from him. "Wait! Help me! Please help!"

Charlie sprang from the rocker and fell hard onto the bedroom floor. He grabbed his throat, expecting sand to fall from his mouth, but he wasn't choking at all. He gathered himself off the floor and looked at the clock on his mother's nightstand. It was 3:45 a.m.

He entered the hallway listening for any sign of Lisa, thankful that his recent startle hadn't woken her. He was thirsty and wide awake. He had walked that house in the dead of night countless times and knew every nook and cranny of it, every dead floorboard and every soft spot. He crisscrossed his way down the steps, through the living room, and into the kitchen.

The refrigerator door had the same quirks as the rest of the house. He took it back as slowly as possible, keeping its squeaking shrill to a minimum. The carton of OJ looked like a lost friend and acted like one, too, as he gulped down the last half of it in seconds.

The boys would need OJ in the morning, and maybe some fresh air would do him good.

A deserted Roosevelt Boulevard made for a peaceful drive. He could see a 7-Eleven sign a few blocks ahead and thought better of it, considering his recurring nightmare, but he knew it would be his only option this time of night.

From the parking lot, he could see the inside was well lit. Apart from the clerk sitting behind the counter reading a magazine, the place was empty. He laughed and shook his head. "Must you tempt fate?"

He entered the store and glanced at the clerk, who paid him no mind—something he found odd since it was four in the morning. He probably had a gun behind the counter.

He stopped short of the freezer doors on the back wall and studied his choice of orange juice brands. He recognized the big green Tropicana lettering as the one in the fridge at home and reached for the door handle, then abruptly stopped.

The cool air emanating from the freezer doors kept him still. He took his open hand and planted it against the door's face. It was true…it *was* comforting. With his hand still planted, Charlie glanced over his left shoulder at the clerk still reading his magazine, then turned straight ahead and closed his eyes.

If he could ever will an image into his head, let it be now, please let it be now. *Nothing.*

He quickly opened the door and grabbed two cartons of juice along with some milk and bologna. He picked up a *USA Today* and the *Philadelphia Inquirer* and scanned their fronts in search of any new articles on the wildfires out west, but saw nothing. One week in, and it was becoming stale news. Hopefully, there'd be something on the inside pages.

As he left the store, the night felt different, dreary, as if a bad storm was on the rise. The smoky-colored clouds above him looked close enough to reach out and touch. An eerie stillness set in, and he felt as if he were being watched.

A man appeared from the side of the building. He was broad-shouldered, middle-aged, and wide-eyed, wearing a contemptuous smile as if he knew something Charlie didn't. The stranger passed him and whispered, "He's coming."

Charlie yelled back, "What did you say?"

The stranger stopped short of his truck and stared back at Charlie.

"You said something…you whispered it to me. Who's coming?"

The stranger ignored his question and continued toward his truck, which looked as if it had just been driven off the showroom floor of a 1950s dealership. It had a split windshield with a visor above it, chrome bumpers, and a grille and rims that made it shine in spite of the night's gloom. There seemed to be chrome all over it.

"Who are you? Answer me!" Charlie exclaimed.

The stranger jumped into his cab and shut the door, then began revving the engine. Charlie moved toward the truck and stood just inches away, the only thing separating the two of them a sheet of glass. "Who are you?"

The stranger shook his head and cracked a slow grin. The pickup went into reverse; the man rolled down his window and called out again, "He's coming!"

"Who's coming?"

The truck peeled out of the lot, leaving the stark smell of burned rubber in its wake. Charlie stared at the truck's taillights until they fell from sight. His heart was racing, his breathing heavy. Looking down, he noticed his arms were empty. The bag of groceries had slipped from his hold.

Scattered about were a torn grocery bag, two cartons of orange juice, a carton of milk, a package of bologna, and two newspapers. There was something about the chaos on the ground that made him want to cry. A feeling of isolation came over him, and though they weren't more than ten dollars' worth of groceries, he marveled at them as if they were the unfortunate pieces of his young life. Just the thought of picking them up, rebagging them, and taking them back home made his stomach turn.

He wanted to vomit, but instead Charlie knelt down on the damp blacktop and slowly began placing the items back into the torn bag, one by one.

CHAPTER 9

Jake pushed aside the veil-like shade and peered out at his new backyard, deep in the woods of Pennypack Park. There wasn't an armed guard to be seen, and if he never saw barbed wire again in his whole life, he'd be thankful. Rays of sunlight broke through the dense treetops above him. He took a deep breath and smiled, glancing over at the empty bottle of Jack Daniels. A hangover had never felt so good.

Planting his feet firmly on the floor, he sat upright and glanced at the ceiling. If it were only six inches higher, he'd be in good shape. Looking to his right, he found his reflection in the mirror hanging on the bathroom door. "You should be used to tight quarters, old man."

He walked sideways to clear the entranceway into the kitchen area, where he had use of a small range, a small fridge, and some counter space. He poured the remnants of a Styrofoam cup into the pot atop the hot plate and opened a can of spam while he waited for his day-old coffee to come to a simmer.

As he ate breakfast, something metallic caught his eye. The glare of sunlight through the window showed some wear and tear on its barrel. Jake had seen plenty of guns over his years being incarcerated, but never any within reach. His heart picked up pace as he stood above the .38 Smith & Wesson. It had been a long time since he'd held one. It was acting as a paperweight. He pulled the note out from under the gun, careful not to touch it, and read its words.

Jake - Hope you found the trailer OK. Stay as long as you need—the .38 was left in the camper by the previous owner; it's yours if you want it. Take care. JR

There'd been a day when the feel of a gun in his hand was as normal as a wallet in his back pocket, and he preferred not to think about the reasons why. Throwing the note to the side, he picked up the .38 and studied it. What had once felt normal was now distressing.

Why couldn't JR have just taken the damn thing? Why did the owner have to leave it behind? He cursed its existence and hastily threw the gun in a drawer and slammed it shut.

CHAPTER 10

Charlie heard Lisa running through the house downstairs.

She called up the steps, "Where's my cat tail? Did someone take my cat tail?"

He didn't answer; he had his own issues to resolve. After several futile attempts to position his two boys with their grandmother for a picture on Halloween, he grew adamant. "All right, that's it! Now everybody look here. Ma! Look at me."

Eddie pulled a candy wrapper from Billy's hand and held onto his shoulder so he wouldn't move.

"Hold it, that's it!" He'd done it: one Darth Vader, one very small bunny rabbit, and one mentally ill woman, all captured in time thanks to his Polaroid. Although his mother had looked at just the right moment, he knew better than to think it was anything more than pure accident. He ripped the picture from its cartridge and studied his production.

"Hey, Boone boys? Let's go. Charlie, you know the drill. Get down here to answer the door while I take pictures."

The words weren't fully out of Lisa's mouth before the first knock hit the door. Eddie shot down the steps with Billy right behind him.

Charlie slid the picture into his chest pocket and went to work securing his mother into her rocking chair with the seatbelt he had made a year earlier after she'd almost fallen down the steps while wandering.

"There you go, Mom. Sit and rock, just like the old days."

"Who are you?" she mumbled.

No matter how many times he heard it, the bluntness of her question always startled him. It was her matter-of-fact tone that was most unsettling. "I'm Charlie, Mom," he said, going back to the strap. "I'm your son."

"Did you say Christopher?"

He turned on the TV and switched it to *Wheel of Fortune*. "Remember *The Wheel*? That's what you used to call it. You always loved *The Wheel*."

"Where'd that little boy go?"

"Downstairs."

Charlie stood at the top of the steps, hesitant to go down. It was the same nonsense every year: a small assembly of ghosts, goblins, and their parents exchanging fake pleasantries and bogus smiles. It was the time of year when the Boones were popular with the neighbors. The Boo Radley stigma their home had developed over the years had become neighborhood legend.

They filed in as if they were in line for a carnival fun house, eager to sneak a peek at the crazy lady living on the second floor who hadn't seen the light of day in over ten years. The lurid tales stretched far and wide, a realization he was painfully reminded of each Halloween.

After a few more Polaroids, he followed Lisa off the porch steps and into the street, where the boys stood with a convoy of other trick-or-treaters and their parents. The two bent white ears sticking out of Billy's head put a slight smile on his face.

"You're coming, right?" Lisa asked.

"Nah, you guys go on. I'll stay here and hold down the fort."

"You sure?"

"Yeah, I'm sure."

"You OK?"

"I'm fine, just a little tired."

Lisa smiled and looked down at her boys. "All right, boys, let's go." She called over her shoulder, "We'll be back in an hour."

He kept a close eye on them until they fell into the shadows ahead. A sensation, not much different from the one he had had a few nights earlier outside the mini-mart, came over him. He glanced down either end of the block and was amazed at how deserted the place had become in a matter of seconds. He quickly retreated back up the porch steps and into the house.

The newspapers by the recliner were piling up. He picked one off the top and fell back into the chair. A cool breeze cut across his body from the door he'd left open.

He welcomed the cold air. It was a slight reminder that he was still alive, that he could still feel things. *How can someone be constantly tired but never able to truly sleep?* If he could catch a short nap, he'd feel better. Charlie closed his eyes, but the black there was quickly replaced by a bright light. The cold air was gone, heat…

There's a pool of water on the horizon. He moves toward it headfirst, but it takes every ounce of energy to do so. Only one arm to pull him along…but why? Where's his other arm?

His legs are there; he can feel them, dragging behind him. He feels no pain—just thirst.

A shadow flashes above him. A plane? Someone to rescue him! Please! Please be some-one with water. His nails dig into the hard clay surface, and with every pull of his body, he finds chunks of desert. This thing moves; it's behind him.

"Who's there? Help me! I can't crawl anymore." It's a large shadow. "Who are you?" He flops over on his back, but it's hard to make out. "Come closer, I can't see!" The head is dark, its width strange. "I'm thirsty, please help." It walks with caution… "My God! What are you?" It's a bird…an enormous one with feet the size of his own.

One more descends, then another. They gather and make a circle…their eyes…there's nothing in them. They're black and hollow. They're reading his own…he can feel it…too close…flipping over on his stomach, he scrapes and claws, but then there's the first tug on his back…then a bite to the ear, then his neck. He screams, "Stop! Get off me!" He kicks, but nothing moves anymore. He's paralyzed. "Please God, no!"

Charlie leaped out of the recliner and in one swift movement latched onto his prey's neck with both hands. They both collapsed to the ground, where he kept a firm grip around the boy's neck, saliva dripping from his mouth.

The choking cries of a young boy finally started to register. Sweat dripped down his brow and into the boy's face. Charlie looked into the boy's eyes…he was killing him.

He quickly released his hold and rolled over. The boy let out a huge yelp and then gasped for air. He jumped up off the floor and ran out of the house, scream-ing. There were two others with him, standing in the doorway, their mouths agape.

What happened? What the hell happened?

Charlie jumped to his feet, slammed the door shut, and locked the dead bolt. He ran to the window and looked out but saw nothing in the pitch black. He pulled the shades closed and ran to his bedroom and shut the door behind him. His heavy breathing filled the room. His heart was racing.

"My God! What the fuck just happened?"

Charlie slid down the back of the door. The Polaroid he had taken earlier ejected itself from his shirt pocket, scratching him in the chin. He picked it from its place and stared at the outline of his mother and the two boys and started to cry.

———

It was half past midnight when Lisa entered the kitchen. She threw her pocketbook on the range. There was a long silence between them.

"They're not going to press charges," she said.

"I saw a gun," he whispered.

"A toy gun, Charlie! It's Halloween, for crying out loud."

"It was a mistake. I was in a deep sleep."

Lisa laughed. "Yeah, a deep sleep? Like that's even possible."

"He was standing over me."

"He was a kid! A fucking child, dressed up as a cowboy."

"I understand that! It was an accident. Accidents happen."

"Yeah, well, lucky for us accidents happen. A severely bruised neck easily could have been something different…I mean God, Charlie, you could have killed him!"

"The police agreed these things happen."

"Oh, don't kid yourself. If the kid's parents weren't half nitwits, your ass would be in jail right now. Holy shit, don't you get that?" She buried her face in her hands. "I can't even imagine what's being said right now."

"Why do you care what they think?"

"Because you don't! That's why. And as a result, we all suffer."

"They're not nice people," Charlie whispered.

"And how would you know? You don't even know these people."

"Yes, I do! You saw how they paraded through here tonight, like we were some fucking freak show. They can't even look you in the eye. They're looking over you, around you, not listening to a word you're saying, in hopes of a slight glimpse at the crazy lady who eats bugs for breakfast and sleeps in a straitjacket!"

"Spare me."

"I won't. They come here once a year for their own demented amusement, and you allow it. You should be ashamed of yourself."

"Fuck you, Charlie! What I do, I do for our children, and you should too."

"So we're not friends with our neighbors," Charlie screamed. "Is that what this is about?"

"No! It's about…" She was holding back tears. "It's about being normal. Some days…some days I just want to have friends, to be friends with our neighbors. To wake up and know…" She stopped.

"To know what?"

Her words came slow. "To know everything's gonna be OK that day, everything's gonna be normal!"

Charlie fell silent. The whole house fell silent, as if its usual creaks and groans had stopped to listen too.

Lisa got up from the table and stopped in the doorway of the kitchen. "I dropped the boys off at Mrs. Spinks's down the road. They're staying there tonight. We're gonna have to tell them something in the morning…*you're* gonna have to tell them something."

He looked up at her. "Whatever they're saying, they've said much worse. Don't worry what they think."

"I used to feel that way, Charlie." She shook her head. "But not anymore."

CHAPTER 11

He had the same feelings of contempt, staring out the passenger-side window, as he had had on his boyhood trips to Trenton. He was going for one reason only—to appease Lisa.

"Where is this lady?" he asked.

"Chinatown," Lisa replied.

He laughed. "Chinatown? Seriously?"

"If you're gonna be an ass about it, we might as well turn around. You've got to be open to this, and trust me; she's legit. I wasn't going to tell you, but I came down here last week by myself."

"Why?"

"Because I wanted to check her out…I wanted to see for myself."

"And?"

She took her eyes off the road and looked to him. "She said a lot of things. She said that she saw better days ahead for me, for me and my family. That the sun would shine bright on all of us even though it's not that way now."

"And she calls herself a psychic? A homeless gypsy could have told you that. Hope you didn't pay for it."

"I believed her, and this woman doesn't advertise…there's no big neon sign out front. She's very spiritual; I could feel it. She studied my hands and said the women in my family have had it rough. They've all had crosses to bear, that I wasn't the only one.

"She told me I wear a strong face, but deep down inside, things are different. She said I wear that face for the protection of my family and myself. She told me to let go."

"And that sealed it for you? She passed your test?"

Lisa turned right at Eighth and Vine and parked the car. A pile of trash sat on the curb just outside Charlie's door. He looked over to her. "There's no turning back, huh?"

"You promised."

She was right. There was no big neon sign out front. But even if there had been, it wouldn't have mattered. Just getting to the place from street level was a maze. Through a back alley, over a crossway, up three flights of dark steps, and down a long corridor. The whole place reeked of cat urine.

"You came down here on your own?" he asked.

Lisa knocked on the door. "Desperate people do desperate things."

An old Chinese lady opened the door and waved them in. She nodded and smiled, then pointed to the back room. Everything in it was red: the carpet, the curtains, even the dozen or so lit candles.

She pointed Charlie to a chair across from a small table. "Sit."

He did as she said. Though he couldn't see Lisa, he knew she had sunk into the shadows somewhere behind him.

"You're skeptic?"

"A skeptic? I don't know, maybe just suspect."

"You don't trust doctors."

"No, I don't."

"Me neither. What brings you here?"

He hesitated for a moment and then looked over his shoulder for Lisa, but she wasn't there.

"She's behind the door...can't hear us."

He looked the old lady over. Her face had some wrinkles but was still noticeably smooth. Her mouth lay flat, no smile, no frown—and her eyes were inviting.

"I'm here because my wife asked me to come."

She nodded. "Your wife cares very much."

"Me too."

"Hmm." Her eyes squinted as she studied him. "I believe you." She continued to stare at him.

"What is it?" he asked.

"Crazy…I don't see it."

Charlie laughed. "My wife…she thinks I'm crazy. She told you that."

"Do you?"

He fell silent. "Some days, yes."

"You see things. What is it you see?"

"Where do I start?"

"What troubles you most?"

"It's all troubling when you don't know what it means."

"Have you ever been to a psychic before?" she asked.

"No…why?"

"I saw something…like you've been touched."

"Touched by who?"

"Not by who, by what."

Charlie grew a big smile. "You think I'm psychic?"

"There's something in you."

He leaned in. "Maybe I should be reading your palm."

"I don't read palms, or minds. I study you and say what I feel…say what I see in my mind."

"And what does all that mean for me?"

"A tortured soul, a hard fate."

Charlie scooted to the end of his chair and whispered, "You see death?"

"Not death but alone. I see unhappiness, confusion, anger. Where I see you, you died years earlier."

His jaw line tightened. "I guess it's not always good news at these meetings."

Her eyes narrowed. "You came here to tell me something. Say it."

He took in a deep breath. She was right. "I used to see things as a child. These visions. It was evil…and it was coming. Things never made sense. Still don't, but…"

"But what?" she asked.

"Tell me what they are," he whispered. "Tell me what they mean."

"They're scattered, frightening, they're a part of you. But there's one that scares you more. Scared you then and scares you even today."

He studied her eyes while they were studying his. She was confident and in control. *How could she have known that?*

"It's a dream. I've had it as long as I can remember. It's dark in this place, but I know I'm not alone. There are people with me—it's some sort of room, and there are children too. They're all lying on the floor. I see their names; they're written before me in the black."

"What are they? Tell me their names."

"Darrell, Darwin, Clyde, Harry, Beatrice, Lula." He paused. "And then everything slows down; it gets real quiet. I can only hear my own breathing, and I fall asleep."

He looked back up at her. "But this cry wakes me—it's a child. It's so loud and so bad, you wouldn't even think a child could make it. I get up and walk to the door, but I'm careful where I move. I'm careful not to move...like not to step on anyone. I can hear this crackling under my feet too, and the closer I get to the door, the louder the crying gets.

"I open the door, and there's this huge field. It just goes on forever, and then I see him. I see this little boy, he's all alone, he's crying like..."

"Like what?" she asked.

"Like he just lost his mother."

"Are you that child?"

There was a second-floor window above the pantry roof; it was always unlocked. He'd go in and out of it as a child. The gun cabinet was in the hallway, next to his grandfather's bedroom, and the bullets were in the drawer. He'd loaded and unloaded every one of those rifles a dozen times. He could be up there in forty minutes, and it'd all be over...that window was unlocked—damn sure, he knew it was.

"Mr. Charles?"

"Hmm?"

"The boy, is he you?"

Charlie nodded. "Yes."

She reached over and rested her hand on his. "We can't stop what's inside us."

"And what's inside me?" With his other hand he reached over and gripped her forearm. "Please, tell me *something* that makes sense to me! Tell me what this is."

"I can only say what I see and feel...I can't lie."

Charlie let go of his grip and sat back. "Can't lie about what?"

She answered with only a slow shake of her head.

"OK, then. Let's say that's how this goes...bad. What am I supposed to do to change it?"

"Keep yourself open to everything around you." She gripped his hand. "Do what's in your heart, son, not your head. Our mind will take us to trouble; our heart will lead us out."

CHAPTER 12

The young girl behind the checkout handed Lisa her change as she threw the last grocery bag into the cart. Billy sat in the bag cart playing with a Pez dispenser while Eddie strung a yo-yo at her side. She grabbed the receipt out of one of the bags and began to read through it as they exited the store:

2 gallons of milk
2 cartons of orange juice
3 dozen eggs
1 loaf of Wonder Bread
2 boxes of Cheerios
2 packs of bologna
1 jar of peanut butter
1 jar of jelly
2 packs of singles cheese
1 frozen chicken
10 cans of tomato soup
6 boxes of macaroni & cheese
1 boiled ham
1 sack of potatoes
and 1 Pez dispenser

The screeching of the tires was so loud that a barrage of store employees came running out of the Acme. A dense stench of burned rubber filled the air while a cloud of smoke lifted above everyone's heads. Taken by the wind, the receipt in her hand drifted peacefully across the parking lot.

She stood inches away from the grill of the truck, motionless, her hand covering her heart. She felt for Eddie on her right side and landed her hand on his stomach. Billy was winding up for a hysterical cry.

The sun's glare off the windshield was too strong to see him. She wanted to say something but couldn't even speak; she could barely breath. She grabbed Eddie's hand and moved away from the front of the truck, chastising herself along the way. "Jesus Christ, Lisa, what the hell are you doing?" She felt her oldest son's resistance. "Eddie? Stop staring. Get in the car!"

Jake Mott sat stone-faced and still behind the wheel of his truck, a bead of sweat on his forehead caused by his racing heartbeat. He looked into the eyes of the little boy, and all he could think of was going back to that place he'd just come from. That little boy's stark blue eyes and the look of terror in them he would never forget.

CHAPTER 13

His nervous energy was building, stacking up as quickly as the folded news-papers on the living room floor. He was buying five papers a day—the *NY Times, LA Times, LA Daily News, USA Today,* and the *Philadelphia Inquirer*—and still Charlie couldn't get enough information on the fires out west.

They didn't have cable; it wasn't in the budget—but he certainly considered making the purchase, sure that cable news was providing plenty of coverage on it. Now that his Saturday hooky forays were out in the open, he found himself stopping off at Circuit City and watching CNN rather than going to St. Patrick's.

Being three thousand miles away from the wildfires he was obsessing over was enough to make him scream, but instead he collected the newspapers on the living room floor and took them to the basement. It was time to do some-thing. It was time to plot its course.

He taped the corners of the newly bought map of California to the base-ment wall and ran his hand down its middle to smooth out any creases, then began plotting the fire's path of destruction with little red thumbtacks.

To the left of the map he secured an old corkboard that he had found in the attic and placed each article in chronological order, highlighting town after town that was being engulfed in flames. What had begun as a forest fire was now destroying the lives of thousands of people, and each red thumbtack that he placed on the map represented another town lost—towns such as Riverhead and Dunnshead.

Once finished, Charlie took a step back.

"Why?" he asked. "Why is this so important?"

He gathered up the newspaper clippings lying at his feet and threw them in the trash. Glancing back at the fire mural he'd just built, he was reminded of something he once saw in his mind's eye—hundreds of people running from a wall of fire—and though he was sure of nothing, he hoped whatever was possessing him to map this natural disaster with such detail was also responsible for that vision years earlier. It was the only thing that made sense...it was the only hope he had.

A twinge of optimism engulfed him. He'd soon find out what all this meant. He was sure of it, not only in his heart, but via the prophecy of a stranger in the middle of the night.

"He's coming," he whispered.

CHAPTER 14

C harlie sat in the office of his boss, Randy Knox. The photos on the wall portrayed an avid fisherman, a happy family man, and an athlete: having played two seasons with the Philadelphia Eagles before being cut. His old jersey hung in a frame above his chair, next to a picture of him with Jaworski and Harold Carmichael. Charlie leaned in toward the desk to view one photo of Randy standing by a lake, a large fish hanging from his hand.

"Hell of a fish, ain't it?" Randy closed the door behind him and took a seat at his desk.

"What kind is it?" Charlie asked.

"Bass, was a bastard coming in. Lake Michigan, last year." Randy shuffled some papers around on his desk. "Look, Charlie, you know why I called you in here."

"No."

"Well, you should." He picked up a piece of paper on his desk and held it in front of him. "I got a call from a Robert Wilson. That name ring a bell?"

Charlie thought for a moment. "No, should it?"

"He was on your bus last week, elderly black man. Says you borderline harassed 'im."

Oh yeah, I know him—but harassed? I never harassed anybody.

"I don't know what you're talking about."

"Bullshit you don't!" Randy opened up his desk drawer and pulled out a file. He jabbed its cover with his index finger. "You know what's in here? Let me save you the time from guessing. Five complaints...count 'em, five." He opened the folder and began skimming through it. "I seem to have a short-ass memory, so I decided to do some checking up on you. Dating back four years, I got five complaints. And four of the five were by males…all black!" Randy put on his glasses. "Driver stopped bus, got out, and proceeded to *chase me* down Sixteenth Street."

Charlie remembered it well. It was a snowy day in February. He'd seen the man from a block away standing just inside the bus shelter. As he approached, the man's face seemed distorted, but a closer look showed just a bad case of pocked skin. The two made eye contact long before Charlie even stopped, but he was sure the man said something to him before even entering. *Follow me* was what he heard.

"I thought he said something to me…and I was *walking* down Sixteenth Street, not running."

"I don't give a damn if you were skipping, and where the hell does it say you can leave your vehicle unattended?"

He was about to answer, but Randy didn't let him. "Second one."

He already knew the second one. He knew them all, for that matter, and could provide more detail than Randy would ever want to know. "You don't have to go through each one."

"Well, I'm glad for that." Randy shut his file. "Now what the hell is going on out there, son?"

"What? I can't talk to the passengers on my bus?"

Randy ripped the file back open. "Driver stopped bus with only me on it and said nothing. I asked him was everything OK? He said yes and continued to drive, repeated same action a few blocks down the street. Once again I asked him if everything was OK, driver stared at me and said nothing. Finally driver stands, turns to me, and says, 'What are you doing on this bus?'" Randy shut the file and pushed it away for good. "Eye contact? Son, that's borderline insane. Now I don't give a damn what you wanna call it; I should have fired your ass for that alone."

"I apologized," Charlie said softly.

"You what?"

"I said I was sorry."

"Well, isn't that nice? By the time you had him shaking in his goddamn boots, what did it matter? Now, I wanna know something right here, right now. Do you got a problem with a black man riding your bus?"

He shook his head. "I'm not a prejudiced man."

"Guess what? I don't think so either, but there's a pattern here, and I need answers."

Randy's need for answers had Charlie feeling as if there was an ultimatum coming. "They looked suspicious. You're telling me I can't keep an eye on suspicious people?"

"And who the fuck are you, Superman?" Randy rubbed his eyes. "Listen, you know what I think? I think one of these days you're gonna blow, Charlie. You're gonna snap, and when you do, guess whose ass is on the line? Mine." Randy pointed to his file. "It won't take five minutes for some lawyer to rip this file apart and see where the problem was. Now look! I've looked the other way on this shit, and I've done so because you're a good employee—you're here every day, you're on time, and I never hear from ya…but make no mistake about it, this is a problem." Randy stood up at his desk.

"It won't happen again, I promise."

"Son, you haven't taken a day's vacation in eight years. Did you know that?"

"I work. I need to put food on the table. I got kids, I got a wife who depends on me."

"Yeah, well, I work, too, but I also take time. Hell, Charlie, you've never even called out. I mean you haven't *missed* a single damn day of work in *eight years*, forget about vacation. How's that possible?"

"I don't know."

Tucking his shirt back into his pants, Randy sat down. "Two weeks' leave. That's what I'm giving you."

"What?" Charlie asked.

"Two weeks leave of absence."

"What does that mean?"

"It means you have some free time on your hands. It's a leave of absence… for personal reasons, requested *by you* to me."

"Wait a second. What does that mean?"

"Wait nothing! You want a suspension in this file? Because that's the alternative, and that'll leave you one mistake from being gone." Randy picked up a pen and started writing in his file. "No, this is how we do it, leave of absence. I've cut you some serious slack in the past, son, but this I gotta do. This is my ass too!"

"I've got a family. I got two young kids, a sick mother; I can't afford to lose this job."

"Then you stop this nonsense! You hear me, Charlie? I want it stopped."

Charlie bit his lip.

Randy sat up, his tone much lower now but still stern. "I can't take one more call like this. I got my own family to worry about. Two weeks. Go unwind, take a deep breath." He closed Charlie's file and looked up at him. The two of them sat silent for a few moments. "Go home and clear your head, Charlie. Get it right, then you come back here free of this shit."

CHAPTER 15

R andy's words were taking hold with every silent second that passed. He would rather hop a bus to Trenton right now than go home and tell Lisa he'd been put on leave of absence without pay. He pulled himself together long enough to grab some personal items from his locker and was out the door.

He passed his exit and continued driving up I-95 without direction or purpose. He could drive forever right now, clear out of state and across the country even, without ever stopping, not even once for gas. Just the thought of speaking to another human being right now seemed too much of a task.

A barrage of cars and trucks passed him while he cruised the far right lane at fifty miles per hour. Like the eighteen-wheeled rigs that sandwiched his truck, Charlie felt the walls of his life closing in on him. His nerves were shot, and his psyche was bordering on collapse. Confusion and anger weren't the norm anymore…now helplessness was setting in.

He had read an article about panic attacks and recalled the warning signs: shortness of breath, hot and cold flashes, a racing heartbeat. He'd been afflicted by every one of them at one time or another, but at the moment, all three were taking hold of him.

He stomped his foot on the gas pedal and pounded his fist on the dash. He wanted to scream but held it in.

The car's sudden burst of speed found it kissing the back of a horse trailer. A shiny brown colt stared back at him. The horse's large snout hung out the back of the trailer. Charlie locked in on him…the animal had a kind face and big brown eyes that said, "I'm here." Charlie wondered if the colt, like him, wanted nothing more than to run free at that very moment. A moment of calm came over him. He slowed down at the next exit and got off.

A mile down State Road, Charlie found himself at the entrance of Pennypack Park and turned in. He'd never been in the park before but had heard of a particular spot that looked out over the Delaware. Randy had mentioned it before as a decent local fishing hole.

Just a half mile from the entrance, he found it without much effort and parked his car at the waterfront. He got out and stood at the rail overlooking the river.

It hadn't been a full week since the Halloween incident, and no doubt this thing with the job would be the straw to break the camel's back.

He closed his eyes and pleaded for something to come to him. A sign, an image, an answer…direction. Black was replaced with static white, and then the image took form in his mind. It was him, an old man sitting in the same house he lived in now, the only house he'd ever lived in. He looked straight ahead in a daze. His skin was wrinkled and hung from his body like a worn-out dishrag. Stacks upon stacks of newspapers covered the floor at his feet. There were no signs of life in that home, and he knew that. No grandchildren ran about; the two sons he loved so dearly were noticeably absent. Most alarming? The realization that the woman he loved was gone too, long gone, having walked out on him years earlier and taking all that was ever good about him with her. The Chinatown psychic was right. *Alone…unhappy, angry.*

Lisa's words popped into his head. *It's on you…you better get this thing right.*

There was no doubting her this time, and the thought of losing his family only to grow old and bedridden like his mother was devastating.

Looking down on the Delaware, Charlie knew now was the time to do something about it.

Embrace it. In that instant he made an oath that the isolation and abandonment in his vision would not be his destiny. In that moment, he committed himself to finding out the truth, to solving the mystery that was his life. His life was falling apart, and it was only up to him to put it back together.

He opened his truck door to leave and was startled at the scratching of limbs coming from a dense tree line about thirty yards in front of him. Though there was no stiff wind to be felt, the woods behaved otherwise, casting what sounded like a deep whisper over his head. It called his name: *Charlie.*

Scared yet understanding, he looked over the thick, dark woods, took a cautious breath, and, unable to see anything that resembled life, answered its call. "Show me, and I'll follow."

CHAPTER 16

H e stood in front of the mirror in their bedroom going over it in his head. It had never taken him so long to get undressed before. How much would he share with her about his leave from work? No matter how he painted it, she'd be suspicious.

"Eddie was digging for worms in the backyard today," Lisa said. "He said something about you taking him and Billy fishing this Saturday."

"Yeah, I thought I'd try to do something fun with them for once. Seems like we never do that kind of stuff." He turned to face her. "Right?"

"I think it's a great idea, and I agree you should try to do that stuff more often. Eddie would really love it...where are you taking them?"

He thought of the pier he had stood on earlier that day in Pennypack Park. "There's a spot over in Pennypack that might be good."

Lisa smiled. "That sounds fun. Maybe I'll come too, and we'll make an afternoon of it. I can pack us a picnic lunch."

It was nice to see her smile. It seemed like weeks since they'd last shared a light moment. "Let's do it," he replied.

"Yeah! Let's. I think there's an old picnic basket in the basement. I'll have to pull it out."

"You know what else I've been thinking?" he asked.

She looked over to him.

"This family needs a vacation, babe."

"Vacation? That would be awesome, but we can't afford a vacation, Charlie."

She was right. They lived week to week, and if they had a mortgage to pay, they'd be underwater, but none of that mattered to him right now. "Randy gave me some time off today. He said it was mandatory that I take it, actually…two weeks."

She stopped folding the laundry. "What for?"

"He said I deserved it. Said I haven't taken a single day off in eight years. Did you know that?"

"Eight years? I knew it'd been a while, but that's long. Well, you're a hard worker, and they're lucky to have you. And they damn well better remember this come review time. I mean, the time off is nice, but a pay increase is what we really need."

He ignored her comment, knowing full well he was already one of the highest-paid drivers. "Who knows, maybe I'll even find something better, making more money."

"Find another job? You sure everything's OK at work?"

He hesitated before speaking. "Everything's fine. My file's clean, my attendance is second to none. Randy said it's long overdue."

Lisa returned to the laundry. "Your job is so important to us. If you want to find something else, that's fine, but what would you do?"

"I don't know…driving that bus is starting to take its toll on me, though."

"Well, I feel for you, but let's just make sure we have something lined up that's secure before you do anything, right?"

He didn't respond; he had something else on his mind. "You think Eddie thinks I'm a good father?"

"I think Eddie thinks you're a great father. You get up every day and go to work. He knows what you do for us, and he respects you for it."

"I'm a bus driver. What's so special about that?"

"It's not what you do; it's how you do it. You come home every night with a smile on your face for those two boys, and that doesn't go unnoticed."

He looked up at her. "They're all I got. You and them."

She smiled. "I know."

"I'm gonna get this thing right, babe. I promise. You mean too much to me."

She grabbed his hand. There were times when he'd find himself in complete awe of her. Pinch yourself kinds of moments—not just for her beauty, but because she was really his wife. How had he ever been lucky enough to meet her, let alone marry her?

"What is it you want?" he asked. "If you could have anything at all, what would it be?"

With a tenuous smile she replied, "Be careful what you ask."

He recalled his vision on the pier at Pennypack Park, the vision of that lonely, withdrawn old man sitting in the living room of this very house. He couldn't afford to lose her, not ever. "No I'm serious, very serious. What is it?"

The grin on her face told him she was hooked. "Well, I've always wanted a big white house. I mean a *big...white...house*. Stark white, with a huge black door and big black shutters on all the windows, with a wraparound porch and a big yard for the boys to play in. And away from everybody—I mean no neighbors, somewhere in the country, because you're right, Charlie. Our neighbors aren't very nice people."

The smile fell from her face, and she briefly looked down to her side. He cursed the reality check she was having.

"But let's focus instead on what I have," she said. "I have two beautiful children, and I have a husband I love very much, and that, Charlie, is truly all I need."

"I would never do anything to intentionally hurt you."

She stared down at the folded-up shirt in her hand. He'd seen that face before. It was a mix of disappointment and uncertainty. She was right. It wasn't just taking its toll on him anymore, but on her as well.

"The wildfires, Charlie. What are they for you?"

He paused. "When I first saw that headline, it was like a little piece of me filled in. Like one small piece of a giant puzzle found its home."

His answer didn't get it done; she still wore that look of disappointment.

"Listen," he said, grabbing her chin. "I won't grow old and alone in this house or any other house without you. I'm gonna figure this thing out, and we're gonna be fine."

She cracked a smile and nodded.

"And the reality is I don't have to go to work for the next two weeks, so maybe you and I can catch up on some lost time too...do something fun."

"Hmm, now that sounds tempting. There is a party on Friday night. It's Marny's thirtieth birthday."

"Marny? The girl from the salon?"

"Yeah, you've met her before."

"I didn't think you went there anymore."

"I don't." Lisa laughed. "Now I go to her house. She cuts it for half price in her basement. Anyway, I wasn't going to ask you because you usually say no at these kinds of things, but I think I'd like to go."

"Where is it?"

"Jerry's."

"Jerry's? Holy shit, I haven't been there in years. You swore me off the place."

"It's been a long time for both of us." She reached for his hand. "I know you hate these things, but I think it would be good for us. It would be good to get out and socialize."

"What about the boys?"

"Mrs. Spinks was so good to them on Halloween. I know they'd go back. She feeds them whatever they want, and Eddie plays that pinball machine in her basement."

He reached over and pulled her onto his lap. "You want me to go?"

"Yes, I do."

"Will there be any costume wearing at this party?"

She laughed aloud. "All toy guns will be checked at the door, Mr. Boone."

"Then I'm in." He leaned in and kissed her on the lips.

CHAPTER 17

"**B**ear!"

It was Eddie's call coming from the backyard. He'd only been up a few minutes, but he already knew it was pure chaos downstairs.

"Bear! Where are you?"

He found Lisa standing in front of the phone waiting for the rotary dial to finish. She looked panicked.

"What's going on?" he asked.

"The dog's gone."

"Who are you calling?"

"Who do you think I'm calling? The dog catcher."

"How'd he get out?"

"Easy. He jumped through the screen." Lisa pointed to the storm door leading to the backyard. Bits of gray tape dangled from the broken mesh screening. "Remember that? You said you were gonna fix it last summer, but instead you taped it."

"Shit," he whispered under his breath.

"Eddie's devastated. Go outside and keep an eye on the boys. The last thing I need is for them to wander off."

———

Jake could hear the cracking of twigs and crumbling of leaves just under his window. He imagined what it might be, picturing it in his mind. Maybe a squirrel or a raccoon, though it sounded a touch bigger than an animal that size, and raccoons didn't whimper like that. Then he remembered he could just as easily go outside and have a look for himself. Acknowledging that old prison habits were hard to break, he closed his Bible and put it to rest at his side.

He swung open the door and looked down. A small black puppy stared up at him, sitting nicely at the foot of the steps to the camper door. He hadn't petted a dog since Vietnam. He bent down, swiped the puppy off the ground, and brought him inside.

It sniffed around at his feet, every once in a while stopping to look up at him, and then finally rested itself just below the kitchen counter. Jake grabbed a can of day-old catfish on the counter and put it down on the ground. The puppy buried his face in it.

"You're one small fella. Just a few months, I bet. What the hell you doin' out here?" He noticed a tag tucked underneath the backside of the dog's collar: "Bear – 10 Nebraska Lane." He scratched at the phone number etched into the dog tag.

"Bear, huh?" He considered ripping the tag off its collar and throwing it away. A companion would do him some good, especially the kind that couldn't talk back. But he'd decide on that later. For now, he'd enjoy the company.

CHAPTER 18

The dog had been missing all day, and with nightfall near, Charlie feared the worst. Lisa wasn't talking to him, nor was Eddie. The whole family sat around the kitchen table hoping for that knock at the door. Eddie was doing everything in his power to hold back his tears—Charlie could see it in his eyes.

If I had only fixed the damn screen. The phone hadn't finished its first ring when he sprang to pick it up. "Hello?"

The voice on the other end was deep. "You looking for a dog?"

His heart picked up. "Yes, we are!" He gave a quick nod to the rest of the family seated at the table. "You have him?"

"Yeah, I got 'im."

The voice wasn't exactly full of compassion, which struck Charlie as odd. "Wow, you don't know how much this means to us. Where are you? I'll come get him."

"No," Jake said abruptly. "I'll come to you. Where's Nebraska Lane?"

"It's off Boulevard, near Mayfair."

"Mayfair? Don't know it. I know the Boulevard a little. There's a 7-Eleven somewhere; I was there the other day. You near it?"

"Yeah, I know it well. It's not far from me."

"OK, that's where I'll be."

Charlie stood in front of the mini-mart, not far from the same space where he'd dropped his groceries a week earlier. He recalled the strange man he had encountered that night and thought it odd he was back at that very spot waiting for another stranger. "He's coming," Charlie whispered.

A beat-up black pickup pulled into the far end of the lot and abruptly stopped, creating its own space as it did so. Charlie knew he had the dog, but the man's appearance wasn't what he expected. In retrospect, he looked much the way he sounded: mean.

"Hello?" Charlie called out.

"Puppy?"

"That's me." He cautiously approached the truck.

Jake pointed across his own chest to the passenger side of the cab. "There he is."

Charlie was just close enough to see the top of Bear's head. Finally, some of the day's anxiety lifted. A few steps closer, and he saw all of Bear.

"Yup, that's him. I can't thank you enough."

"No mind," Jake mumbled. "Go on, you can get 'im yourself."

He walked around the front of the truck and opened the passenger-side door. Bear jumped to the ground, and he leashed him. "Well, like I said, thanks for bringing him baa…" He paused and took note of the scars on Jake's face: the few around his chin, one at the corner of his right eye, and one across his left cheek. From there, he went to Jake's eyes, where he stayed for some time.

"Something wrong?" Jake asked.

He shook his head ever so slightly. "Have we met?"

Jake eyed him up. "You ever spend time in Georgia?"

"No."

"Then we haven't met. Listen," Jake said, "shut the door. I gotta go."

Charlie stepped away from the door and looked down at Bear, who was scratching at his feet. "But the dog, where did you find him?"

"The park," Jake replied.

"The park? Which one?"

Jake reached across the front seat and slammed the passenger-side door shut. "Pennypack Park."

Charlie's heart skipped a beat. That wasn't possible. "Pennypack Park? That can't be. That's at least five miles from where we live. Getting there on foot is next to impossible, let alone a dog crossing highways."

"Well I don't know what to tell ya then, but that's where I found 'im. Maybe you should keep a closer eye on 'im."

"But I wasn't in the park! No one was in the park! Not Pennypack Park, not with him."

"Then maybe someone picked him up off the highway and took him there. Maybe he got a ride. Point is, be happy you got 'im back."

Jake put the truck in reverse and began backing out.

"Wait! What's your name?" Charlie asked.

"It's not important."

Charlie watched him pull out of the mini-mart and speed off down the boulevard. Déjà vu, no—but something wasn't right about any of it.

CHAPTER 19

He hadn't been to Jerry's Saloon in years but certainly knew it—and its owner, Jerry—well, and he figured little would have changed at the locals' bar where much of the neighborhood gathered. Its two cracked windows, half-lit neon sign, and dim interior made it one broken toilet away from an official dive bar, but the makeshift kitchen was known to turn out great food at a great price.

He fell in behind Lisa, allowing her to navigate through the crowd, sidestepping and weaving their way to the back room. Every few feet, she stopped to exchange a quick pleasantry while he patiently stood behind her taking inventory of the place.

Most of the crew at the bar hadn't changed—perhaps just a few more wrinkles on their punch-drunk faces. He recalled those days, sitting right there beside the rest of them. It was nothing but the booze as he remembered it, providing him just the right numbing effect he needed to dismiss what was happening to him. That is, until Lisa put an end to it.

And then there was Jerry, with his bushy white hair and rosy-red face. He was the glue and tape that held the rickety bar stools and paper-thin walls together. As if someone had tipped him off, Jerry looked up from the cash register, wad of money in hand, just in time to catch a glimpse of Charlie's face.

"Holy shit?" Jerry mouthed. He stopped what he was doing and yelled over the crowd, "I'm either seeing a ghost, or I've died and gone to hell."

Charlie nodded his head and yelled back, "It's been a long time."

"That's an understatement."

Charlie motioned to the back room where the party was going on. "I'll see you in a bit."

"There'll be one here waitin' for ya."

He followed Lisa to the back, where she and a slew of other women huddled around Marny. He watched Lisa dive into the social fray with excitement. They were so different that way, but it made him feel good to see her happy.

He bent down to her ear. "I'll be at the bar." She gave her approval with a nod and a smile.

He scanned the crowded bar for any sliver of an opening and found one on the corner. No hurry—Jerry would see him in a minute.

In the foreground of his mind, he could hear those faint piano notes, prompting him to look for the old baby grand that used to sit on the far wall. Though he couldn't see it through the bodies, he hoped it was still there. There had been many Friday nights that culminated with Jerry sitting down at his broken-down piano playing Springsteen's "Racing in the Street" for a small crowd of lingering drunks.

The sweet melody had become a sort of closing signal for those still left in the place. He could clearly recall the deftness with which Jerry had mastered the Bruce classic backed up by the whispers of a group of hard-luck men sitting at the bar.

Jerry walked over with a wide grin. "I never thought I'd see you in here again. Looks like you haven't changed a bit, though."

"Haven't changed? Shit, I feel fifty!"

"Well, I always said you were older than your years." Jerry smiled. "Charlie Boone, the *old soul,* has returned. You know, I'd bet the cash in my register it's been every bit of six years."

"You're probably right."

"How the hell you been?" Jerry asked.

"Not too bad. You?"

Jerry held his hands out to his sides. "I'm still here, brother. Can't be too bad, right?"

Charlie leaned into the bar as if he were sharing a secret. "Hey, you uh… you still doing the song?"

The old bartender smiled from ear to ear. "Wow! It's been a while, but yeah, on rare occasions it comes out."

"Man, I'd love to hear that one more time."

"Well, you stick it out tonight long enough, and maybe you will."

"Then you better get us started," Charlie replied.

"I thought you'd never ask." Jerry poured two shots of tequila. "You remember these, don't ya?"

Charlie grimaced. "I don't know how I did it."

Jerry picked up his shot and handed Charlie the other. "Here's to old times. It's good seeing ya."

They knocked glasses and tilted their heads back. Charlie braced his swallow by gripping the bar in front of him. "Why did we do that, again?"

Jerry laughed. "Consider it a toast to your wife for keeping you out of here as long as she has. What the hell brings you back?"

Charlie motioned to the back room. "Friend of my wife's."

A waitress threw a tray of specials atop the bar and yelled for Jerry as loud as she could, then disappeared into the mass of people. Jerry retrieved the food, divvied it up, and then lapped the bar for drink orders.

The shot of tequila came to rest in Charlie's stomach, allowing the beers to flow much easier, and Jerry kept them coming. It didn't take but a few rounds to slip right back into old conversations while the majority of the bar around them sang backup to "Free Bird" blaring from the jukebox.

"You look happy," Charlie yelled. "You know that?"

"Some days, yes, some days, no. But this is the thing: I'm still doin' it. This beat-up old place was my destiny!"

Destiny. "Funny you say that. I've been thinking about my own recently."

"Oh shit, you're not gonna start talkin' heavy on me, are ya? It's only been two beers!"

He laughed. Jerry was certainly a friendly face and at one time a good friend... it was good to see him. Friends weren't something Charlie had many of.

"You remember some of them conversations we used to have back in the day?" Jerry asked.

"Conversations about what?"

"Oh hell, you name it. We'd sit up half the fucking night." Jerry poured a couple more drafts. "We talked about it all, life, death, what it all means."

He drew a blank. He recalled more than a few marathon nights—long Fridays at work followed by six hours of heavy drinking at Jerry's, only to stumble home and wake up hung over with Lisa in his ear.

"You were funny, Charlie. Always lookin', always in search of something, that's what you used to say." Jerry looked up from the register with half a smile. "You were searching for the truth."

"Yeah, well, I'm no closer today than I was then."

"News flash! Stop looking, 'cause you ain't gonna find it." He rinsed a handful of glasses and hung them on the drying rack. "The only truth in this world is you get one chance, so make the best of it."

"You got it figured out, huh, Jerry?"

"Hell no. I'm as fucked up as they come. Life passed me over in a rice field somewhere in Asia, and I've been trying to catch up ever since."

Jerry's words rang true. Charlie was sure life had passed him over somewhere in Trenton as a child.

"You remember the last night you were in here?" Jerry asked.

Charlie shook his head. "No, should I?"

"You were in a bad way that night, man. Really hung up on something, but you wouldn't talk about it. You just kept saying that you saw something at work that threw ya off."

"Wait a second. Was there a snowstorm?"

"You got it. A real bad one hit us that night. People weren't leaving their houses. But you were in. You remember now?"

"Yeah, I remember it. Septa shut down for four days." He pushed for the memory of the vision he had seen that day, but nothing came to mind.

Jerry chuckled. "I was wondering what'd happened to ya. One of the guys finally told me Lisa dug her nails in. We sat here though till two a.m., and you were telling me some heavy shit. Stuff about your mom, your grandfather. Who you had plans on taking out, by the way." Jerry paused. "You said that somewhere deep inside, you knew what it was like to kill a man, said you knew that feeling."

Tequila was starting to move around in the pit of his stomach.

"And?"

"And nothing. You asked me if I ever killed anyone. Then we got talking about an old buddy of mine from 'Nam, a guy I hadn't thought of in years but was pretty close to at the time." Jerry shook his head. "Funny thing, too. Son of a bitch just reached out to me a few weeks ago."

"You don't sound too happy about it."

"Ehh, I don't know, Charlie. I like to keep life simple anymore. But...I guess if I can help out an old friend, I should, right?"

He couldn't even picture a gun in Jerry's hand, let alone him actually pulling the trigger. "It's not an easy thing to kill a man, is it?" he asked.

"Hardest thing I ever had to do." Jerry paused. "And every time I did it, a little something more seeped out of me."

Looking at the creases on Jerry's face, Charlie felt something stir. *It's easy for some people to kill.*

"Your friend...the killing was easy for him."

"Jake? I don't know what makes you say it, but yeah...didn't seem to bother him." Jerry picked up his beer and downed what was left. "I know how to make a good Manhattan and pour a clean draft and I don't pretend to know much else. But I also know that killing another human being...that ain't for young people to do. Those things stay with you forever."

Jerry was right about forever. He may not have ever killed anyone, but he certainly saw death enough in his own head to make it feel as if it were a part of him. His body was warm, and his face tingled. He was drunk.

"We all got our crosses to bear," Jerry said.

Charlie nodded. "That's the truth...we're just trying to find our way."

"Not asking for much, are we?"

"Not asking for the world," he replied.

"Just some pretty girls in Camaros," Jerry said.

Charlie laughed. He immediately picked up on the Springsteen reference, a line from "Racing in the Street."

"You always had a simple way of putting things."

"Yeah, well, so did Bruce." Jerry poured two fresh beers. "Do me a favor, huh?"

"What's that?"

"Don't be a stranger."

"I'll try my best."

Jerry held his beer in the air. "To each his destiny."

Charlie picked up his beer, wondering if the simple act of touching glasses would do just that…seal his fate. "To destiny," he said. He finished what was in his glass. "I'll take another."

No! Not the desert again, but thank God it wasn't him this time. The stranger was dragging himself through the desert sand a foot at a time. His pants were torn, and his shoes were gone. The bottoms of his feet were burned red and swollen from the sun.

Dried-up trails of blood clung to his face. Blisters the size of quarters hung from his lips. His nose! Where was it? It was completely gone.

Who are you? And why am I here? Who are you?

"Hey, let's go, party's over." He could feel a hand pushing down on his right shoulder. "Come on, let's go. Move it out."

Her voice sounded miles away. He picked his head up from the bar and took a second to gather himself, then staggered to his feet. "What the fuck was that?" he asked.

A lone waitress stood behind the bar pouring herself a drink. "That was me waking your ass up. This ain't no motel. I wanna get home too."

"No," Charlie replied. "What was *that?*"

"Go home; you're fucking drunk."

He looked around. The place was empty. "Where's my wife?"

"She left with a band of people hours ago." He noted the enjoyment in her voice. "Looked like they were moving the party to one of the young fellas' places."

"What about Jerry?"

The waitress grabbed her purse from the bar and headed for the door. "He's in the back. Told me to wake your ass up."

Charlie took a deep breath and exhaled. He rubbed the corners of his eyes. That face, he couldn't get it out of his head. He grabbed his Septa jacket off the barstool and left. The last few hours were a blur.

Some fifty steps away from the roadside bar, Charlie heard Jerry and those solemn piano notes of "Racing in the Street." He stopped and considered going back, but didn't. The words struck him still. *Wow!* Jerry Ryan was singing his heart out with a passion that rivaled any he could ever recall.

CHAPTER 20

*T*hose solemn piano notes pulled him back into the bar. He entered and saw Jerry playing the piano. But his attention was on the back room. Pop Grey was sitting at a table
alone. He looked up and winked.

"Charlie?" It was Jerry calling him.

Jerry was standing on a bar stool. "What happened to you? I waited!"

"I couldn't stay," Charlie replied.

"Where you goin', Charlie?"

"Heaven, I hope, but I don't know…you happy, Jerry?"

"Of course I'm happy."

"I love my wife, and I'll always look after her," Charlie yelled up at him.

"You better get this thing right, Charlie. You're losing time! She's not gonna wait forever."

"Lisa?"

"Destiny, Charlie! Make your own, or you won't just lose your mind. You'll lose your
family too."

"It's not true! Don't say that!"

"Sorry, Charlie…there's no hot rod angels here."

He fell from his dream state into another abyss. He was semiconscious,
but he didn't know where he was. Was this death? He was in a state of lifeless
awareness that wasn't sleep at all, or life…then the voices started in, some
heavy, others soft. They each called from their own dark space. It was hell.

*Let me out!…Maybe this was just your stop, and you didn't know it….No, I don't
belong here….Charlie, is that you?…Mom? I hear you; where are you?…Tonight I sleep—
it was a whole family; they died in a house fire…Who? Who died?—Your family. I almost*

killed them, almost killed them all! Please stop, please let me be, I beg you…your road ends here, right here, right now!

———

She paid the cabbie and rushed up the walk to the porch steps. The neighbors didn't need any more gossip material than they already had. Lisa Boone coming home from a night out at eight a.m. would rival even some of the most lurid tales of her mother-in-law.

She dropped her pocketbook on the den floor and entered the kitchen. A Tylenol and a glass of water were the only things she'd been able to think of since waking up an hour earlier on Marny's couch.

The faucet's cold water felt good against her fingers So much so that she bent down and splashed her face and then poured herself a tall glass. The Tylenol was upstairs in the medicine cabinet. She turned to leave the kitchen and noticed the basement door was open, and the light was on at the bottom of the steps.

She stood at the top and called down, "Charlie?"

The more she concentrated, the more clearly she heard a slight gasping sound. It was someone's labored breathing. The glass dropped from her hand as she descended the steps two at a time.

"Oh my God…Charlie!"

He lay in the fetal position on the basement floor. Sweat dripped from his forehead, his eyes were wide, his breaths were short and difficult.

She fell to her knees and cradled his head in her arms. "What the fuck? Charlie! Baby, look at me!"

His eyes finally began to take focus. She wiped the sweat from his forehead. "Oh baby, what's wrong? What happened?"

Charlie rolled over, out of her grasp, and squeezed his temples with his own hand. "I'm not dead."

"Dead? Oh, Charlie, what happened here? You looked like you were dying."

He pulled his hand from his face and looked up at her. She'd never seen him so mad. He grabbed a bottle of detergent on the basement floor and then stood up and threw it. The bottle's plastic cap hurled across the room, and thick, blue detergent seeped down the basement wall. He turned and stared at the fire mural on the far wall…his life was falling apart.

CHAPTER 21

It took him fifty dimes, two days, and two hundred miles to find it. Time, basically, but Jake was looking at time in a whole different way these days. He had plenty of it—the rest of his free life.

Georgia State housed a computer in the prison library, to be shared by all eight hundred inmates. Jake had never been on it, yet he was sure that a computer was exactly what he needed to find what he was looking for.

A handful of phone calls directed him to a place called University Park, home to Penn State University. It housed the largest public computer database of maps in the state of Pennsylvania.

The tree-heavy highway of Interstate 76 made for a colorful ride on the early November day. Thick patches of brown, red, yellow, and green sat under a bright-blue sky as he navigated the narrow and curvy terrain. He had crossed half the state by midmorning with the windows down and Willie Nelson playing in the tape deck.

He recalled a particular night in '68 when he'd met the famed singer, who was playing to a small crowd in a Nashville bar. Nelson had commented on Jake's size, a joke of sorts, saying if he ever made it big, he'd give him a call to come bodyguard for him.

It had been just months since Dr. King's death in Memphis, and things were volatile, not just in the South but all across the country. Jake's size wasn't the only thing that made him stand out that night. He was also the only black man in the place, a fact that reminded him today what he had known then but paid little mind to. He had gone south to an all-white bar in Nashville in search of trouble, and trouble he found.

A couple of white boys came calling when he left the bar. He ducked into a dark alley, and they followed. What had happened next was unfortunate and ugly.

He dismissed the rest of his thought, tucking it deep into his memory as only he could do, since a permanent erasure of that night wasn't a possibility.

Back to listening to Nelson, Jake thought him to be a good man and one who didn't see the color in people's skin. These were the types of things he wanted to think about these days—only the good in his life, yet very little of his past fell into such a category.

It was noon by the time he reached College Park, and he was impressed by its fairy-tale-like setting. It was his first time on a college campus. What a different world than the one he knew. Throngs of kids walked past him with books in hand and eager smiles on their faces.

Much like that night in Nashville, he felt out of place. His age, his size, his worn-down cowboy boots and stiff blue jeans all spoke of a man from a different time and place.

The library was a gray stone building that sat near some soccer fields. A couple of students pointed it out to him. Taking to the steps, he had hope that he may catch a glimpse of the little hole he'd been dreaming of, the one he had dug on a hot summer day three decades ago, never thinking he wouldn't be returning until some thirty years later.

He approached the scholarly looking woman behind the reference desk. Her gaze met him halfway as he approached. Her eyelids twitched, and she stepped back on her heels. One thing he always had was that sense of fear in others—even with a four-foot counter acting as a barrier between them, the poor woman was scared to death. *No offense taken.*

"Can I help you?" she asked.

"Yes mam. I need a, uh…I mean…I'm looking for a map."

"What kind of map?"

"A map of California. I called yesterday and spoke to…uh…" He pulled a piece of loose-leaf from his shirt pocket. "A Ms. Hannigan."

"Oh, that's me." A smile broke on her face.

"Oh, good. So where is it?" he asked.

"Umm, I have to confess, I thought you were a student…are you?"

"No, ma'am, I'm not. Is that a problem? Can you still help me?" Her brief hesitation had him fearing he had wasted a trip.

"Absolutely, I can." She stepped out from behind the counter and motioned to him to follow her.

The computer lab was unlike anything he had ever seen before. The walls and floor were painted white, and everything in it looked too clean to touch. It was a quarter full with students. Ms. Hannigan stopped about halfway in and looked around the room and then up at Jake. "Perhaps I'll put you in my office. The door's always left open, and it's just off the main entrance. I think you'll have a bit more privacy there."

He also felt the stares, and while he knew her suggestion was a good one, he still trusted no one. "That's not necessary. Right here's fine by me."

"No, really, I think you'll be more comfortable there."

He nodded. "OK then, if you want it that way."

She led him behind the reference counter and into a small office. "Have a seat at the desk, and I'll get you set up." He did as she asked and then watched her click the mouse and start typing. "Have you ever used one of these before?" she asked.

"No, I have not."

"OK. Well, I'm going to get you where you have to be. And then I'll be right outside that door if you have any questions." Her instructions were soft and friendly, as if she were talking to a third grader, but he didn't mind it. It was a rare feeling of comfort. As promised, she got him settled in, and he was thankful for the privacy she was sure he'd enjoy.

A big green outline of the United States sat on the screen before him; he stared at it for several seconds waiting for further instruction, but it never came. He looked at the palm-size clicker she called a mouse, moved his right hand over the top of it, and clicked. Somehow he ended up in New Mexico. After a couple more clicks, he found the letters he was looking for: CA.

The outline before him first appeared all white atop a light-brown screen, then more lines slowly appeared atop patches of green and dark brown. Seconds later, hundreds of lines began to cross the screen, forming nothing more than one large squiggly mass of confusion. He'd never seen anything like it and was transfixed as the state of California continued to build itself on the six-by-six-inch screen in front of him. His mind wandered between the small screen and those torrid days out West. For years, he had thought about going back out there if he ever made it out of prison, and now here he was, taking the initial steps toward revisiting that tumultuous time in his life.

He considered himself a strong man, much stronger than the weak, immoral man of his youth. But even now he questioned what a return to California may cost him.

"One thing at a time," he said aloud. "Just one thing at a time."

He studied the map, getting his eyes as close to the screen as possible, but he was still unable to make heads or tails of any of it. He sat back and rubbed his eyes while continuing to think about those unpleasant days out west.

"How can one man do so much harm?"

After several seconds he answered his own question. "He wasn't alone."

"Mr. Mott?"

Ms. Hannigan peeked her head through the doorway.

"Yes."

"Did you find what you were looking for?"

He looked back down at the screen and contemplated his short future. With one short answer, yes, he could get up from the chair, return to the camper inside Pennypack Park, and start a new life while trying to forget his old one.

But what did it matter anyway? He had driven all this way to map a bag of money. What else did he have to do with his life? "No. Is there any way I can look closer at the map?"

"Sure you can." She entered the room and took over the mouse.

Alone again, he made the first click on what he thought to be Los Angeles. Three clicks later, he was able to make out the small block lettering on the screen, which read LA.

He knew Big Bear Lake to be about a hundred miles east of downtown LA. He moved the mouse a few inches in that direction and clicked. A slight mist of sweat developed on his palm and brow as he watched the San Bernardino Mountains take shape before him. He knew that mountain range well and remembered riding out of the foothills on that hot spring day on his bike as if it had been yesterday.

With every click of the mouse, he became more familiar with the patterns developing on the computer screen.

Towns such as Riverside and Moreno Valley appeared before him; there was a time when he had known those places well. He followed Route 10 through the Redlands and then Banning. Banning brought a smile to his face. He'd spent four straight days there with a nineteen-year-old Mexican girl he'd met at a strip joint. Those four days alone had gotten him through his first four years in prison.

Picking up Route 62, he pictured the open road in his head just as it had been back then, a straight run through the Yucca Valley and then Twenty-Nine Palms, ended by a scenic fall into the desert. The desert…he would never forget that god-awful day in the Mojave.

Seeing Danby Lake come up on screen meant Vidal Junction was the closest town east. It was there, near Vidal, where his old friend, the man he had left to die in the desert, may very well still lie killed.

Jake took a deep breath and returned to that stretch of land between El Casco Lake and Calimesa, for there lay what he truly was looking for buried three feet in the ground. He pulled the piece of paper from his shirt pocket and began to scribble down points of interest and general landmarks.

CHAPTER 22

The boys were long gone upstairs, and the kitchen table looked as if a bomb had hit it. Lisa stared silently at the crumpled-up napkins, corn-bread droppings, and sloppy-joe-stained plates.

"Eddie didn't say much," Charlie said.

"He hasn't said much all day. He's been upset ever since I picked him up."

"Well, he can't be that upset. He ate all his food."

"No, that's you. You don't eat when you're upset...I do."

"So he takes after you, then?"

"He may have my resolve, but he has your eyes and looks."

"Well, if he has your resolve, he should be just fine." Charlie took a sip of iced tea. "Still hung over?"

"If exhausted and completely full is hung over, then yes, I am." She pushed her plate away. "Why are we having this conversation?"

"What's wrong with our conversation?"

"I mean why are we avoiding the obvious, Charlie?"

He pushed his plate aside and sat back. "There is no obvious."

"I want to know what that was this morning because it wasn't right. You should've seen yourself, it was like..." She shook her head. "I can't even explain it; it was horrible."

"I was drunk. The combination of that and what's going on in my head just got a hold of me."

"Bullshit! That was more than a drunken sleep. That was something else entirely."

She noticed him glance at the bag of unread newspapers he'd bought that afternoon.

"You've got to take your medicine tomorrow, and I'm calling Murphy's office on Monday, and that's that." His silence prompted her to get up from the table. "I'm tucking the boys in. I'll be down to clean up later." Halfway through the living room, she heard him call out.

"Do you remember the night we drove home from the shore?"

Wow, the shore. The very place they'd forged their relationship. She hadn't thought of those days in years, nor the memorable drive back.

They paid $250 for a beat-up Datsun and headed for Nebraska Lane. It broke down on some back road off Route 9. Dusk turned to night, and it got cold out.

She could rattle off her emotions on that very night: vulnerable, uncertain not only about the night but her future. Lying on the ground, she'd turned to Charlie and said, "I can't say when it was, and I'm not sure how it happened, but I dreamed of you before we ever met. I was probably alone and scared, lying in my bed...but I dreamed of you." She remembered the kiss he had planted on her and the passionate love they'd made alongside a run of beat-up railroad tracks.

Now stopping in her own tracks midway through the room, she was unable to reply. She saw Charlie standing in the doorway.

"Do you?" he asked.

"Of course I do," she whispered.

Charlie walked over to her and took hold of her arms. He pulled her body into his and kissed her. His hand ran down her back and, though she thought better of letting him proceed in the middle of the house, she quickly lost any inhibitions. It had been way too long since he had touched her that way.

They fell back onto the couch and made love.

———

Lisa stood in the boys' bedroom doorway. She caught a glimpse of Eddie's eyes studying her, so she entered the room and knelt down at his bed. She ran her hand through his hair. "Can't sleep?"

"I don't wanna live here anymore," he replied.

"Why?"

"Because I don't like it here. It's always dark."

While she wouldn't classify it that way, she understood what he meant. For her, it was the constant unknown that was always lingering, hovering over all of them and capable of striking at any moment. Eddie's perceptiveness never ceased to amaze her.

"I'm sorry for leaving you this morning."

"That's not it," Eddie replied. "I'm sick of this place."

"Sick of what, Eddie?"

"Just everything."

"Well, talk to me. If you're not specific, how can I fix it? And I will fix it, but you have to tell me what it is you're upset about."

"We were supposed to go fishing today! And I knew it. As soon as I heard him say it, I knew I shouldn't get my hopes up. He never does anything with us."

Her heart was breaking as the words fell from his mouth. "Oh, Eddie, I'm sorry. But that's Mommy's fault. It was all my fault. I had Daddy out late last night. He didn't want to go, but I made him, and we got in really late. That's why I was so late picking you up this morning. I even lost our car, and your father had to go look for it this afternoon."

"How do you lose a car?" Eddie asked.

"It's a long story."

"Dad lost our car?"

"No, Eddie, I lost our car, and if your dad had things his way, he would have been up early with you today fishing."

"He forgot. He didn't mention it all day."

"Listen to me. Your father loves you very much, and he'd do anything for you. He works very hard for this family. Do you know his work made him take this time off because he hasn't taken a single day in all the years he's been there? That's eight years of perfect attendance. Imagine never once taking off from school since you were in kindergarten or even before that."

Eddie shook his head no.

"I know it's hard to believe, but your father's going to be home for almost two full weeks, and I know you're going to be doing plenty of fun things with him."

"I have school."

"Well don't tell him I told you, but he said he's going to take you out of school one day and do whatever you want."

"Really, he said that?"

"You bet he did." She smiled. "He said you deserved it for always being such a special young man. Now get some rest, and we'll talk in the morning."

Eddie nodded his head and closed his eyes, willingly accepting her tuck-in for the night.

———

Having just clipped a new article out of the *Los Angeles Times,* Charlie dug for a single red thumbtack in the pencil holder and placed it on the town of Calimesa. He stepped back and looked at the small bell curve he'd plotted over the last few weeks...something inside him suggested this would be the last of his tracking of the California wildfires.

CHAPTER 23

Charlie threw the bag of balls over his shoulder. "Let him go; he's just having fun."

"But Billy's trying to keep up with him. He follows him everywhere."

"That's what's nice for them. They'll always have each other."

Lisa picked out a spot on the grass near the water and unfolded a few blankets. She watched Charlie walk to the far end of the field, where he gathered the boys up and brought them down to the water's edge. She didn't need to hear Eddie's words to know how happy he was; his movements alone said that.

Her surroundings were quiet, the park empty. She breathed in the fresh air, took note of the unseasonably warm day, and smiled. She had had a good conversation with Dr. Murphy this morning and felt good about Charlie's future, their future. Things were going to be OK, things were going to be just fine.

———

With the sun going down and the wind at their backs, Charlie spent two hours with his boys catching fish: eight of them, to be exact. He sat with Eddie and Billy in their room before going to bed that night and rehashed the day's events. From the very first bite to the last two that got away, they replayed it all.

It was the first time in his life he had bonded with his oldest son, and he was thankful for the opportunity.

CHAPTER 24

"*Charlie?*"

He knew this ground. It was a stretch of road that led back to the bay down the shore at whale beach. The very spot where he and Lisa had shared their first kiss.

"*Charlie?*"

That voice again, it was behind him. He turned but saw no one. He looked for Lisa, but there was no sign of life anywhere.

"*It was a good day, huh, Charlie?*"

"*What do you mean?*" *he asked the voice.*

"*You went fishing with your boys. It was a good day.*"

"*Best day of my life.*"

"*But now you have to go…isn't that right?*"

"*Go where?*"

"*Calimesa.*"

"*What about it? Is it there? Is that where I'm supposed to be?*"

"*The names of the people in your head…the bodies you step over.*"

"*Yes! Who are they?*"

A car turned off the main road, headed his way. It slowed down just enough for him to see the passengers inside. He didn't know the driver, but Lisa sat in the passenger seat. She was laughing, she was happy.

"*Wait! Come back! Lisa!*"

Standing alone again, he listened for the voice, but nothing came. He looked for another car but saw nothing. Fear! Lisa was gone, but she was happy. He took off toward the bay, running as fast as he could. He wasn't going to stop for anybody or anything. Reaching the water's edge, he dove in.

Charlie sprang up in bed as if someone had thrown cold water on him. Calimesa! What was is it about that place? What was there? And Lisa—who was she with? He jumped out of bed and ran for the basement.

He labored over the newspaper clippings, looking for any names he recognized from the names in his dream, but there was no Darrell or Darwin, Clyde or Beatrice. Not even the slightest hint of a connection in any article.

He stared at his map of fire, zooming in on the town of Calimesa with the vision of Lisa fresh in his head: the smile on her face, the laughter coming from the car that had passed him by. Passing by—that was what his life was doing to him right now. He glanced over at the hollow cinder block and cursed what sat behind it. In one swipe, he ripped half the map off the wall and threw it to the floor.

CHAPTER 25

Jake sipped what was left in his glass and gently placed it back down on the table. "Cold floors, hard beds, hard pillows, no privacy…that's prison. Second week in, I woke up with a set of feet dangling in my face. Son of a bitch hung himself. Damned if I heard it. He'd been in ten years. I was staring down thirty. Didn't eat that day; don't think I ate for a week. I was angrier than hell."

"How did you get through it?"

"It's all mental in there, a big mind game. I took it over for a bit, had things my way, but that gets old too. But that's enough about me. Listen, I came up here to say thanks. It's been nice to have somewhere to hang my hat."

"Don't mention it. It's just a beat-up old camper. I wish I could have done more for ya."

"You've done plenty. So, what the hell you been doing with yourself, Jerry?"

"Charlie?" It was Lisa calling from upstairs.

He stood before the den window looking out at the front yard, knowing it was a childish grudge he was holding, but he couldn't help it. He didn't want to answer her.

Not only was her expression in his dream was still bothering him, but she had followed through on her promise. He was scheduled to go back to Murphy's office in two Saturdays.

Trapped in a box, that's what this was. Every aspect of his life was being controlled, and he didn't know how to get any of it back.

"Charlie!"

He called back, "*What?*"

"I ordered dinner from Jerry's. They said it would be fifteen minutes."

"Jerry's?"

"Yeah, I forgot how cheap it was there. I thought it would be a nice treat for all of us."

He looked up toward the sky. "It looks like rain."

"There's an umbrella hanging inside the closet door."

He ignored her offer and threw on his Septa coat. A brisk wind hit him in the face, and a light rain began to fall. He zipped up and headed for his car.

The crowd inside Jerry's was light. Jerry walked out from behind the bar when he entered. "Damn! Twice in one week? I know I told ya not to be a stranger, but this is a little much, don't ya think?"

He wasn't in the kidding mood. "Lisa ordered food."

"Ahh, by the way, what happened to ya the other night? You were my only audience, and ya deserted me."

"Waking up on the bar wasn't how I expected to end my night, but I still heard you, Jer…it was one of your best."

"I'll take that," Jerry said.

Charlie looked around. "Light crowd, huh?"

"Must be the rain. Yell if you need anything."

Jerry disappeared into the back room with a couple of whiskeys in his hand. A waitress took Charlie's name and headed into the kitchen. She returned seconds later. "Hey, honey, you know what you ordered?"

"No," he said.

"Well, would you mind calling home? Dumb cook's been taking orders the last twenty minutes without writing names down. Must be high on grass."

Charlie dug into his pocket and pulled out a dime. He glanced over at the built-in phone booth in the back room. It was empty. He got up from the bar and entered the back room; Jerry sat at a table by himself on the far wall.

"Drinking alone?" he asked.

"Waitin' for a buddy of mine. He's in the john."

"I just gotta make a quick call home," Charlie said.

"No bother."

He put his dime in and dialed the home number…it was a busy signal. He hung up and dialed again, but a second time, it was busy. He sat back and looked over the hundreds of scribblings, some etched but most written in the tiny wooden cubicle. *Why is everything in my life such a wait?* He laughed as if it was anything but funny, and then Charlie heard a voice he recognized.

———

"It's nice to do your business in privacy. You take it for granted, you know?" Jake retook his seat. "I've only been out a week, but it already feels a year."

"If time only went by like that inside, huh?" Jerry replied.

"You ain't shittin'."

"Then I take it you have no plans on going back."

"Not if I can help it."

"So what are you gonna do, Jake? I mean, what are you gonna do about work?"

"Not sure. As much as I've heard it's a changed world, I don't see many people hiring an old ex-convict, black no less."

"Well, you're just gonna have to give it some time. I could probably find some part-time work for ya 'round here—just dishes and stuff—it wouldn't be much, but it'd be something."

"I appreciate it, but I don't think it'll be necessary." Jake took a long sip of his whiskey and put it back down. "There is one thing I've thought of doing. Thought of it quite a bit, actually."

"What's that?"

"When I got back from 'Nam, I hooked up with a guy that I ran with for a little while. We did our fair share of traveling—never in the same city twice, never stayed more than two nights. Shit, I think we crisscrossed half the country at one point."

"Should I ask?"

"No, and I thank you for not asking." He paused before continuing. "There was a stretch of time when I'd slowed down enough to actually plant my feet, and I found myself in LA working for a guy named Ronnie Wood. Wood owned a nightclub. It was an odd place, a real mix of people: bikers, Hollywood types.

The guy was printing money, though, plus he had a million-dollar book he was running out the back room."

"A million? Holy shit, that's a world of money."

"Word was he was backed by some guys from Vegas. I don't know if he was or wasn't. Didn't care much, either." He took another sip of whiskey. "So, one night Ronnie told me to lock the place up and come into the back office, said he needed me to move some safe around for him. So I do what he says. I lock the place up and walk into the back." He could still recall the empty beer bottles, countless, that he'd have to kick away to make a path to walk in at the end of every night.

"And?" Jerry said.

"So I walk into his office and I find him dead, right on the floor...dead as can be in the middle of the fucking floor."

Jerry's mouth dropped, and his shoulders shrank. "You gotta be shittin' me."

"Now, I ain't no doctor, but I was the only one in the place, and he didn't kill himself."

"So how'd he die?"

Jake shook his head. "Damned if I know for sure. Maybe the cocaine he snorted all day finally caught up to him. Whatever it was, it left me in a situation: a dead man on the floor and a bag at his feet."

"What bag?" Jerry said.

"A bag, a big bag. I looked over and saw the safe he was talking about. Thing was half the size of me. Then I looked back down at the bag. Half a second later, I had the thing torn open, and I was a-countin'."

"How much?"

He just stared into Jerry's eyes.

"How much, Jake?"

"I never counted all of it, but it was somewhere around three fifty."

"Three hundred fifty or three hundred and fifty *thousand*?"

He answered his question in a roundabout way. "I didn't stay another minute. I had the bag zipped up and tied to my bike, and I was moving ninety miles an hour out of town before I even realized what the hell happened." Jake shook his head as if he still didn't believe it. "Potluck, nothing but pure potluck."

"Where did you go?"

"Drove far out of LA and stayed out. Spent seven days holed up in some wooded shack in the foothills. I was thinking, *be patient, no need to rush things.* Wanted to make sure the dust had settled before I even drove out of the mountains. Ronnie Wood was no angel, but he still had friends, both good and bad. But I wasn't overly worried about the law."

"So what did you do with the money?"

"I spent a little of it. Not much, though. Never really had time to."

"So?"

"So I ended up burying it. I buried it three feet in the ground." He paused. "And then I drove to Mexico."

Jerry sat back and took in what he'd just heard. "That's quite a story, Jake."

"Yes, it is."

"I'm not sure I wanna know the answer to this, but why you tellin' me?"

He shrugged. "Didn't know I was going to. Guess I just needed to share it with somebody at some point. I ended up going away shortly after that. I know it's been a long time, but I felt like I knew ya well in 'Nam, and, well, what you did for me when I got out...I just figured you were about the only person I could trust."

Jerry smiled. "Yeah, well, dodging bullets ten thousand miles away from home will match up the unlikeliest of people."

Jake sat silently thinking of 'Nam, a time and place he'd rather not go to—the very place he blamed for most of his failures.

"Jake?" Jerry said.

"When I first got in, there was an old convict I warmed up to. It's been so long I can't remember his name, but he said something that always stuck with me. He said, 'Once a crook, always a crook. You can be good for years at a time and do nothing, but deep down inside, it never leaves. Deep down it sits, and it'll rise whenever it damn well pleases.' When he said those words, I knew what he meant. I'm trying my best to become a God-fearing man, but sometimes I doubt there's no more criminal left in this old boy."

Jerry picked up his whiskey for the first time and gulped half of it, then sat up in his chair. "We've all made mistakes, Jake. Hell, that's what life's all about. It wasn't us who put us over there to do what we did, and God knows what we did wasn't any good. Now, how some of us dealt with the aftermath was different than others, but so be it...there's only one judge and jury, and you're not there yet. Now, if you came here to get something off your chest, then that's fine; I think I've obliged. But if it's my approval you're lookin' for, to go chasin' a bag of money...well, you sure as hell don't need that. You've paid your debt to society. Twice, no less."

Jerry's kind words did little to heal the deep scars he still felt. "Three feet deep near El Casco Lake, just outside a town called Calimesa. There's been a hell of a wildfire coming out of the foothills, though, started last month in Rialto, about thirty miles west of San Bernardino. I heard it's charred up some seven thousand acres. Mighta ripped right through that range. Mighta ripped right thru Calimesa."

"It did not."

The soft whisper coming from the other side of the room seemed to be in desperate need of air. Its maker stood perfectly still, his eyes wide, his heart appearing to be beating outside his chest. "It stopped short, and it was three thousand acres, not seven. A crosswind came from the north and took it south to Gorgone. It just missed it, though...it just missed Calimesa."

Jake recognized him from the 7-eleven. "And what makes you the expert?"

His gaze firmly fixed on Jake, Charlie replied, "Because I've been tracking it, tracking it every day for the last three weeks of my life. I've held vigil over its path. Every town it's destroyed, every river it's crossed, every life it's taken, I've got it all...in my basement."

Jerry spoke. "This, ah, this is Charlie Boone, Jake. A neighborhood guy. Charlie, this is Jake Mott, old friend of mine. Jake and I served a couple years together."

"You wanna hear about it?" Jake asked.

"Hear about what?" Charlie replied.

"'Nam."

"No, but I just overheard you speaking."

"You always listen to other people's conversations?" Jake asked.

"Only when I've heard them before."

Jake looked to Jerry. "What's this guy talking about, Jerry? Sounds like nonsense."

Charlie spoke up. "Your conversation, your voice. I overheard all of it some ten years ago, and now I know why...it makes sense to me now."

Jake fidgeted in his chair and pulled his back up.

"You remember me, tell me you do." Charlie said.

"You two know each other?" Jerry asked.

"Seems that way," Jake mumbled.

"You're shittin' me! What the hell are the chances of that?"

Jake said nothing.

"More than I think we even know," Charlie replied. He stepped closer toward the table. "I'd like to talk with you."

"I'm not in a talkative mood. Besides that, I'm a private man."

Jerry stood up and put his hand on Charlie's shoulder. "Hey Charlie, listen, your food's probably done, huh? Let's go get it, get it home to the kids."

"I got to talk to you about some things...I *need* to talk with you!"

Jerry put his other hand on Charlie's chest, trying to direct him to the front bar. "OK, but not tonight, Charlie, huh? The little ones are waiting to eat, right? Come on, let's go."

Jerry walked him out of the back room and into the main bar. "Listen, man, that was a private conversation we were having back there, and Jake's not the friendly type. Now come on, Charlie. Your food's up. Go on home."

Charlie looked back at Jake sitting at the table. "There's a reason why, Jerry."

"What the fuck are you talking about, Charlie?" Jerry asked.

"I have to talk with him. Jerry, listen! You don't understand; this means everything!"

"Hey, stop it! You're soundin' crazy. Now I'm not gonna be so nice about it in another second. Forget about what ya heard back there Charlie and get home."

———

Jake purchased some packaged goods before saying good-bye to Jerry and then made his way home for the night. It was half past nine. He spent the short trip back to the camper with the radio turned down. He was deep in thought. It was good to see his old friend again. The years had been better to Jerry than to him—maybe not physically, but certainly mentally. Jake was in good shape for his age, and considering the hard years of his past, he had aged reasonably well. Jerry, on the other hand, liked his liquor, and it showed. Still, Jake envied him for the sense of peace he seemed to have.

His last thought before turning down the dirt drive that led into the back-woods of Pennypack Park was of Charlie Boone. He didn't like him and hoped that he'd never see him again.

Charlie slowed his car to a crawl before watching Jake's pickup make a right turn down an old dirt road. While it wasn't the entrance to Pennypack Park he was familiar with, he knew enough of the area to know the dirt road was a seldom-used back entrance to the park. Certain things were beginning to make sense. Absorbed in the moment, he kept close watch on the pickup's taillights until they disappeared into the dense woods.

CHAPTER 26

She'd been yelling all morning, and all he could do was take it.

"How many times do I have to say I'm sorry?"

"How about as many as it takes? You go to pick up food for your children, Charlie, never mind me. What about your kids, who are home hungry while you're having beers at the bar!"

"Keep it down."

"No, I will *not* keep it down. I am *done* hiding things from them. He's smarter than the two of us put together. He sees right through our lies, all of our bullshit. I'm not gonna lie anymore."

"I was gone an hour."

"Two. You were gone two *fucking* hours, for a place that's five minutes away."

"They were busy," he said.

"Bullshit. I spoke to Jerry. He said you left over forty minutes before I called. Now where were you, Charlie? Where did you go?"

"I drove around."

Lisa picked up the closest thing within her reach—Billy's plastic juice bottle—and threw it at him. "Don't lie to me, you son of a bitch."

Eddie and Billy ran into the kitchen. Their frightened eyes said it all. The happiness and normalcy of yesterday's family outing seemed to have been stripped from the home in just one day.

He needed to say something, but the truth wasn't an option. It killed him to do so, but he had to lie. "I'm sorry, Eddie. I stayed longer than I should have. Time got away from me. I met one of Jerry's old war buddies, and time just got away from me."

Lisa walked behind Eddie and rested her hand on his shoulder. "Come on, Eddie. Mommy's gonna drive you to school today. Get your coat on."

Eddie glanced up at him with a look that said it was OK, that he understood, and Charlie needed it.

"I'm taking Billy with me, and we're gonna be out all day. You can take care of your mother yourself."

"Hey, Eddie?" Charlie called out to his son. "Whatta ya say we go out to dinner tonight? We'll go to Ponderosa for that all-you-can-eat buffet. That one we saw on TV. Sound like a deal?"

Eddie nodded. "Yeah, that would be great."

Lisa sneered at him on her way out of the kitchen and mouthed back, "We'll see."

With the slamming of the front door, Charlie retreated to the basement and began pulling down what remained of his wall of fire. Though he took little satisfaction in destroying the mural that had consumed him, he found comfort in the thought that he was one step closer to knowing why. The previous night's encounter with Jake Mott had brought clarity to the last three weeks. The wildfires, his drive to Pennypack Park just days earlier, the voice he had heard coming over the tree line, the faceless stranger he'd been seeing his whole life…Bear disappearing only to be found by Jake himself. *This was it. It was all about this man.* A mild spark ignited in the pit of his stomach. For once in his life, he truly felt alive.

CHAPTER 27

"Charlie?" Lisa said in a whisper.

He'd been up all night listening to the storm, wide-eyed but still. "I'm here."

"What was that noise?" she asked.

"Our doorbell."

"Our doorbell? Our doorbell doesn't work…it never has."

"It used to work, years ago."

Lisa squinted at the bedroom window. A driving rain bounced off the plate glass front. "The doorbell hasn't worked in ten years. You're telling me in the middle of a typhoon it's going to start working?"

He got up and grabbed for his jeans lying on the floor.

"Where are you going?"

"I'm gonna go answer it."

"Are you out of your mind? There's no one down there."

He put his hand up. "Allow me the moment, please. It's been decades since I've answered a doorbell in this house." With a playful grin on his face, he continued. "It may never ring again."

He watched her glance down at the lump at her feet, which was Billy.

"What time'd he come in?"

"Couple hours ago. I'll be right back."

Nightlights from Eddie's and his mother's bedrooms cascaded into the darkened hallway. He passed each door, stopping just enough to make sure they were both in bed.

He took to the steps expecting to find no one, assuming a strong wind may have knocked some loose wires tight again. Unless, that is, it was Jake Mott coming to call on him.

He glanced at his watch (it was 1:55 a.m.), unlocked the dead bolt, and opened the door.

The stranger looked to be in his midsixties. He had fine-looking, boyish blond hair and was dripping wet. He stood motionless on the porch with an odd grin on his face as raindrops pelted off his body. The darkened backdrop was lit up from nearby lightning, while the rolls of thunder were so loud Charlie felt the house shudder.

"Can I help you?"

"I hope so. My truck broke down just up the block there." He pointed to a flash of red hazards about two blocks up on the opposite side of the street. Charlie could just see it from his semidry perch in the doorway. He recognized those taillights as ones he'd seen in the past too. Even in the dark of night, he could make out the rounded, boxed body of a split-windshield 1950s pickup.

"What kind of pick up is that?" he asked.

The stranger replied with a grin, "A dead one. Bought it off an old friend for a few dollars. Guess it serves me right. Anyway, I'm sorry to bother ya, but you were the only porch light on."

Whatever band of wires had restored themselves must also have controlled the porch light, because like the doorbell, it hadn't worked in years.

Lisa called down the steps, "Charlie, who are you talking to?"

He stepped back into the house and looked up the narrow staircase. She stood at the top with one hand holding her robe shut. "Someone broke down in the storm."

"Who?"

"I don't know who he is."

"Who the hell would be out in this weather?"

"I don't know."

"Are you trying to scare me, Charlie?"

"No, I'm not trying to scare you. Look out the window and see for yourself, pickup truck half a block up." Seeing her run from his sight, he returned his attention to the stranger. "What's wrong with your truck?"

"Not sure. I'm thinking just a jump might be the fix. It stalled out on me and now won't even turn over."

Charlie looked over the man's shoulder and into the street. It seemed as if a foot of water was flowing down the block like a whitewater rapid. "How the hell did you even drive in this?"

"Wasn't easy."

Is this a dream? He reached around the side of the door and pushed the doorbell in—sure enough, it went off.

"When the bell strikes it's time to go," the man said.

"What does that mean?" Charlie asked.

"Hopefully it means I can make it home tonight. Can you help me?"

"Sure, I can help," he said. "I'll come have a look with you. If it's a jump you need, then I'll try to bring my car up. Just let me get my boots and a flashlight."

The stranger looked as if he'd just been given second life. "Oh, bless you. You're an angel. I'll wait for you here."

Charlie closed the door and walked away, but after a few steps went back and locked the dead bolt, an action he knew the stranger could hear, but he felt better knowing it was done.

He grabbed his snow boots off the cellar steps and threw his fisherman's raincoat over his shoulders. He checked the flashlight before throwing it deep into his pocket and then grabbed his own keys off the kitchen table.

Lisa called down the steps as he approached the door. "Where are you going?"

"I'll be two minutes."

"Absolutely not, Charlie! Who is this guy?"

"The man needs help, Lisa. I'll be right back."

"I don't give a damn what he needs. Who's out in a storm like this at this hour?"

It's a good question. "He said we were the only porch light on the whole block."

"Porch light? That light hasn't worked either."

"I know it hasn't." The expression on her face said it all: don't go out there. "He seems friendly enough. Keep an eye from the window."

"Charlie!"

He opened the door and stood still. The porch was empty. He looked both ways, but there was still no sign of him.

Lisa stuck her head out. "Where'd he go?"

"Maybe back up to the truck, but I don't see it anymore. The taillights are gone." He looked back at Lisa and asked, "You did see a truck up there, right?"

Lisa slowly nodded. "I did."

Charlie descended the porch steps into an unrelenting, pounding rain. "He may have lost his lights if the battery went totally dead."

"So what?"

"So, I'm gonna go check it out!"

"Would you look at it out here?"

"I told the man I'd give him a hand. What if that was me who was broke down or even you and the kids? I'd want someone to help me out, and so would you."

"And out of all the houses on the block, he had to knock on this one? That spells weird right off the bat."

"What the hell is that supposed to mean?"

"It's the shittiest house on the block."

"What's shitty to you might be inviting to others. Now go back inside and sit with your kids. They're probably scared half to death."

He moved swiftly toward the curb as raindrops the size of quarters pummeled his body. A strong current passed underneath him. He grabbed hold of his footing and trudged his way across to the other side. Up on the sidewalk again, he took his flashlight from this pocket and aimed in the direction of the truck, but there was no dark outline, no red eyes blinking in the night.

He turned back toward home. True to the stranger's words, his was the only house lit on the block; not even a single street light was on. He stayed there in the middle of Nebraska Lane, standing in a foot of water while rain continued to pour from the sky, staring at his lit-up house. It was all too surreal.

"Fantastik," he whispered.

A muffled pounding sound came from inside his bedroom window. It was Lisa, motioning for him to get inside. Baffled and even a bit disappointed for reasons unknown, he walked back into the house and locked up.

He sat on the recliner near the window, looking out at the worst storm he could recall in years. *Is it possible that a messenger has been sent?* His mind was fixed on one thing: Jake Mott.

He looked down at the set of keys in his hand and clenched them. He knew exactly how to get there, and over the last three days had made the trip half a dozen times in his own head. But what would he do once he got there? What would he say?

He went into the kitchen and took the bottle of Nyquil from the cupboard, filled three quarters of a coffee mug, and downed it. Slurping cold water from the kitchen faucet, he visualized the canister of sleeping pills inside the medicine cabinet upstairs. He'd bought them off a co-worker for fifteen bucks sometime last year, swearing only to use them in the direst need. Perhaps tonight he would; morning couldn't come fast enough.

He fell back into the recliner and kicked his feet up, hoping the Nyquil would set in before he had to take anything else.

All he saw was land, field after field. The wind was blowing in his face, and the scenery was more beautiful than he could ever imagine. Cattle grazing, horses galloping, silos the size of city buildings, broken-down barns, and mended fences. He was in middle of America, and he loved it.

But he wasn't driving. It wasn't his truck he was in, either. His truck didn't have cracked-up black seats. His were cracked blue.

Looking to his left, he saw his driver for the first time. It didn't quite matter how one looked at Jake Mott, by profile or straight on; his pained expression and hard look were constant.

Jake looked over at him and nodded his head, as if to say, "We've made it."

"You hear that?" Charlie asked.

"Hear what?" Jake replied.

"That chopper." He looked out his window and up at the clear blue sky. "I hear it. It's a Bar-M. You ever seen one?"

"Seen what?" Jake asked.

"A Bar-M chopper. You ever seen one?"

"If it's a flying angel, then it pulled me out of the jungle many years ago."

Charlie looked back at Jake. "I've never been on one, but that's my ride to heaven."

Yelling over the gusts of wind cutting through the truck's cab, Jake yelled back, "I've got ink."

"What is ink?"

"A tattoo. I got a Colt just over my left shoulder. Only pet I ever had. He watches over me."

Charlie shook his head, entranced at the tranquility of the landscape.

"Thanks, by the way," Jake yelled back.

"For what?"

"For coming on this trip."

CHAPTER 28

He awoke with that groggy feeling that only Nyquil can leave behind, but there was no fuzziness about what he'd dreamed. If there was ever a sign he thought he should follow, it was that dream, and he had little doubt about it now.

Dawn had broken, and the torrential downpour of a few hours earlier had calmed to a light rain. Still sitting in the recliner, Charlie stared out the window.

From where he sat, he caught a glimpse of a small hole near the steps where the living room wall met the floor. He hadn't noticed that hole in years but recalled being a small child, his face pressed up against it as he struggled to catch sight of something in the darkness on the other side. How unfortunate that he was still struggling to catch a glimpse of something in the darkness.

The very thought of being in the same chair and having the same thought ten years from now was devastating. *Destiny! What will mine be?* According to Lisa's psychic and his own vision, his destiny was sitting alone in this house a very old man, alone and no closer to the truth.

When the bell strikes, it's time to go. Well, this was his time; the bell had struck. If he didn't act and confront Jake Mott now, the mystery that was his life may never be solved.

Standing up, Charlie looked around the room and at that moment vowed two things: he would not die old and alone in this home, and another day would not pass without his speaking to the man whom he believed could free him of it all.

CHAPTER 29

Drops of water against a tin roof: it was a new sound to him as he lay in bed with his feet dangling off the side. They were coming down by the hundreds, light and steady. The cool air creeping in through the small window made the hot, fly-infested air of Georgia State Prison seem a lifetime away.

He looked forward to hitting the road and making his way out west but was unsure when. In the end, he'd decide to go when the moment struck, for the regimented schedule of prison life was no longer a part of him.

Grabbing a few of his dirty T-shirts off the floor, he swung open the camper door and, after a few shakes, draped the first shirt over the empty flower box that hung from the side of the camper, just as his momma had done when he was a boy growing up in Texas.

He repeated the process with another shirt but then abruptly stopped. There was a presence. It was instinctive—the knowing, almost as if he had eyes in the back of his head; years on the run could do that to a person.

Jake brought his arms to rest by his side and leaned slightly inside the camper, just in case he needed to make a grab for Jerry's gun. In his youth, this would have been done already, but for the moment, he'd try a different way.

"Can I help you?" he asked.

"I just walked up when you opened the door. I was about to knock."

He asked again, this time emphasizing his words. "Can I help you?"

"I'm not here for trouble," Charlie said.

"Then why are you here?"

"Because I can't get you out of my head."

"Sounds like a problem of yours, not mine."

Charlie looked down at his feet. "I tried everything in me not to come here, but I couldn't stay away. I can't stop thinking about what happened at Jerry's, and sure as I'm standing here, I know what I'm doing is the right thing."

"And what is the right thing?" Jake asked.

"Coming here. I need to talk to you; there are things that have been happening to me, things that point to you...things we need to discuss."

"What in the hell are you talking about, son?"

"I mapped three hundred miles of a forest fire I knew nothing about. It consumed me for three weeks, and for the life of me, I couldn't explain it. Then I met you, and when you asked about it that night, for once things made sense. Things clicked for me, and that's just the start of it...I've been searching for something my whole life, and Sunday night at Jerry's, I found it."

Jake threw his T-shirt back over his shoulder and descended the small camper steps. He stopped just short of Charlie's feet. "Now, you listen to what I'm about to say, 'cause I ain't gonna ever say it again. I don't know what you want from me, but if it's money, then go on, drive yourself out to California and get it. It's all yours. But keep in mind one thing: there's reasons a man like me goes away for thirty years, and one of 'em ain't to be browbeaten by some punk who's probably never done more than throw a sissy punch his whole sorry-ass life. Now, I'm a private man, and I don't appreciate you coming here. So I suggest you get back in your truck and don't ever come back here." Feeling confident he'd done enough to scare Charlie off, Jake turned around and headed back toward the camper.

"I don't want money, and I don't have an agenda," Charlie called out.

"Then go home," Jake said over his shoulder.

"I wish you'd reconsider."

He stopped at the camper steps and turned. "Reconsider what, fool?"

"I need to go to California with you. I can help you share the driving."

"Son, you don't even know me. I just got out of state prison not three weeks ago, and you wanna hop in a truck and drive across country with me? What the hell for?"

"Because that's what I'm feeling. There's a reason we met at the bar, there's a reason you found my dog. There's reasons why our paths crossed! And I'm here to find out why."

"Shit, you *must* be on crack, and I don't got time for it."

"It is what it is," Charlie said adamantly.

"That's right, and it's *fucking* crazy! Why in hell would I go with you any-where? I don't like the way you look, I don't like the way you talk, and we sure as hell ain't the same people. I'd eat you up and spit you out before we left the state. Now go home and leave me the *fuck* alone."

Jake climbed the camper steps and reached for the door.

"You have a picture of a colt on your left shoulder blade!" Charlie's tone was authoritative; there was conviction in his words. "It's some sort of pet for you. He was yours, and he looks after you...he looks over your shoulder."

Jake stood still in the doorway; a chill ran up his spine. With his back to Charlie, he slowly turned. Speaking softly, he said, "Say that again."

"Ink, you called it."

Jake could see the water collecting in Charlie's eyes, as if the boy's emotions were getting the better of him.

"It's a tattoo. He meant something to you, and now he looks after you. He watches over your shoulder."

Jake's mouth went dry. "And just how do you know that?"

"You told me," Charlie said, his voice was fluttering. "Last night you came to me in my dream and you *told* me that! You also thanked me for coming on this trip with you."

There wasn't a person in the world who knew about his tattoo. He had gotten it from some second-rate artist on a backwoods road when he got back from the war. Even in his prison years, it was hardly ever noticed, hidden by his dark skin. He stood silent and confused.

"Have you ever done something that you knew wasn't normal, but it felt right to do anyway? Well, I've been doing that my whole life. Mixed messages, crossed signals, visions, dreams that make no sense...but coming here, after seeing you the other night—not only does it seem normal, but I know it's the right thing."

Jake couldn't get past the colt reference. He was falling to pieces inside. He wanted to run inside the camper like a little girl and cry. Staring straight ahead, he said, "Sounds like you need help, son. Sounds like you need more than I'm capable of giving. Now, I don't know how you knew what you did, but I don't want nothin' to do with ya. So don't come round here no more. That's it. No more."

Jake stepped inside the camper and shut the door. Peering out a small window, he watched Charlie drop a sealed envelope in his truck and then leave. He grabbed for the whiskey bottle on the counter and uncapped it, took a long swig, and then another. Pulling Jerry's gun out of the drawer, he threw it onto the counter. His heart was racing.

CHAPTER 30

A t four thirty in the morning, the dense brush of Pennypack Woods made the already-dark camper pitch black. Three empties sat on the kitchen counter, while the fourth rested against his stomach as he lay in bed. A slight change in position caused the empty fifth of Jack Daniels to fall to the floor and dance around in a circle before coming to rest on the beat-up linoleum. Awoken by the noise, Jake abruptly sat up. Something large scampered away. He was familiar with that sound too. Living with rodents hadn't bothered him in prison, and it wouldn't bother him on this night either. He gave his eyes a good rub and felt for his forehead.

He didn't remember anything after the second fifth but knew he could thank Charlie Boone for his drunken sleep. His mouth was bone dry, he had a splitting headache, and his first thought was of the crazy white guy who'd called on him that evening.

He went back to Georgia State, but only to get Charlie off his mind. He looked at his wristwatch; it was 4:30 a.m. Three hours till first call for breakfast. The menu would be the same: watered-down scrambled eggs, stale bread that became even harder when toasted, and some brown stuff they pawned off as hash browns.

As bad as they were, he could actually go for some right now.

He stood up as best he could in the small space and stepped inside the bathroom. He lit the two candles he had bought from Save Right. Cupping his left hand, he poured water from a gallon jug, splashed his face, and then took a few swigs.

That old boy had rattled him earlier, rattled him enough to put the thought in his head. He looked down at his right hand and wondered if it could even do the job anymore. Pulling a trigger seemed a much bigger task than it had thirty years ago. He hoped it couldn't. Even prayed at times that he'd never find out.

His mind grappled with a vision of Charlie Boone, standing out there in the rain, staring at him.

Jake stopped what he was doing and placed the jug of water on the sink. He reached behind him and pulled the bathroom door shut. It was just enough so that his naked back showed in the slim mirror on the door. Looking into the small mirror above the sink, he stared at the outline of the colt planted on his left shoulder blade and gave it a name. "Thunder," he whispered.

He reached over his shoulder, rubbed the colt, and then remembered the sealed envelope that Charlie had thrown into his cab. He grabbed one of the candles off the sink and made his way to the truck.

———

Charlie glanced over at the digital clock in their bedroom. It was 8:43 p.m. They rarely received telephone calls, especially that late at night.

He picked up on the second ring. "Hello."

There was silence at the other end of the line, and then he heard Jake's voice. "You said something about doing stuff you know ain't right but you do it anyway because it feels right to do."

"Yes, I did."

"That kind of thinking can get a fella in trouble."

"I guess some things we have no control over," Charlie replied.

"That's the young speaking."

"Maybe."

"Yeah...maybe." Silence took over the line for what seemed like an eternity. "I'll be down at Jerry's."

Charlie got out of bed. Barely able to get it out, he asked, "When?"

"Now."

CHAPTER 31

C harlie stood in the entrance to the back room. Jake sat in the same seat he'd been in that past Sunday. He was stoic as always, and he had a whiskey in front of him.

"Thanks for calling," Charlie said.

"He was a Caspian," Jake replied. Staring into his shot glass he continued, "A rare breed of horse, arguably the oldest breed that still exists, but that's not what made him special. That horse had heart. That horse had feelings...no different than yours or mine. He was shot dead by some crackers out joyriding from town. He was shot because he was owned by niggers. That horse was the only true friend I ever had. I buried 'im myself, and from that day on, I stopped feeling things. I put 'im on my shoulder when I came back from 'Nam."

Charlie whispered, "What was his name?"

Jake looked up from his shot glass, his eyes went wide, and his expression softened. "Thunder," Jake replied. "He was born wild on the side of a dirt road we called Thunder." Jake motioned to an empty chair across the table from him. "Have a seat."

———

"You wanna drink?" Jake asked.

Charlie shook his head no.

"You don't drink?"

"I do drink. But I think I want a clear head for this conversation."

"A clear head, huh? Well I came here to drink, and that's what I'm gonna do." Jake took another sip from the rocks glass sitting in front of him.

"Why did you call me?" Charlie asked.

"Because you asked me, remember? The sealed envelope you left behind. It said, 'How to get ahold of me' in big letters. You left your address and your phone number." Jake shook his head. "Stupidest thing I ever saw."

"Stupid? Why?"

"Do I have to keep reminding you? We don't know each other. I've spent half my life in prison…you don't know what I'm capable of, son."

"I trust you," Charlie replied.

Jake shot him a look of disdain. "Well, you shouldn't! That's your first mistake. Trust anyone but yourself, and you'll wind up dead. Shit, you can't even trust yourself at times."

"Why did you call me?" he asked again. "I'm glad you did and I knew you would, but I wanna hear it from you."

Halfway to his mouth, Jake put his glass down. "What are you, by the way? Some kind of psychic or something?"

"I'm just a guy looking for some answers."

"Answers to what? For the love of God, what answers can I possibly have for you?"

Charlie remained silent. Several moments passed as both men continued to stare at each other.

"I did three tours," Jake said. "I came home for good on the *Forestall*, it was January 1968, touched ground in San Diego. I was twenty-two, had a little money in my pocket…shit, by that time, I thought I'd seen the world over. Thought I had all the answers, too. Wasn't back four hours and bought myself a cycle." A slight grin took hold of Jake. "A Harley, Shovelhead. It was the most beautiful thing I'd laid eyes on in years, silver polished and chrome all over. Never rode a bike before, but I didn't care. Learned how to drive it on my way out of the lot.

"I drove straight out of the city…nowhere to be, nowhere to go, and not a care in the world. About an hour into the hills, I was coming round a sharp bend and lost control…ran right off the road through a fence and finally stalled out in some high grass." Jake fell silent for a moment. "There I was, lying on the ground in a foreign field, and for the life of me, I thought I was back in Vietnam. Then, all the sudden, I felt this nudge on the back of my neck. Kind of woke me up. I turned around, half expecting to see a rifle in my face, and right there staring back at me was a little filly."

"A filly?"

Jake took a sip of whiskey. "A female horse. They're an amazing animal, horses. I shoved the bike off me, got up, and rubbed her snout." Jake smiled. "Then I smacked her ass and watched her run. Damn if I didn't feel like I was right back in Texas watchin' old Thunder. I sat there and watched that horse run for hours.

"Next town I hit, I tracked down an artist and paid him good money to put Thunder on my shoulder. It'd been too long since I'd thought of that colt… just way too long." Jake picked up the rocks glass and finished off what was left.

"Before last night…before I told you what I did…when was the last time you thought of him?"

Jake looked him in the eye. "Every stinking, rotten day."

Charlie sat up in his chair and leaned in. "Why did you call me?"

Jake studied him before answering. "I don't know. Maybe I was curious, or maybe I just had to know for myself that you're nothing more than a crazy shit looking for a payday."

"I'm not, and I'm not looking for a payday. What I dreamed was real, and you know it."

Jake peered out into the bar area before pulling a fifth of JD from his coat pocket and pouring himself another drink. "I didn't come here to talk about me. I wanna know who you are and what you want."

"You believe in destiny, Jake?" Charlie asked.

Jake sat back and looked at Charlie. "Destiny?"

"Yeah, destiny! Fortune, fate."

"Oh, I know what it is. I may not be schooled, but I'm an educated man. And I'll tell ya there's another word for your *destiny*, in case you weren't aware."

"What's that?"

"Doom! You believe in doom, son?"

Even sitting down, Jake was a large man. There was a callousness to his tone that made Charlie second-guess his even being there. But like an old dog, he knew the ex-convict could sense fear. If he was going to get anything out of this meeting, he'd have to stand his ground.

"I'm not afraid of you," Charlie whispered.

"Well, you should be."

"You've said that before."

"Are you testing me, boy?"

"Don't call me boy. My name's Charlie Boone. Now, whether you believe it or not, there's a reason why we met, and I'll be damned if I'm gonna let it pass by without doing something about it."

"You talk nonsense, you know that? I knew guys like you. They'd throw them in lockup for months at a time." Jake shook his head. "Every time they came out, they were just a little worse off, too. They should do us all a favor and just take 'im out back and shoot 'im like a maimed dog. That's what I used to say."

"That might scare me if you really believed it, but you don't. You're a better person than that."

Jake laughed. "You think so?"

"I do...I can read people."

Jake leaned in. "Then read this: don't *fuck* with me!"

"That's not why I'm here. Last night when I told you about my dream, that shook you."

Jake's eyes squinted as he focused in. "Shook me? Nah, that didn't shake me. But it did get me wondering about who you were...who you know, what you care to know about me—but some dream you claim to have had? Nah, that didn't shake me. Fact is, I don't trust you very much, and I think you're a nuisance, putting your head into other people's business where it don't belong."

"You wouldn't be here if that were true."

"You're a disturbed kid," Jake shot back.

"You're wrong."

"I'm never wrong...not about my gut."

"Let me ask you something. Did Jerry Ryan know you had a tattoo of a dead horse on your shoulder?"

Jake sat silent.

"Listen to me. I've been seeing things my whole life, things that made no sense to me, and I've had a lost feeling, like a piece of me has been missing and I'll never be complete without it. But that night, right here in this room, when I heard your voice and I heard your story, when I saw you, I felt something.

That's why I can't stay away, and I won't." He fell silent before continuing. "I'm going to California with you because that's what I'm supposed to do."

Jake took a long, slow swig of whiskey and then placed his drink back on the table. "You done?" he asked.

Charlie nodded.

"Good! Now save me your cosmic, psychic-ass bullshit. You got a line of shit on you as good and long as I've seen. Talk to me straight and maybe we'll get somewhere, but leave the other shit behind!"

"I am talking to you straight."

"Bullshit you are! You're talking nonsense."

"I'm going to California with you. I've waited too long for this, and I'll be damned if it's going to pass me by."

"Man, what the *fuck* are you talking about?"

"It's everything! It's my life...my family...my wife! I need this." He pointed to his chest. "Me! I know what this is; you don't. I got to make it right because if I don't, I'll lose them all."

"Let's get something straight right now! You and I ain't goin' nowhere together, ever."

"Why?"

"Because I said so, damn it, that's why!" Jake sat up in his chair. "You're nothing but a kid who ain't ever seen the harder part of life. Wet behind the ears, down on your luck, and need a little money in your pocket. That's what this is. I'm no fool. You probably got a wife and kids at home who don't know you're even here. You have a hard time feeding 'em; maybe you're out of work. So you hear about a little money tucked away somewhere, and crazy thoughts start running 'round your head. Thoughts you probably ain't even capable of."

"You done?" Charlie asked.

Jake didn't reply.

"My life's been far from easy. I've struggled more than I care to tell and survived it all. And as far as luck's concerned, well, I've never had any. I do have a wife and kids at home, and they love me very much. I've spent more time in this place the last five days than I have the last five years, and I don't give a shit whether you're chasing a bag of money or a bag of rocks. That's not why I'm here."

"Then why are you here?"

"Because I'm close to finally piecing it all together. Because you came to me in my dream and told me about a horse I knew nothing about. So don't sit there with that look on your face and tell me that I'm fucking crazy, because I'm not. I'm stone-cold sane, and if you have the balls you say you do, then you'll look me in the eye right now and tell me otherwise. But I know you won't because I read you, and you know it's not true. You know I'm not crazy."

"You always this way?"

Charlie didn't reply.

"I've seen crazy. I've looked it in the eye more than I'd like to talk about and more than you'll ever want to know." Jake sat silent. "You're not crazy, but you are stupid. But I don't gotta do shit, understand me? I'm a grown man, and I'll do what I want, when I want. It's obvious you don't know much about respecting other people's business."

"Respect? And what do you know about respect? Did you get thirty years for respecting other people, or was it something else that got you sent away all that time?"

Jake clenched the rocks glass in his right hand. "Another day and another time, and those would have been your last words. But tonight you'll go home to that family of yours. I'll grant you that."

"I don't need any favors from you."

Jake stiffened. "I wouldn't give you a drop of water if it was your dying wish. How's that?"

A reference to the desert dream, or just a coincidence? "Look, I didn't come here for this." He sat back in his chair. "Fact is, I don't wanna be here any more than you. Home with my wife and kids, that's where I want to be right now. I'd love nothing more than to get up from this table and go home. Walk into my house, shut the door, crawl up next to my wife, and forget all about you."

"So do us both a favor and do it."

Charlie took a moment to answer and then whispered, "I can't."

"Why?"

Charlie looked him in the eye. "Because I'd be back. I'd be back again and again and again, knocking on your trailer door looking for answers."

Am I connecting with him? It doesn't feel like it. "Look, Jake, I didn't choose this—these were the cards I was dealt. My life didn't turn out like I thought, but it's not too late to act. I still have a chance to do something about it, and you have a chance to help me."

Jake laughed aloud. "Wow, that don't sound quite right."

"What doesn't?"

Jake's grin quickly vanished. "I don't help anybody...I don't got that bone. You think meeting me is your redemption? Your chance to make something of your sorry-ass life?"

"I think a lot of things, but there's three things I know. My family is the best thing I've ever done, I love my wife with all my heart, and I belong on this trip with you."

Jake glanced over the table as if the answer to all this craziness lay somewhere amid the scribbled graffiti that was carved into the wooden top by the hundreds of patrons before them. And something caught his eye, tucked away in the corner of the table nestled between some profanity-laced tirade and a random phone number.

It didn't take long for Charlie to see it too. It was book and verse only, and Charlie read it aloud. "Matthew seven, verse seven."

As if he were reading the words right off the table, Jake said, "Ask and it will be given to you; seek and you will find, knock—"

Charlie interrupted him: "And the door will be opened. For he who asks receives, he who seeks finds and to he who knocks"—Charlie paused—"the door will be opened."

"How long you been reading?" Jake asked.

"A year or so. You?"

"About the same."

"I never would have taken you for a Bible man."

"You either," Jake replied.

"Then I guess we were both wrong about each other."

Charlie looked back down at the verse inscribed on the table and said, "I think there are times in your life when something great happens, something unexplainable...something *fantastic.* And when it does, you can't let it pass by, because it may never come again, and then all you can do is wonder *what if?* I don't want to be that person...I can't. I have too much at stake."

"Fantastic, huh?" Jake said.

"It's a powerful word."

"Mean something to ya?"

He nodded. "Little bit."

"I once knew an Indian who claimed to tell the future. Said he could tell it because he saw it. He saw it in flashes, amid the blackness behind his eyes." Jake shook his head. "Son of a bitch hung himself."

"Maybe he didn't like what he saw," Charlie replied.

"Yeah…or maybe he was just crazy." Jake sat up in his chair. "What do you see? You see the future?"

"I'm not sure. I'm still trying to figure that out. But I did see you coming, and what I see ahead is resolution to all of it."

"Resolution to what?"

"Maybe to both our burdens."

Jake sat back in his chair, considering the possibility.

Charlie read the expression on his face. "I don't think I'm the only one looking for redemption."

Jake said nothing, but the wheels were turning.

"You look like you got something you wanna ask me, Jake, but you're not quite sure how to ask it, or maybe you're not sure you'll like the answer."

"I only believe in what I see. Call me a hypocrite if you want, but my only reason for picking up the Book was to learn a little bit about hell. Because if there is one, that's where I'm goin'. And now you're asking me to believe in something I can't see or understand. You want me to believe that there's something bigger happening here than you and I know about?"

Charlie nodded. "That's what I'm saying."

For the first time, Jake noticed Charlie's piercing blue eyes. He recalled seeing a similar pair not too long ago. They, like Charlie's, were blue as the sky and intense. Even now he saw the boy's face, his unwavering stare, looking out the back window of that green station wagon as they pulled away. Looking at Charlie, Jake realized that not only did they share the same eyes, but there was a strong resemblance too.

"How many kids you got?" he asked.

"Two. Two boys."

"Your oldest boy, he look like you?"

Charlie shrugged. "I guess, a little bit. Why?"

Jake didn't believe in those kinds of odds. He put his hand up. "Never mind, it's not important."

Fact was he didn't want to know if the three people he had almost killed days earlier were Charlie Boone's family. He'd rather not have to debate that one in his head. Instead he told himself it was all nonsense and poured himself another drink of whiskey and took a long sip.

Naïve! Who was this kid claiming to know that their meeting was something more than just two strangers passing? Who was this kid invading his space, fucking with his head, and making him lose sleep? He wondered if Charlie would even still be sitting there had he any idea of his past. The evil years. The years when he'd beat a man just for looking at him wrong, beat 'im so hard that he left him to die wherever he fell. Or break a man's finger for not passing the sugar at a diner counter and then follow him home and shoot him dead because he called him a nigger too.

These were the types of things he was capable of. Not talking about destiny, fate, or whether the stars that night were aligned for such a meeting. In the end, and as much as it pained Jake to admit it, Charlie Boone didn't even belong at the same table. He was too civilized for Jake, who at the moment felt like being back in his cage of the last thirty years. Those solid steel bars were the only thing that could keep him sane, keep him from transgressing, keep him from killing again. Could he...could he kill again?

To say the act was never premeditated would be a lie, but more often than not, it was just instinctive. It was always quick and effortless. The only warning of what was to take place was that knot that would develop in the pit of his stomach and then travel up his chest and throat, where it would then park itself, waiting for the shots to be fired, and then he'd be left standing in the chaos he'd created with the taste of death in his mouth. A dry, metallic taste that made him want to throw up.

It would be about this time when his heart would slow to a whisper, and he'd get on his bike and ride for days.

He thought about the lives he'd taken and the destinies he'd stolen, not just from the individuals themselves but from their families too. He had stolen the destinies of many; mothers and children too, and here was this kid sitting before him who knew none of it, was naive to it all, and Jake hated him for it. Hated him for even thinking that it could be Jake who would lead him to his own destiny, a destiny he thought would be something great.

He now had a splitting headache. He'd heard enough and wanted to go home to be alone. "Calling you was a bad idea, and I regret doing it." He reached for the bottle of JD on the table and put it in his inner coat pocket.

"Why?" Charlie asked.

"Because I do," Jake shot back. "Just take it for what it is."

Charlie was wide eyed, and his face was getting red. "But what about my dream? What about Thunder?"

"I'll chalk it up to a good guess."

"Bullshit you will. You *know* that's not true."

Jake stood up from the table. "You need help, son, and I suggest you find it, 'cause you ain't gonna get it from me."

"The dream, Jake! You came to me in a dream. I *saw* you coming!"

"You're a piece of work, you know that?"

"You're lying. You're lying to me, and you're lying to yourself. Something's eating at you…what is it?"

"Stop it!" Jake said. "Stop talking crazy. I got a damn headache, I don't feel well, and I don't wanna hear ya no more, got it? I don't wanna hear no more of your nonsense."

"That's not true."

"It is true! Don't tell me what I know, boy. I know what's true and what ain't."

"We're not ending like this. Don't shut this out because it's too much for you to handle. I have too much on the line. Now you got something to say to me, so say it."

With a look of beseeching, Jake leaned in. "Listen to me. I'm not going to California. There is no California."

"No…that's not it."

"It was all a big lie, you hear me? I made it all up. There is no money."

"Don't…don't you do this to me."

"I have nothing for you. Never did and never will."

"I stood on a pier and heard my name. It *came* from your woods."

"I don't wanna see you ever again."

"You came here tonight because you felt something, and now you're gonna ignore it. Why? Why are you doing that?"

"Because I'm tired, that's why. I'm an old man who wants to be left alone."

"I won't stay away."

"Well, you better. Trust me on that."

"You're scared."

Halfway out of the back room, Jake turned around. "For the love of God, never in all my life have I met anyone like you. You won't shut up. You just won't quit."

"You're a coward, Jake Mott. There's a part of you that thinks I might be right, and it's too much for you to handle. All you been is cooped up in a box for three decades, and for it you don't know what's up or down."

"I don't know what's up or down? You got it twisted, son." He turned to walk out. "You belong in a straitjacket."

"You're fucking scared, man. That's all you are and all you ever will be. You've been running your whole life, and now's no different."

In one swift movement, Jake stopped, turned, and slammed his hand down on the table. "God damn it, I'm scared of nothing, fool. Hear me? Nothing!"

"Then ask me! Ask me whatever it is! Ask me anything!"

"All right! You *sorry* son of a bitch. Your car. What kind of car do ya drive?"

Looking confused, Charlie fell back in his chair and sat silent.

"Well?" Jake yelled. "Answer it! You, your family. What kind of car do you got?"

"I don't understand."

"What are you, dumb? I asked you a question; that's what you wanted me to do...so answer it!"

Charlie hesitated. "I...I drive a pickup. It's a white pickup, it's a truck."

As if all his emotions—anger, exhaustion, and even relief—were sprawled out on the table before him, Jake looked at them and gathered himself. He stood upright and took a deep breath. "Just what I thought. Nothing but a bunch of bullshit; nothing but a waste of my time."

Heading out of the back room, Jake heard Charlie whisper, "My wife...she drives a green station wagon."

Jake stopped just short of the crossway into the main bar area. Standing still and silent with his back to Charlie, he considered two things; first, what the chances were that all of this was pure coincidence, and second, if he did turn around and sit back down, would he regret it?

C. A. McGroarty

An uneasiness began to develop in the pit of his stomach, an uneasiness that had the makings of a knot. Angry at Charlie for making him feel it, and as confused as ever, he spoke softly, though firmly, just over his left shoulder. "I don't think you and I should meet anymore. I think it's best you stay away from me. Far away."

CHAPTER 32

"Are you fucking kidding me?" Lisa reached up and turned the lamp on next to her bed.

"Shh, don't wake the kids," Charlie replied.

Lisa whispered, "Are you crazy?"

"No more than two weeks, that's it...could be less."

"I don't give a damn if it's two days. You're not going anywhere with this man. And what the fuck are you talking about, anyway? You can't just walk in here when I'm half asleep and tell me this shit."

"Babe, listen to me."

"No, absolutely not. We are *not* having this discussion, you are *not* doing this." She leaned over to turn the lamp back off, but Charlie grabbed her arm.

"No, Lisa...you don't understand. I have to do this. There is no option."

The tenseness seemed to fall from her body. She sat up and fell back into her pillow. "You give me one good reason why, Charlie," she said.

"Because this is it. This is the one that's gonna make everything right."

"I've stood by you on a lot of things."

"And?"

She shook her head and let out a deep sigh. "And I'm tired...I'm really, really tired." She leaned in again and shut off the lamp.

Charlie undressed in the dark and climbed into bed. He was mentally exhausted but too excited to sleep. *How am I going to sell Lisa on this trip?*

———

"There's fire on the mountain!" The sun was shining bright on a brand-new day, and those were the first words Charlie whispered into his mother's ear.

He knew Lisa kept a hanging calendar on the inside of her closet door. The idea of keeping a calendar for anything was foreign to him. A man who had woken every day and gone to work for the last eight years of his life didn't need a calendar. But things were different now. He had a plan. He was going to California and needed to know how many days of complete freedom he had left.

No doubt he'd have to go in and talk to Randy tomorrow to request some additional time off; perhaps another two full weeks, maybe even three. With his record of service, he was sure Randy would give it to him. But if he didn't, then he'd walk. As confident as he was that he'd be accompanying Jake Mott cross-country, he was equally confident he'd land on his feet upon his return.

About to close the closet door, he caught a glimpse of something blue. He recognized that color—it was a sky blue with distinct, though faint, black-and-white pinstripes running through it. He hadn't seen it in years but knew exactly what it was. It sat on the top shelf, buried by some sweaters. He reached up and pulled it down, bringing the sweaters with it.

There it was, right in his hands—a piece of his own childhood. He looked at it was if it were treasure and whispered, "The gypsy box."

There'd been a time when his mother would take it everywhere she went, not much different from the pocketbooks the other mothers on the block wore over their shoulders. Looking at the gold stars on the cover, he remembered his mother naming it the gypsy box after she bought some spiritual rocks and cleansing salts at a flea market. Over time, it had come to collect anything she considered valuable, which meant it housed nothing but junk.

He contemplated opening it up, unsure of whether or not he'd want to bear the heartbreak of what may lay inside, its inventory a painful reminder of his mother's state of mind.

He placed the box on his bureau and opened its top. "Holy…!" He couldn't believe his eyes. The brushed black steel was lying dead center in the box. It was the handgun his grandfather had given his mother years earlier.

It was some time before he actually picked it up from its resting spot, but he finally did and gripped it in his right hand.

He had often held it as a child, but it had been years since he had last seen it.

"Charlie?" Lisa called from the bottom of the steps. "You up?"

"Yeah, I'll be right down."

He grabbed the single bullet that lay in the box and then wrapped it and the gun in a sock and tucked it under some shirts in his dresser drawer. Returning the gypsy box to its place in Lisa's closet, he hastily stacked the sweaters back as best he could without calling attention to any of it.

CHAPTER 33

He'd been aimlessly driving around town for hours when he began taking notice of the details around him. Details were on his mind because that was what Charlie Boone had on him. Charlie had resurrected something near and dear to his heart, and that was a place no single human being had been able to go in quite some time.

Idling six or seven cars deep at a red light, he noticed a clan of people waiting at a bus stop. It was one woman's green belt that first caught his eye; the man standing next to her wore a red Budweiser cap, but the *B* was missing. Then another woman's silver tooth glistened in the day's sun. Details were something he had never concerned himself with in the past, but there they were; it was the details in all of those people that made them different from one another.

Some details could be seen by the naked eye, others couldn't. Some things that make us different are covered up, only to be seen in the privacy of our own homes. Things like tattoos.

The people he gazed at abruptly vanished as the Septa bus they waited for pulled up. Jake stared at the 7-Up advertisement plastered to its side and read the Septa logo, recognizing it as the same one Charlie Boone wore on his jacket.

What else might this kid know about me?

Details...of late he could remember the most minute of them from the people he'd killed. Things like what they wore, the color of their eyes, a birthmark, a small deformity, or even dirt under a fingernail.

Picking up speed down the Roosevelt Boulevard, Jake felt weak. He longed for the eight-foot bars and three cinder-block walls of a prison cell. The act of doing time had always suppressed his feelings of guilt, but now that he was a free man, all of that was gone. He was free to go anywhere he liked and do anything he wanted. He was free to experience life, yet he wasn't prepared to do so. Surely there was another penance out there for him. Another penance for him to pay, and perhaps then his heart and mind would find peace.

He needed redemption from his past, but he wasn't ready to start his future. Could this kid be his new penance, his redemption?

He pulled into Mert's Liquor Store. He'd been drinking a lot lately, but it was there, in an empty bottle of Jack Daniels, where he found it OK to think about what still comforted him… *Thunder.*

CHAPTER 34

Washing the last of the dinner dishes, she glanced down the basement steps and could see Charlie looking out the basement window. *Innocence*...it popped into her head. The side of Charlie's profile suggested his own and reminded her of the very first day they'd met. They were both seventeen. She had just started working at Iggie's Sandwich Shop on Federal Street to save up for a car. She knew Charlie's face from high school but barely ever saw him around...and when she did, he was always alone. She'd ask other people about him but the answers were always the same: he was a loner; he was a loser, a weirdo.

She was surprised to see him walk in that day, but it turned out Iggie knew him well. He told her Charlie had been coming to his shop since he could barely see over the counter to order and *always* ordered for two people. And he was right. Without fail, he'd show up twice a week and order the same thing: two cheesesteaks with raw onions, yellow mustard, ketchup, and pickles. "You mean a hot dog?" she asked him the first time.

"No, a cheesesteak."

"Who puts mustard on their cheesesteak?"

He just stared at her red faced and awkward...she'd embarrassed him but didn't mean to. The next time he came in, she apologized and asked him out...he ran out of the store without his order. She laughed out loud at the memory.

He stayed away from the shop for four weeks, then finally showed up and said he was sorry for running out that day. And that if she'd have it, he would like to take her to a movie. She remembered going home that night, resting her head on her pillow with a permanent smile, full of excitement about their first date. It took him six months to bring her home to meet his mother.

Innocence—he had had it then and still did. She always thought she could protect him, pull him out of his shyness, and free him of what'd been a tough childhood. She couldn't say he was still shy, but as far as everything else? She'd failed.

"What are you looking at, Charlie?" she asked.

"The boys," he said. There was a long pause before he said anything else. "They're getting so big. They're gonna be men before we know it."

She cringed at the thought of her boys growing up and leaving the house. "Dare I say this house may need another baby?"

Charlie shot out of the basement with a large sack in his hand and placed it atop the kitchen table. "You know what? I think you're right."

She grabbed a sponge and wiped down the counter. "I'm kidding, Charlie. Don't get me wrong; I'd love it, but another mouth to feed is the last thing we need."

"No, I'm serious. Couple pigtails and some little bobby pins is exactly what this house needs. A little girl."

She turned and faced her husband. "Sometimes you can say the most beautiful things." She motioned to the sack on the table. "What is that?"

"Nine thousand dollars," he replied matter-of-factly.

"Excuse me?"

"I think it's nine. I lost count a couple of years ago, but it's no less than nine."

"Whose money is it?"

"It's *our* money."

She pulled the two purse strings at the top and opened up the bag. A handful of tens and fives spilled out onto the table. "Charlie...what the..."

"It was my mother's. I came across it years ago. I started adding to it when I was twelve. Probably only had a couple thousand in it when I found it."

"But where did you have it all this time?"

"In the basement, hidden behind some cinder blocks in the wall."

"You think the basement is a good place for nine thousand dollars?"

"Yeah, I do."

She pulled out more fives and tens intermixed with some twenties and even a few hundreds. "My God, what were you saving this for?"

"Hard times. If I ever got laid off. No matter how bad things got, it'd be a long while before you and the boys went hungry."

"And what about you?" she asked.

Charlie smiled. "And me too."

It pained her to ask the question because she feared the answer. "Why are you showing me this?"

"Because it's time...this is *our* money. It's always been. Since the day you walked in this house, I haven't taken a dime from it that hasn't gone toward the well-being of this family." He grabbed her hand. "I can't do this without you. It's two weeks, probably less. Two weeks! It's gonna be a flash in the pan, and I'll be back before you know it."

"Why is this so important to you?"

"Because if I *don't* do it and I ignore this, I'm afraid of what might happen."

"It just makes no sense."

"To you it doesn't, but I've been waiting for this my whole life."

She broke her hand free from his grip. "You're asking my approval for you to go on a trip across country with a man you hardly know because you think he's going to help our situation? You think he's going to bring some sort of resolution to your problem?"

"You need to trust me," Charlie said.

She got up from the table and faced the kitchen counter with her arms folded. "I pray all the time to understand you, Charlie, but deep down, I know I never will."

The boys' playful screams coming from the front yard carried through the exterior walls. She looked toward the den. "You hear them out there? Those are our two boys, and they're very real. Their well-being is all that consumes me, and part of that well-being relies on your being here...on your having a job!"

"So what are you saying?" he asked.

"I've had enough heartache in my life. I just don't want any more." She paused. "I'm just tired of it all, and I don't know how much more I can take."

Charlie rose, grabbed his Septa jacket off the back of his chair, and left the house. A few seconds later, she heard his pickup pull out of the drive.

She buried her face in her hands and started to cry.

CHAPTER 35

S itting in a booth at the Roosevelt Diner, Charlie gripped his mug of coffee as he anticipated Jake's next move and considered his own.

Knowing he didn't have Lisa's support was debilitating, but it didn't change how he felt or overshadow his fear of letting Jake Mott pass him by. His destiny was on that trip to California, and he wasn't going to miss it.

What Lisa didn't and couldn't understand was that they were all going to be better off for it. Unfortunately for both of them, he just didn't know how to communicate it. His feelings made little sense; that much he could agree with her on. But none of it changed the realization that he'd be leaving for California the day after next. Why he knew that to be the day he was unsure, but it made him wonder whether or not Jake had come to the same realization.

He pulled a pen from his pocket and began writing the letter he had come here to write, with the hope that she'd understand just a little bit more the reasons for what he was about to do.

"Would you like another cup of coffee, son?"

Charlie sat motionless. "Huh?"

"More coffee?"

"Oh...no, thank you."

"Then how 'bout something to eat? You've been sittin' in this booth all night with no food in ya."

Charlie looked down at the pages of loose-leaf he'd been hovering over. He knew his heart and soul was on that paper. "What time is it?" he asked.

"Eleven ten."

"Holy shit!" He pulled a five-dollar bill out of his pocket and threw it atop the table. Hastily folding up the letter, he scribbled Lisa's name on top of it and put it in his pocket.

———

She pulled a kitchen chair up to the living-room window, where she had sat all night waiting for him. There were no more fingernails left for her to bite. If she could only go back to their earlier conversation, perhaps she would've said something different; perhaps she would've agreed.

Charlie had never left the house during a fight, and it killed her to think that he might not return. It was a painful reminder that, independent or not, she needed him more than she realized.

The headlights of his truck hit her square in the eyes. She ran to the door, where she waited patiently. He wasn't even through the doorway when he handed it to her.

"What's this?"

"Sorry…the night got away from me."

"What is this, Charlie?"

If it was a good-bye letter, she didn't want it. She'd take back what she said; they'd sort through it.

"It's a letter. It's everything, start to finish. It's the truth as I know it."

"The truth about what?"

"About me, about us, this house, my mother." Charlie hesitated. "It's the truth about what I'm gonna become if I don't do this."

With nothing left to say, Charlie retreated to their bedroom for the night. Alone again, she entered the kitchen, took a seat at the kitchen table, and unfolded the letter.

Several minutes later, Lisa carefully folded up the nine pages and placed them next to her heart. Staring blankly at the lime-green wall in front of her, she contemplated the secrets Charlie had written down. She looked back down at the letter in her hand, closed her eyes, and whispered an Our Father.

CHAPTER 36

With a map of the states laid out before him, Jake tried to plot his trip but could never get out of Pennsylvania without bringing the tip of his index finger back to Philadelphia and tapping it up and down. Charlie Boone was in his head.

Though his body wanted to get moving, his instincts told him otherwise—and did so without explanation. He contemplated the idea of staying in the trailer indefinitely, away from other people, free from the temptations of society, free from Charlie Boone, but then he was reminded of Charlie's own words: "Because I'd be back again and again and again."

What on earth did he have that Charlie Boone wanted? It was a question he had asked himself a hundred times over the last couple days, and the only answer he could come up with was money.

He considered Charlie's take—that it was more than just chance encounters that had brought them together, that there were signs that couldn't be ignored.

There had been a time in his own life when signs, right or wrong, had meant something to him, but it'd been years since he'd thought of or put stock in any of them. The only signs in prison to follow were the ones pointing you in the right direction, the direction that kept you out of trouble. But in the game of life, Jake knew that signs were very real, and being out in the world again was a reminder of how complicated life could be. Signs could sometimes help people make decisions—important ones, too.

The Book he'd been reading for the last year and a half put a lot of credence in signs, so much so that it said there would be six of them that would foretell the coming of the end.

So maybe there was something believable to what Charlie was telling him. Suppose the kid was right, and Jake chose to ignore him, writing him off as a crazy bastard. *What if he was wrong?*

He was reminded of the soothsayers in the backwoods of Praire, Texas, when he was a boy. They were elderly black women who seemed to be neither auntie nor momma to anyone. It was as if they were born out of the very ground they lived off of. They seemed to live in this woods forever, eternally eighty years old, coming out to tell their tales only in the latter months of the year, once cotton picking season was over. As he remembered, it was about the only time of year that plantation owners would put up with their voodoo magic and fireside hysterics.

He recalled many nights traipsing through the thick brush of Rollins's Plantation with his momma, en route to another reading. She put as much stock in the soothsayers behind their home as she did in the Good Book.

He could see his momma now, sitting on the porch of his boyhood home, his uncle Sam and aunt Rae standing beside her just as they did on that April morning when he left for boot camp.

He'd caught a ride into town with Carl Rollins, the youngest son of John Rollins, on the back of his pickup. Young Carl was the third-generation owner of the Rollins farm, where just as many Motts had been picking cotton as Rollinses had been selling it.

Even through the cloud of dust, he saw the pained look on his momma's face as they drove away. She disapproved of his joining the army; she had already buried a husband and two other sons. Jake was all she had left.

She wrote him often in the service, but he rarely replied. The few times he did respond, his letters were no more than a couple of sentences long, reciting where he was that week and how bad the killing was. Certainly not the words a mother wanted to hear from her son a thousand miles away from home.

What a hardened and bitter man he had become. What had happened to the innocence he once had?

It had been a simple time. He'd wake at dawn to roosters in the backyard. He'd rise and have breakfast and give his momma a kiss on the cheek before heading out to the fields with his uncle Sam. There he'd spend a hard day's labor—ten or twelve hours—picking cotton before heading home at dusk.

Uncle Sam wasn't much of a talker, but he had a gift; he was able to fix a farm tractor or cotton spreader quicker than anyone in town. It was a gift the Rollinses valued, and for it, the Motts always had jobs on the farm in addition to a place they could call their own.

He wondered if things might have been different had he never left. He could have stuck by his uncle's side, pooled their money, and built that brand new home his uncle Sam and momma always talked of on the very lot the Rollinses had given them. But those were just daydreams now, a reality that never was, a very possible outcome to a very simple situation.

Instead he'd chosen a different path, and look where it had ended him: an old convict with not a pot to piss in who, like his momma, would probably die alone.

That last thought pained him the most. Not only had he not *seen* her in thirty-some years, but he hadn't spoken to her either. Their last communication was shortly after his return from Vietnam. She successfully tracked him down long enough to get him a letter or two. Much to his regret, he never replied.

A pack of smokes, $847, an old pair of boots, a set of bike keys, and those two letters were all he had when he entered Georgia State Prison on that hot summer day, and all he had when he left it.

Pride or stupidity? Staring at the yellow-tinged envelope before him, he asked himself which one it was that had kept him from answering his momma all these years.

Pride, of course, as he was ashamed of what he'd become. However, later in life, he had nothing but stupidity to blame for all his stubbornness...for all his mistakes.

What he wouldn't do to have a place to call home. To have a place to go where people knew him, a place where people called him nephew, cousin, or even son. A place where people knew his smile, knew the things that made him laugh, knew his nuances and made fun of him for them, such as the way he'd always rub his chin when he felt that something bad was about to happen. His uncle Sam always razzed him about that one.

It all seemed like a lifetime away, as if it were someone else who had experienced all the good his childhood had to offer. *Where did I go wrong?* While he wasn't sure, he believed it was on that summer day when Thunder was shot dead.

Jake drew a straight line with his red marker from Philadelphia to Praire, Texas. Perhaps it was time to face some hard truths. Truths like what his mother's fate had been and whether or not she still believed she had a son.

Regrets and what ifs were the things that had made up his life to date, but might he be able to change all that now? Maybe a trip cross-country could do just that. Perhaps this was his chance to take some of his life back.

That was all he wanted. A chance to redeem his past so that he might live the remainder of his days undisturbed by his own guilt. A chance to live in peace.

It had been years since he'd done a good deed for anybody. So long that he didn't even know where to begin. Sitting in the darkened camper, Jake asked aloud, "How?"

He answered in a whisper: "Charlie Boone."

CHAPTER 37

They hadn't spoken since Sunday at Jerry's, and for all Charlie knew, Jake could be halfway to California. But somehow he knew that wasn't the case. He felt confident that today would be the day Jake would call.

There had been no mention of the letter when Lisa had come to bed the previous night, just uncomfortable silence. But now was the time to confront her.

She sat at the kitchen table, gazing out the back door watching Billy and Bear play in the backyard. Charlie took a seat across from her.

She smiled halfheartedly at him.

He kept silent.

Lisa looked to her husband. "I've had the same question in my head all day."

"What's that?" he asked.

"What happens now?"

He took a deep breath. "I'm leaving the day after tomorrow."

She stared blankly into the center of the table and looked as if the fight had been knocked out of her. "You spoke with him?"

"No...but I think that's the day."

"You've never been away from home," she replied.

"Because I never had to."

"You feel that strongly about this?" she asked.

"As strong as my love for you, and that's my problem. If I could let this man walk out of my life, I would. But I can't do that, it would be the greatest regret of my life."

"What did you say he was, the one to make this thing right?"

He reached over and gripped her hand. "I'm doing this so that once and for all I can know in my heart that I'm *not* just my mother's son." He tightened his grip. "I *know* what's at stake, and I won't let you down."

"Two weeks?"

"Two," he said.

"Your love is unconditional. It always has been, and that's not something I can say for myself. If this is the way it has to be, then you go do it, be done, and get back here where you belong." She paused. "We'll be waiting."

He hadn't expected to ever hear those words from her mouth. He really was the luckiest man on the face of the earth.

It took a few rings before he realized what he was hearing. He looked over to the receiver attached to the wall. "That's him."

They both stared at the receiver, which seemed to get louder with each ring.

"Answer it," Lisa said.

He didn't move.

"Answer it!"

He stood up and grabbed the phone. "Hello."

"You say you drive for a living, right?"

"I do."

"Well, someone to share the driving with wouldn't be all that bad."

"It's a long ways."

"I'm not much of an eater. We stop when I say we stop and go when I say we go."

"It's your trip. I'm just along for the ride."

"I'm an early riser too."

"I hardly sleep," Charlie replied.

"OK, then. We leave day after next, first thing in the morning. I'll pick you up at seven a.m."

"Ten Nebraska Lane," Charlie blurted out.

"What's that?" Jake asked.

"My address."

———

Lisa poked her head into Mrs. Boone's bedroom and found Charlie sitting in the rocker. The single lamp on the nightstand cast a dim light across the room. "I was wondering where you were. You want me to leave you two alone?"

"No, come in," Charlie said. "The kids in bed?"

She entered and took a seat on his knee. "They are."

"It's nice to watch her rest....I was just remembering her laugh and how loud it was."

"She did laugh a lot. It was sometimes hard to find the humor in what she was laughing about, but at least she seemed happy."

"You hope so, right? You hope she was happy at some point."

"I'm sure she was, Charlie. We shared some nice moments together. All of us, as a family. Those first couple years, anyway."

"Yeah, few and far between, though."

She kissed him on the forehead and rested the side of her face atop his head. "You better talk to Eddie tomorrow when he gets home from school. He's gonna wanna know why."

"I've been thinking about that. What do I say?"

"I don't know, but whatever you do, don't lie to him. He's too smart for that."

CHAPTER 38

He threw the last few items remaining on the bed into a small duffel bag: socks, a couple of T-shirts, and plenty of underwear. For the most part, he could get by with the clothes on his back.

Lisa laughed. "That's all you're taking?"

"Yeah, why?"

"Not much, is it?"

"That's the beauty of it." He glanced at himself in the mirror before opening up the medicine cabinet. "I think I might grow a beard."

"Hmm, that sounds sexy!"

"Yeah?" He pulled the bottle of aspirin out of the medicine cabinet and closed it quickly, purposely avoiding the bottle of Prozac on the shelf.

"I overheard your talk with Eddie."

"You're right," Charlie said. "He's a smart kid, smarter than me. Those boys deserve the best, and when I get back, I'm giving it to them."

"I will say, you do seem happier these last couple days."

He kicked an old pair of boots out of the closet and picked them up off the floor. "I am happier, and you should be too."

Lisa picked at the quilt she was lying on.

"What's wrong?" he asked.

She shook her head. "I know I can say some pretty shitty things sometimes, but it's just frustration talking. I want you to know that. It's times like these that I realize how much you mean to me and how much you mean to this family, because we could never go on without you. I may say otherwise at times, but it's just not true."

He smiled.

"Do you remember our vows?"

"Sure I do."

"No, I'm not talking about the ones we said to the judge at city hall. I mean our *real* vows."

"That's what I was talking about. The Spectrum, Bruce…it was a great night."

"That was our real wedding night. I mean, when we said those words, it felt more real than anything else we ever said to each other." She stood up. "Could you say them if you had to? Could you give me that promise again?"

He grabbed her hand. "We said we'd walk together, and come what may, then come the twilight, should we lose our way, and if we're walking a hand should slip free, I'll wait for you, and if I fall behind, wait for me."

In turn she replied, "We swore we'd travel, side by side, and we'd help each other stay in stride, but each lover's steps fall so differently…I will wait for you, and should I fall behind, wait for me." She fell into his arms. "I'll never leave your side, Charlie Boone."

CHAPTER 39

I t rained hard that night, with no signs of letting up come morning.
Hearing a beep outside the house, Charlie brushed aside the bedroom curtain. Jake Mott's black pickup sat idling at the curb.

He darted down the steps and out the front door.

Lisa called out from the kitchen, "Why is he beeping, Charlie?"

He moved headfirst into the thrash of rain and reached the pickup in a few large strides. He opened the passenger side door. "Come in for a cup of coffee."

"Don't need to. Already had a cup."

"Then how 'bout some eggs?"

"Already ate, too."

He was hoping not to be so direct. "My wife would like to have a cup of coffee with the person I'm about to drive cross-country with. Is that asking too much?"

Jake glanced over at the green station wagon sitting in the drive. "What the hell is this, the first day of school? I wanna hit the road. I told you seven a.m. sharp, and it's seven a.m. Now let's go."

He was getting soaked. "It's one cup of coffee."

Jake stared out the windshield.

"I'll see you inside." Charlie shut the door without giving him a chance to respond and took off for the house.

The screech of the porch door announced Jake's entrance.

Lisa called from the kitchen, "We're in here."

He followed the voice to the kitchen doorway. Charlie sat at the table, and Lisa was in front of the stove cooking. She turned and extended her hand with a smile. "Hi, I'm Charlie's wife, Lisa."

He stood silent for a moment waiting for her to recognize him, but much to his relief, she did not. He shook her hand. "Hello, I'm Jake."

"I know you are. I've heard a lot about you, Mr. Mott. Please, have a seat."

He scanned the small space and met the eyes he feared the most, the ones he had seen in the parking lot that day.

Eddie was already locked in on him. The kid looked paralyzed, unable to even chew the bite of food in his mouth.

Jake spoke up. "Uh, no...thank you, ma'am. Really, I'm fine. I'll just wait outside."

"Nonsense. Have a seat."

He remained standing and still; now all eyes were on him.

"Really, Mr. Mott. Have a seat." The forcefulness of Lisa's tone reminded him of some of the guards and how they'd say something to make a point, as if it was best for you if you did. He carefully slid into a chair so as not to brush his wet jacket up against the table. As if things weren't uncomfortable enough, the kitchen seemed way too small for all the people in it.

Eddie ever so slightly inched his chair away from the table and a little farther away from Jake.

"How do you like your eggs?" Lisa asked. "Not that it matters, 'cause scrambled's all I got."

"Uhh, I'm OK, ma'am. Just a cup of coffee is fine."

Lisa threw a heap of eggs on a plate and put it down in front of him. "I take it Charlie didn't tell you we were having breakfast together. Well, that's OK...here you go; they're nice and hot. You'll want them later, trust me."

He slowly picked up the fork but in no time was gobbling up the eggs in spoonfuls.

"So, Charlie says you used to work for the railroad?"

Jake absently looked at Charlie, who just shrugged. "Uhh...that's right... the railroad."

"Are you enjoying retirement?"

He momentarily stopped eating and looked at Charlie. "I think so."

"Well, that's nice." Lisa pulled a chair up to the table and took a seat next to him. "How old are you, Mr. Mott?"

"Fifty-three, ma'am."

"Really? You don't look it." Lisa smiled. "You must not have any children."

"No, I don't."

"Well, they seem to take years off your life, but it's all worth it, as I'm sure Charlie will tell you."

Still conscious of Eddie's stare, Jake wiped his mouth. "Well, we should probably get going. Sounds like the rain's died down a bit."

"Yeah, you're right," Charlie replied. He stood up from the table and for the first time noticed the look on Eddie's face.

"Thanks for breakfast, ma'am. It was kind of you."

"My pleasure, Mr. Mott."

"Just call me Jake, please."

"OK then, Jake. Perhaps when you boys get back two weeks from today, I can make you dinner."

Jake smiled. "Perhaps."

"Hey, Jake, just give me another minute, huh? I'll be right out."

Charlie smiled at his oldest son but received nothing in return. He sat back down at the table. "I don't want you looking sad, Eddie. I'm just going on a little trip, and I'll be back before you know it."

Eddie looked away. "I'm not sad."

"Oh…OK. Well, I'm glad to hear that, because I want you to take care of things around here while I'm away. Keep a lookout for your brother and your mom for me. It's gonna make me feel good knowing you're back here keeping watch over everybody."

"Do you like Mr. Mott?" Eddie asked.

"Well, sure I do. Mr. Mott's a nice man. How 'bout you? You like him?"

Eddie bit his cheeks and stared into his father's chest.

"Hey, son, everything's gonna be fine. I promise."

"No," Eddie said. "I don't like him, and I don't want you goin' with him."

Charlie got up from the table and knelt in front of Eddie's chair. "Now, Eddie, listen to me. Mr. Mott and I have some business to take care of. Remember what I told you yesterday? It's for the best that I'm doing this; it's for the family. Now I'm gonna be back here before you know it, and when I do, we're all going away. We're gonna pile in that wagon and go on a trip of our own…just the four of us."

"Where?" Eddie asked.

"Wherever you want, buddy, I promise that. Wherever you wanna go, I'm taking you, because you deserve it." He leaned in toward his son. "Things are gonna change when I get back, Eddie. You wait and see."

Charlie gave him a kiss on the cheek and hugged him as tight as he could. "I love you, son."

The rain didn't stop Lisa from seeing Jake out to his truck, where she grabbed him by the arm and turned to face him. "Jake?"

"Ma'am?"

"You take good care of my husband, now. You promise me that."

Thrown off by the request, Jake stood speechless for a few moments. He smiled awkwardly and nodded his head yes, then climbed into his truck and shut the door.

Lisa met Charlie halfway from the truck to the house. Face to face, they stood in the center of the walk-up as Eddie and Billy stared out the front door. "You have everything?" she asked.

"I think so."

She zipped up his coat. "Last night was great."

Charlie laughed. "Can't wait to do it again when I get back."

"I'll be waiting," she replied. They kissed, and she gripped her husband as tightly as she could while he squeezed back.

After she'd allowed him to break free from her arms, she called out as he reached the passenger-side door. "Charlie!"

She was torn. Half of her wanted to run up to him, tell him she loved him, lead him back into the house, and go on with their fretful lives. But the expression on his face reminded her how important this was to him. She'd never understand it, but just maybe this was exactly what they needed.

"I'll see ya soon, huh?"

Charlie smiled. "Before you know it."

With a wave of her hand, she watched Jake pull away and then followed them into the middle of the street. She could do no more than stand and watch as the taillights on Jake's truck fell out of sight.

CHAPTER 40

*H*e *could see his grandfather on the front porch from the top of the drive, awaiting their arrival, cigar in hand. Even from that distance, the man had a presence about him, large-framed with bright-white hair and super-tanned skin. The man didn't look like a grandfather and never seemed to get old either. He looked more like a cartoon character than a real person. He stood up from his rocker and took a big pull of his cigar as they got closer to the porch.*

"Hey, Daddy."

"Hey there, darlin'. How was the ride?" he asked.

"Oh, not bad. Lots of stops. We're used to it, though. Right, Charlie?"

Staring down at the porch treads, Charlie slowly nodded yes.

"There's my little partner," Pop Grey said. "Boy's getting big, ain't he?"

"He sure is."

Pop Grey motioned toward the door. "Shall we go in?"

He and his mother waited in what she called the parlor room while Pop Grey went to the kitchen to "fetch some iced teas." He knew the routine well. This was about the time when she'd start rambling on about childhood memories. The same exact stories, same words used to describe them, and even the same fake laughs prompted at the same time. There was a nervousness about her in that house. It was all very confusing to him.

Pop Grey took a final sip of iced tea and put it down. "Pretty good iced tea, huh? I had the maid make it before she left."

"It is good. Good on a hot day, too."

"Yes, it's downright steamy out there."

Charlie studied Pop Grey, who seemed to be studying his mother. He turned to Charlie, taking him by surprise.

"How about you, partner? You haven't touched yours. Don't you like iced tea?"

Charlie grabbed the glass next to him and took a quick sip, then placed it back on the end table.

"I see you got my favorite dress on," Pop Grey said.

"Oh, you like this?"

"I sure do. I think you look very pretty in it." He turned to Charlie. "Hey little partner, listen up, I've got a present for ya."

"You do? Did you hear that, Charlie? Pop Grey has a gift for you."

"Yup, I sure do."

His grandfather reached behind his chair and pulled out a long rectangular box wrapped in brown shipping paper. He leaned over and handed it to Charlie. "You're gonna like it."

"How exciting, Charlie!" his mother said.

Charlie stared at its wrapping but said nothing.

"Well, go ahead, boy. Open it up."

A tinge of excitement come over him; he never got presents at home. A few quick tears of the wrapping paper revealed a white box with a picture of a BB gun on it.

"Oh my, is that a gun?" his mother asked.

"It's a kid's gun. Shoots little pellets. Go ahead and pull it out of the box."

Charlie did as his grandfather said, ripped open the top cover and pulled out the BB gun, which was almost the size of him. He'd never held a gun before, let alone seen one up close. He stared at it in awe.

"You like it?" his grandfather asked.

He aimed it, as he'd seen on the Lone Ranger, and nodded yes.

"You know, Daddy, I've always thought we should have a gun in the house."

Pop Grey grabbed the canister of pellets and began loading the gun. "Damn right you should. This ain't gonna do it, though. I'll get ya a real gun, something you can keep under your bed." He handed the loaded gun back to Charlie. "You know how to shoot it?"

He didn't, but he'd never tell his grandfather that. "Yeah, I know how."

"Good. Then go on out back and shoot yourself something. There's plenty of squirrels out there, too."

A silence took over the room. All eyes were on him, but he didn't want to leave. He glanced over to his mother; he could protect her as long as he was by her side, and he felt she needed it, even if he didn't know why. She gave him a blank stare and smiled back. "Go ahead, honey. It's all right; go ahead out back like Pop Grey said."

He slowly headed out the parlor door, his grandfather encouraging his every step. "Go on; we'll know right where you are."

It was a big backyard with plenty of trees. His grandfather was right; there were a lot of squirrels to shoot. He watched a litter of them scatter up a tall oak tree when he walked up. He quickly took aim but in the end chickened out.

His grandfather had never given him a present before, which was just fine by him; he didn't want anything from him anyway. Though he liked the gun, he wanted to put it back in its box and give it back, but it was too late for that. With renewed enthusiasm, he cocked the rifle and took aim at a squirrel above his head…and then he heard something.

He had heard these sounds before. The ones he didn't like. They were coming from his mother. They were always coming from her. He brought the gun to his side and stared up at the bedroom window.

The stairs were long and wide, imposing compared to the short flight of steps he was used to at home. He'd never been up them before: strict orders from Pop Grey, and ones he always obeyed. But today something was daring him to climb them.

He started out a little shaky, knowing he could always jump back down into the foyer should he hear his grandfather coming down the hall. The more he climbed, the less likely his quick retreat became. His stomach tightened with each additional step. His small palms were wet with sweat. He was reaching a point where getting in trouble was inevitable.

He could hear his mother's cries a little more clearly now. He looked to his right down a long narrow stretch of hallway. The sounds were coming from a closed door at the end. He tiptoed up, stopping just close enough to reach the door handle. Laughing was mixed in with his mother's cries. They didn't seem to go together. He stood and listened for a while, hearing things he didn't understand. Feeling something slip from his hand, Charlie looked down. The gun. The butt of the gun made a loud knock on the hardwood floor. He let it happen.

Jake gave him a good couple of shoves with his elbow to wake him up. "Hey, get the hell up."

Charlie sat up in the cab and grabbed his bearings. It was dark out; they'd obviously been driving all day. The first thing he saw was a green turnpike sign, but Jake raced underneath it so fast he couldn't make out its wording.

"Where are we?" Charlie asked.

"I thought you weren't much of a sleeper?"

"How long have I been out?" Charlie asked.

"Three and a half hours."

"Holy shit! That's hard to believe. Felt like ten minutes."

"We just crossed into Ohio. Driving in this rain is a real pain in the ass. Slowed me down quite a bit." Jake rubbed at the kinks in his neck. "I'm taking the next exit...I'm tired."

"Feel free to wake me up next time," Charlie said.

"Why?"

"So I can help with the driving."

Shows of kindness were new to Jake. Unsure how to react, he fell silent in response to Charlie's offer. He'd only said that about sharing the driving as an excuse to bring the kid; he hadn't really expected him to help.

"The roads seem empty," Charlie said.

"Does now, but it wasn't. It's getting late; people are done with their business."

"I heard a lot of rigs travel this turnpike."

"Ain't that the truth. Had about fifty pass me when you were sleeping, all going a hundred miles an hour."

Charlie smirked. "Those old boys hit it pretty fast."

"Fast? Might as well be the Indy Five Hundred, was borderline insane. Blowin' down the road with care or caution for no one."

"Like I said, wake me up next time. Remember, that's why I'm here. Those truckers can be ruthless; I deal with them every day."

"Ehh, I'm not worried about no truck driver. Will be a cold day in hell before they run *me* off the road."

He got off at the next exit and pulled into the first roadside motel he saw. The broken-down vacancy light had just enough letters lit to know there was some open space. He put the truck in park and shut off the engine. "Better go get yourself a room before they close up for the night."

"What about you?" Charlie asked.

The kid had only been awake for a half hour, and already Jake was annoyed with him. "What about me?"

"Where you sleeping?"

He slapped his hand down on the beat-up vinyl seat between them. "Right here."

"You're gonna sleep in the truck?"

"That's right, which means you're in my bed, and I'm tired. So go get yourself a room."

Charlie grabbed the duffel bag at his feet and jumped out. Jake watched him walk toward the office with his bag thrown over his shoulder.

"Nothing but a fool," he said aloud.

It was just the first day, and already he was second-guessing himself. Now in the moment of the trip, cryptic signs and coincidental moments seemed to mean very little. Redemption! That was why he had brought him in the first place. "And when is that gonna hit?" he asked aloud.

True, he felt he was doing something good for a change, but already he wanted to be done with him. Sitting peacefully in his truck at the mouth of Ohio, he wanted nothing more than to be free of any and all obligations. Free of having to be there come morning, free of the morbid-looking block of rooms in front of him, free of Charlie Boone. But something was keeping him there, parked outside a seedy motel on a lonely road.

Jake closed his eyes, tilted his head back, and whispered, "Who are you?"

CHAPTER 41

C harlie sat on the motel room floor with the phone by his side, intently listening for any turn of an engine. He had gotten a room just a few doors from Jake's parking spot but didn't want to be caught peering out the window like a little old lady. The way Jake had practically thrown him out of the truck had him wondering if the ex-convict wouldn't just up and pull away—if not now, then maybe sometime in the night, leaving him a state away from home. But while he definitely thought such a scenario was possible, he was more concerned with calling home.

She sat up in bed reading a coverless, cheesy romance novel she'd picked up from a yard sale last summer for a nickel, but her mind was in other places. She'd already read page fifty-four three times, every few seconds noting the time on the digital clock by her side. The first ring brought a smile to her face. "Charlie?"

"Hey, babe."

"Oh, Charlie! Thank God. I was getting worried."

"Why?"

"Because it's getting late."

"Well, that's life on the road, you know?"

She could hear the smile on his face. "OK, wild man. Let's not forget it's your first day."

"It went by quick, didn't it?"

"So does that mean you're having fun?"

"Fun? Not sure, we haven't done anything yet...I did sleep a long time, though."

"You slept?"

"Yeah. Weird, right? How's Mom?"

"She's fine. You know—the same." Lisa sighed. "So, where are you?"

"We're in Ohio."

"Wow, you're that far away?"

"Ohio's not too far. How's everything there?"

"Everything's fine. You're not missing anything here besides a warm bed and a loving wife who already misses you."

"Hmm, don't say that. You'll make me get on the next train back."

"Really?" Silence took over the line. "I just can't help worrying."

"There's no reason to be worried. I told you that before."

"He seemed like a nice man. Is he?"

"Of course he's a nice man. Are the boys up?"

His quick change of subject worried her, but she didn't press. "No, but I can wake them."

"No! No, don't do that."

Just then Eddie lodged his head into the crack of their bedroom door and peeped in. Sitting Indian style on the bed, she motioned for him to come over.

"Eddie was wondering about ya."

Charlie's voice perked up. "He was? What was he saying?"

Lisa held the receiver to Eddie's ear. "Dad?"

"Hey, Eddie! How are you?"

"Where are you, Dad?"

"I'm in Ohio."

"What's that like?"

"Well, I haven't seen much of it yet. It looks nice. It's dark out just like at home. Makes it tough to see, you know?"

"Yeah. Do they have buses in Ohio?"

Charlie laughed, as did Lisa. "Of course they do. You want me to get on one? Drive it home like I do for work?"

"I think you should if you have to."

"Well, that's good advice, Eddie, and I'll hold on to it if I need it, but I don't think I will."

"I'm gonna put Mom back on now."

"Hey, Eddie?"

"Yeah?"

"Sleep tight, huh?"

"You too, Dad."

Lisa watched him as he left the room. "I don't think he could sleep until he talked to you."

"Make sure you tell him everything's OK, huh? I mean, I have, and I know you have, but reinforce it, you know? Every night."

"I will," she said. "Are you sure everything's OK?"

He laughed. "Would you stop it? Now come on…I better get going. I've heard stories about these motel phones."

She didn't want the call to end. "Where is he?"

"What do you mean?"

"Is he sharing a room with you?"

He paused. "No, we have our own rooms. Why?"

"I don't know, just wondering."

"Listen, I'll call you tomorrow."

"Promise?"

"Promise? You'd have my balls in a sling if I didn't."

She smiled approvingly. "Goodnight, Charlie."

"Goodnight."

CHAPTER 42

Charlie stumbled out of the motel room after the third honk and held his hand in the air as if to say "Give me a minute."

Jake sat behind the wheel sipping on a cup of coffee. As promised, Charlie was out of the shower and dressed in short order, and, true to his word, a razor didn't touch his face. He jumped in the passenger seat and kicked away some empty beer cans on the floor. "I thought you said you were in no rush?"

"I'm not, but I'm also an early riser." Jake took another sip of coffee. "There's free joe in the office."

"Yeah, for paying customers only. How did you get a cup?"

Mildly amused by Charlie's sarcasm, he grew a slight grin. "I walked in, poured myself one, and walked out."

"How is it?" Charlie asked.

"It's just my brand: free. You getting a cup or not?"

"No, I'll pass."

"Not rich enough for your blood?" Jake asked.

"Hardly. I'm afraid of what I might say to the old man in there about the crawlers I slept with last night."

Jake grinned, put the truck in drive, and pulled out of the motel parking lot. Charlie studied the empty beer cans still knocking around at his feet. By his side were two empty bags of potato chips. "If I'd known you were having a party last night, I would have joined ya."

Jake shifted his eyes to the floor. "That ain't no party. That's just being thirsty. You'd see some Jack down there if I was having a party."

"Daniels?"

"That's the one."

"Just the thought of it makes me shiver."

"Can't handle the hard stuff, huh?"

"Let's just say it's not my drink of choice."

"Must have been a rough one."

Charlie stared out his window. "Not for me. There was a guy who used to come into Jerry's and sit in the same spot, corner seat at the end of the bar. When he walked in, Jerry would throw a bottle of Jack and an empty glass in front of him." Charlie nodded. "Roland Jones was his name.

"Anyway, this one night, Roland shows up, and the place is packed with wall-to-wall people, and his normal spot is taken, but there's one last spot open at the bar, so he sits there." Charlie looked over at Jake. "Right next to me."

Jake was gaining interest in the story. It had the feel of some of the great drinking stories he'd heard in prison.

"I sat there for three hours and watched 'im finish a bottle and a half all to himself. And that had never been done before, at least according to Jerry—not even by Roland. I mean, he'd come in and finish a bottle or what was left of one, but never did he ask Jerry to crack another. If the bottle was done, Roland went home." Charlie fell silent.

"But then, all of the sudden he just tips over, right in my lap. He's looking up at me, but he's not there, you know? He's out cold."

"Come on," Jake said.

"I'm serious."

"So what happened?"

Charlie shook his head. "It was so damn hot in there with all those people around I could hardly move. People at my back, someone to my right, and then there was Roland taking his last breaths right in my face. I remember this burning sensation in my nose and then the smell of Jack Daniels, and then I had this sharp fucking pain in my head. I started sweating real bad, and this awful feeling come over me, like it reminded me of something."

Charlie fell silent as he stared out the windshield.

Jake glanced at Charlie's profile and thought he saw a bead of sweat on his temple. "Shit, you hadn't even tasted it and it paralyzed you."

"Like I said, it wasn't my drink. If I drank liquor, it was tequila."

"Tequila? Well, I'll give you that…that ain't no woman's drink. I once knew a guy that drank plenty of it. Matter of fact, sounds like he and your buddy

Roland shared the same consumption habits." Jake shook his head. "But this guy…this guy was something else altogether."

"How so?"

"You don't wanna know."

"Sure I do."

Jake looked over at him. "No, you don't."

"Why's that?"

"Son, if the devil himself ever walked this earth, it just may have been him. That's the kind of guy he was, and tequila only made him worse."

"Old friend of yours?" Charlie asked.

He would be lying if he said no, so instead he looked away in disgust and mumbled at his window. "Ehh, it's not important."

"I'm sorry?"

"Nothing," Jake shot back.

"What was he, another war buddy?" Charlie asked.

"War buddy? Shit, that son of a bitch never did *anything* heroic in his life. He stood for nothin', believed in nothin', and respected nobody."

"Sounds like you had a falling out."

"Let's just drop it, huh? I don't even know how we got talkin' about 'im."

"Tequila," Charlie replied softly.

"Yeah right…tequila."

"Those days seem like a lifetime ago," Charlie said. "The tequila days, I mean."

Jake took a deep breath. "I know about lifetimes. They can be a decade or a day. Some go quick, and some don't."

"She's one tough gal," Charlie said, staring out the window.

"Huh?"

"Oh, nothing. I was just thinking about my wife. She's tough. She's been through a lot—with little help from me, no less. She's always supported me." He looked over at Jake. "That's saying something."

"Hmm, can't say I know anything about that. I've never had a relationship last much past breakfast."

Charlie smiled deviously. "How long's it been for ya?"

"Oh, about two hours after getting out of prison. The same amount of time it took me to drive to the nearest city. She wasn't the most beautiful thing, but she worked. I couldn't sleep a wink after it, either. I was so keyed up but with nothing to do, so I walked...walked for hours, just watching my feet go. One foot in front of the other."

"Freedom?" Charlie asked.

Jake was no psychologist, but he'd had enough sessions with a few of the resident prisoners who *were* to know that Charlie's observation was astute. "You get to spending so much time behind locked doors that you don't think much about getting out, 'cause if you do and it don't happen, well...that alone will drive a sane man crazy."

"You never thought you'd get out?"

His jaw line tightened and his lips twisted, keeping him silent for several seconds. He was fighting off a moment, one he most definitely didn't want Charlie to see. He had learned to shed a tear or two in his old age. "Nah, I never did."

"Gotta be a tough thing to go through."

"Prison ain't easy. Made Vietnam feel like grammar school. Gotta be strong there, gotta be strong in prison. You want something bad enough, like freedom...well, you just might get it, but you gotta be mentally tough just in case you don't."

"Like a rock."

"You got it. Like a rock," Jake replied.

"I wouldn't last," Charlie said. "My wife, on the other hand...she would, she's the rock."

It was an odd comment, at least to admit to. "So you ain't strong, huh? You the man of the house, but you ain't tough?"

Charlie laughed in a wired way. "I don't know. I've never thought about it, but I do know my wife's the toughest person I know. Nothing's been easy for her. She lost her mother when she was eleven, and her father was a drunk. He never laid a hand on her but wasn't much of a father either. I might've always put food on the table, but she needs more than that. I'm lucky she stuck it out with me. Her and those boys, they're everything to me."

Jake wasn't used to hearing anyone speak so emotionally about their family. It angered him. Just another reminder of the many voids he had in his own life. At least in prison, you can dream yourself a reality. Once in it, reality can be depressing. Here he was, a few months shy of his fifty-fourth birthday, and he had never fallen in love, never married, no kids. *Is there anyone to say a kind word about me?* After he was buried, would anyone even mention his name? Life had never seemed so delicate to him as it did right then. *Is my mother alive?* As usual, his gut told him no, leaving his heart to ache for the solemn funeral he never attended.

Damn, if he were young again…a teenager riding on the back of Carl Rollins's pickup on his way to boot camp and the rest of his life.

"Jump, kid," he said.

"Jump?" Charlie said.

Jake's eyes locked on the horizon.

Jump off that fuckin' truck, kid. Do it now and run home to your momma. She'll be waiting for you right where she probably stayed till sundown hoping you'd do just as I'm asking now. Jump, and maybe things will be different; maybe you'll have a chance at life.

"Jake? Whatta ya mean jump?"

He turned his attention to Charlie, but by now, his anger was consuming. "Why are you here?" He slammed his fist down on the dash. "Damn it, tell me that boy. Why you here?"

"What are you talking about?"

"I'm talking about bullshit…your bullshit! Your big love for your family, your great kids, the woman who's everything to you, yet you ain't there! You ain't with them. Instead you're here with me! Why? Tell me."

Charlie didn't move; he couldn't. He had never seen rage quite like it before.

"Let me guess: you don't know why. You can't tell me. Well, I'll tell you why. Because you're running. You're a scared kid, and you're running away from your problems."

"You think that's what I'm doing?"

"Goddamn it, I know it. So keep the love stories to yourself from now on, because if any of it was true for one damn second, you wouldn't be here."

"Think what you want, but I got nothing to prove…not to you. My reasons for being here are as selfish as they come. And you're right about one thing. In the past, I may have been running from the thoughts and fears that put me in this truck with you because I was afraid of my own future, but not anymore."

Both panic and confusion set in and bounced around Jake's insides. His gut felt weak, and his mind was overloaded. "Go home," he said softly. "Just get off at the next rest stop and go home to your wife. That's where you belong."

"You think I wanna be here? With some bitter old man who still wishes he was in prison instead of the comfort of my home with my wife and kids? If you think that, then you're stupid and you don't know shit about me."

That was it, Charlie had done it. He'd triggered that anger that had caused so much turmoil in the past. The kind of anger he was hoping he wasn't capable of anymore.

Jake slammed on the faulty brakes of the old pickup. All 280 pounds of his six-foot-two frame pushed down on the brake pedal. It sounded just as it was, steel on steel. The back of the truck fishtailed from right to left as they swerved in and out of the right lane and the shoulder.

It was brute strength that finally brought the shaking steering wheel to submission and the rumbling vehicle to a grinding halt. They ended up on the side of the highway.

"Listen here! I make the decisions on this trip, and your road ends here, right here, right now. I don't know why I agreed to this, but I knew it was a mistake the moment you got in. I don't like you. We're not the same people. Now I've had it with ya."

Charlie sat perfectly still. "I guess it's your truck, right?"

"Yes it is, and in case you forgot, my trip too, something I was doing *by myself* until you stuck your head where it don't belong. And I want you to know something else: the only reason—the *only* damn reason—you're here is because for once in my life I wanted to try to do something good, but you ain't nothing but a sorry-ass son of a bitch that I should've never got involved with."

"No other reason, huh?" Charlie asked.

"None," he replied. His body was finally losing some of its tension. His foot came off the brake pedal, and his body settled back into the seat. "Unlike you, I don't believe our meeting was anything but chance. That there's some greater force at work here don't hold water with me. We're two people that met, two people that knew the same person, and that's it!"

"Then so be it. If that's how it would've turned out, then so be it. At least then I'd know."

"Know what?"

Charlie hesitated. "That I took a fantastic moment in my life and tried to do something with it."

"And what fantastic moment is that?"

Charlie's attention was on the road before them. "All of it…it all pointed to you."

The vibration and vroom of passing cars zooming bounced off the walls of the cab. Both men sat silent for several minutes.

Jake considered what was on his mind and then said softly, "We're all so fucked up. Animals got it right."

"How do you mean?" Charlie asked.

"They got an instinct; they smell things out, look ya in the eye, and know exactly what you're feeling. Not all have it, but most do."

"Thunder have it?"

"Yeah," Jake said, "he had it. I was damn close to keeping that dog when it showed up on my doorstep."

"Why didn't you?"

"Trying to do something good again, I guess."

"Well, you did that. It would've killed my boys to lose that dog."

He recalled Charlie's youngest son sitting in the kitchen the previous morning and could see again the distrust in the young boy's eyes. He wondered why the boy hadn't spoken up then and told his parents about Jake. Looking at the man seated to his right, something told Jake that if Charlie had known, it wouldn't have changed anything. He'd still be sitting where he was, just another sign that he and Jake were destined to meet.

"You asked me if I believed in destiny," Jake said.

"And you never answered," Charlie replied.

"My destiny's already been shaped, son. Been that way for the better part of my life. There are choices a man makes, things he does that just can't buy him that ticket anymore…my ticket's been punched."

"I used to think that, but not anymore. I don't think anything's too late, no matter who you are, good or bad."

Jake looked out the windshield at the flat ground before them and set his eyes on the highway. "What was it you said? You'd be back, again and again?" He let out a slow breath and put the gear in drive. "A man my age needs rest, not heartache."

CHAPTER 43

They hadn't been apart a single night, let alone two weeks, and while she figured she'd miss him, she never expected it to be this difficult. It had been only a day and a half, but she couldn't stop thinking of him. Especially not knowing where he was.

She sat at the kitchen table and collected her thoughts. What an emotional roller coaster the last couple of weeks had been.

It was a minor miracle she didn't have a nervous breakdown through it all; that was the fighter in her. But as much as she was a fighter, she was also a realist, and the thought of Charlie returning to his job upon his return home seemed unlikely.

She knew he wasn't happy driving the bus every day, but her husband's happiness could certainly be compromised for food on the table and clothes on the boys' backs.

The thought of Charlie jobless made her feel vulnerable. How on earth had she allowed him to drive across country with a complete stranger? What was she thinking?

It had all happened so quickly.

She remembered him talking confidently about everything they'd do upon his return: a trip away with the kids, a new job for him, even a new home for her. Being the realist she was, Lisa allowed herself only a moment to consider the possibility of it all, and then she had *the* thought. It had never crossed her mind before that moment, not even for a second, but now, alone, with Charlie hundreds of miles away, not only did she have it, but she felt it. Her stomach turned.

"No," she said aloud. "Don't think that way, Lisa. What the fuck's wrong with you?"

She pressed hard for happy thoughts, like their last night together lying in bed nose to nose, saying their vows again—and the passionate sex shortly thereafter.

She recounted many arguments sitting in the very seat she was in now, Charlie swearing off his medicine and the psychiatrists who had prescribed it. He'd always say that it wasn't his destiny or the destiny he'd allow for himself.

Destiny…he talked about it with such reverence. *What would hers be?*

She surveyed the walls around her. Every piece of peeled wallpaper and every last chip of paint owed its sorry-ass existence to her. She was the glue and tape that held it all together. But the more she studied those walls, the more she saw something else. Peeled wallpaper and cracked paint came to mean a little more than just years of disregard. It was as much a representation of her marriage and the time and energy it took to manage it all—Charlie, the kids, her mother-in-law, her own sanity—as it was neglect.

Maybe it was time to do something, as Charlie kept saying—to take action instead of reacting to what was happening around her. She didn't know how much longer she could bear to live in this house that haunted them both. Except for a new stove, everything in it was the same as the day she had walked in. The only thing she wanted more in life was to move her family into that big white house she had always dreamed of.

Her perseverance knew no boundaries, and if it was a new home she wanted, then why shouldn't she have it? Why couldn't she?

As much as Charlie would say otherwise, they could never afford to buy a new home on his salary alone, and that was if he still even had a job. There it was again: the job. Every time she thought of it, the butterflies kicked up.

There was no more waiting. Starting today, she was officially in the job market. She hadn't waited tables since her days down the shore, but she certainly remembered how good the money was. Even working part time a few hours a day could help them, and perhaps even take some pressure off Charlie.

There were only two things left to do: find a waitressing job close to home, and line up Mrs. Spinks to watch Billy a few hours a day.

She smiled faintly at the prospect of it. The minute he got home, she'd send Eddie down to Leidy's Market for a paper.

CHAPTER 44

He had spent enough time studying the computer maps at Penn State to know his route by heart. I-76 was going to take them straight across Pennsylvania, where they'd cross over into Ohio and then pick up I-70, which they had already done. They'd follow I-70 to Columbus and stay on it through Indianapolis and then over to Saint Louis. In Saint Louis, he'd pick up 44 West and take it into Oklahoma City. From there, it would be Texas, and that was where he'd have to make a decision: whether or not to hit Praire.

The sleepy town of three thousand people sat sixty-five miles east of Lubbock, and Route 27, by way of Amarillo, would get him there. It would take all of a day out of their trip, but he wasn't worried about that. If it was something he was feeling when they crossed the state line, then he'd do it. Otherwise, it would be off to Calimesa.

"I saw a sign for a rest stop a few miles back," Jake said. "I could use some chow."

"Yeah, I saw it too. There's a Roy Rogers there."

"A Roy what?"

"Roy Rogers. It's a fast-food chain."

"OK, I thought he was an actor. As long as they got food."

"Oh, yeah. Good food, too. I don't know about you, but fast food's like going out to dinner around my house."

Jake ordered three roast beefs and piled them high with lettuce, onion, and tomato, along with every condiment in the place he could find.

Charlie got a cheeseburger and fries.

Staring at Jake's tray of meat, Charlie said, "I never knew two pieces of bread could hold so much."

"You've never been in a cell, dreaming about warm beef or the taste of a pickle."

He appreciated the comment and returned to the condiment bar to load up his own sandwich. Returning to the table, he felt a bit manlier than before.

"You been wearing the same clothes since yesterday," Jake said.

"Yeah, so have you."

"Then whatta ya got the bag for?" Jake nodded to the duffel bag at his feet.

"Just some extra stuff—clothes, toothbrush, that's it."

"Important enough to bring in here with ya?"

Charlie held his burger in his hand. It was true he had clothes in the bag, but there was something else too: a loaded gun. He quickly debated whether or not to tell Jake about it, but, uncertain how the ex-convict might react, he decided against it. "Your lock's broken on the truck."

"Think someone's gonna steal your clothes?"

What would Jake do if he knew he had a loaded gun on him? More importantly, what would he think his motives for bringing it would be? Charlie conceded his own doubts about the ex-convict sitting across from him. "Trust no one," he replied. "Remember that?"

Jake grinned. "Yeah, I remember."

"A little dose of your own medicine. Trust anyone but yourself and you'll wind up dead, and sometimes you can't even trust yourself."

"Glad it stuck with you. Maybe someday you'll remember it as good advice."

"Already have," Charlie replied.

He watched Jake work over his last roast beef sandwich. "By the way, I also got a map in the bag. I bought it for the trip. I started to map us a route out west. I didn't finish it, but thought it might come in handy."

"No need," Jake said, shaking his head. "Already got our route."

"Where?"

Jake tapped the side of his head. "I know exactly how we're goin'. If you got a question about it, ask me. Otherwise, keep your map in your bag with your clothes."

Jake finished his food, wiped his mouth clean, and stood up. Charlie thought he saw a hint of a smile hidden behind the old man's cool expression.

"What?" he asked.

Jake kicked the duffel bag with the toe of his cowboy boot. "Damn thing's no bigger than a purse."

Jake's boots. Charlie had never noticed them before, but they were faded black and well worn. A distinct wear too, one he'd seen before. His mouth ran dry and his heart fluttered; there were no two ways about it. He'd seen those boots before. Still staring at them, he slowly replied, "So I'm a light packer. What's your point?"

"None. Just think it's funny looking." Jake started walking away. "I'll be filling the gas tank."

Charlie turned in his chair. "Jake? Your boots?"

Jake looked down at them. "What about 'em?"

"Boots that broken in you didn't just buy."

"Hell no." Jake chuckled. "They've sat locked up at Georgia as long as me. Comfortable as hell, though. I wouldn't trade them for anything. What's wrong? You wanna piss on my boots 'cause I pissed on your bag?"

Charlie fell silent and shook his head. Turning his back, he answered, "I'll see you out there."

CHAPTER 45

Lisa sat at the kitchen table making circles around the black-and-white boxes on the back of the newspaper Eddie had just bought her an hour earlier. There had to be someone out there who was looking for a waitress.

Eddie appeared in the doorway.

"Hey, kiddo."

"Dad call yet?"

"No, but it's still early."

No matter how hard her son tried to conceal his emotions, they always showed on his sweet face.

"Looks like you're thinking about something. What's wrong?"

"Dad said I was the man of the house till he got back."

"He did, did he?"

Eddie nodded. "He said to help around the house."

Half smiling, she eyed the bowl of pea soup covered in tinfoil on the counter. "Well…there's a juice cup in the 'frigerator door. You can take it up to your grandmother along with that soup on the counter, if you'd like."

He grabbed the plastic sippy cup, the one that was his own from childhood, and picked up the bowl of soup. "I'll feed her. I've seen you do it before. I guess I can do it every night until Dad gets back."

"You don't think that's too much for you?"

"No. Dad would want it that way."

"OK then, that would be great."

CHAPTER 46

C harlie glanced at his watch. It was 3:30. "You need a spell?"
Jake shook his head no.

"You've been driving all day, plus yesterday."

"So?"

"So I thought I was here to share some the driving?"

"And you will, when I'm ready to give it up."

"Where are we, anyway?"

"Where are we? Haven't you been paying attention?" Jake asked.

He'd been alone in his thoughts for some time. His mother in particular was on his mind. He kept seeing her plain as day, standing in front of their home, calling for him to come back while he looked back at her from an ambulance window. Dreams were something he had been recalling his whole life, but more than ever, they seemed to be hinting toward a possible future. And if that was true, he didn't like what he was seeing.

He glanced down at Jake's boots. *Is it really possible?* Could they be the very boots of a man who left someone to die in the desert? It wasn't very reassuring to know he and Jake were headed west, and the desert was a stretch of land they'd most certainly be crossing. *What the fuck am I doing here?*

If he had ever had a single stitch of doubt about being on this trip, now was the time to do something about it. He could say he was feeling sick from lunch and had to stop at the next rest area. He knew Jake would resist the request, but he'd push him to do so anyway. And if that failed, at the very least he'd hold out until they laid over for the night. He could catch the next Greyhound out of town, whatever town that may be, and perhaps be home by the next afternoon.

He had come to a point he didn't expect, more torn than ever about what he was doing on this trip. With every mile marker they passed, he was farther and farther from the people who loved him and farther from that home he so often cursed and that now looked so inviting.

He rolled down the window and took in a deep breath. What was happening to him? All of this doubt over a pair of fucking boots. *Maybe I am crazy.*

Was he willing to ignore the signs and go back to his old life of sleepless nights and frantic days? Or would he see this thing through just as he'd persuaded Jake to do hours earlier?

He asked again, "Where are we?"

"We passed Dayton about a half hour ago. We're probably sixty or so miles from Indy."

"Not making bad time, huh?"

"No, good time, actually," Jake replied. "We keep pushing, and we might be able to hit Saint Louis for a layover."

Charlie gazed over at the speedometer. Jake was keeping steady at seventy-five miles per hour. "You feel every bit of the road in this thing, huh?"

Ignoring his comment, Jake remained silent.

"Must be the suspension," Charlie said. "Better take it easy on her if she's gonna stay in one piece."

"You think I'd take this truck across country if I didn't think it would make it?"

"I'm sure she will. I just think she'll fare better turned down a few notches."

"You a mechanic too?"

Charlie laughed. "No, there's not much of me that's mechanical about anything, but I know vehicles. What about you? Good with your hands?"

"Was once," Jake said. "That's about all you do growing up on a farm—work with your hands." He fell silent for a moment and then continued. "Chores before school, chores after school, some fishing in between."

"Simple life. Sounds nice."

"Coulda been." *Just another painful reminder.* "It sure coulda been."

He gave the truck a bit more gas and clutched the steering wheel, turning his dark knuckles a faint white. The speed felt good. Charlie was right. You did feel every inch of the road, but he didn't mind it a bit.

He'd been keeping pace with a sixteen-wheeler for several miles but now found himself right up against the truck's taillights. A quick glance in his side view mirror and Jake jumped into the passing lane. They were past the truck in seconds, followed by two more, and then empty road.

Two empty lanes set out before him, with a darkened tunnel cutting through a small mountain about a hundred yards up. Facing a slight incline before the tunnel's entrance, he hit the gas hard, and then it was pitch black inside the cab. There wasn't a vehicle inside the tunnel, and Jake didn't let up his speed.

He'd driven through plenty of tunnels in his day. "Shadows," he said under his breath.

The word took him back to a time when he'd traveled cross-country on two wheels instead of four, driving over stretches of road for hours at a time. They'd cross two, sometimes three states and not even realize they were doing it, he and his running partner. Thirty-plus years after the fact, and he still couldn't bear to say the man's name, the man he owed much of his own heartache to. They had entered many dark tunnels back then, in every sense of the word. *Shadows*.

It was the name he used to describe the uneasiness he'd feel in such places back then. Dark places, that is. Highway tunnels, the pitch black of a motel bedroom, or perhaps even the side of a mountain absent any campfire. There'd been plenty of those along the way. It was then the shadows would come out. The shadows he'd see plain as day, the lost souls of the many men he had either killed himself or watched his partner in crime kill. Lucky for him, three months of solitary in the early years at Georgia State had finally cured him of that ailment.

He flew down the narrow two-lane stretch of tunnel toward a beam of sunlight, but unlike the years of his youth when he was running from shadows, today Jake was running from years of shame he had yet come to grips with.

Like a slingshot, their vehicle hit the sunlight and began a quick descent out of the tunnel and down a large hill. It felt as if their speed had doubled.

Nestled up against the tunnel exit sat a parked vehicle, and though the blue unmarked car fell from sight as quickly as it had appeared, he knew exactly what it was. Both men shared a quick glance before Jake, stone faced as ever, looked away.

"Was that a cop?" Charlie asked.

He continued to barrel down the highway.

"Brakes?" Charlie said.

Jake kept a steady eye on the crest of the highway behind him in his rear-view mirror. It was taking longer than expected.

"Come on, pig," he whispered. "Come out that shoot and catch me, catch me if you can."

Charlie turned and looked out the back window. The blue top came into sight. Like them, it picked up speed and started a quick descent down the hill. Charlie turned and sat back. "What's that speedometer reading?"

"No mind," he replied.

"Jake! Slow the fuck down. You're gonna get us pulled over."

He never wavered, not even a blink of an eye or a twitch of his hand as he kept close watch on the fast-approaching cop. What was he gonna do when he caught up to them? And what was Jake gonna do in return? He wasn't going back. He wasn't ever going back.

Jerry's gun sat just behind his feet under the seat. It didn't take long for that rush to come back to him, thrilling and intense—so intense that just catching a glimpse of himself in the rearview mirror made him pause. The tightness of his jawline, the look of determination, the cold, dark abyss of his eyes; he knew that stare all to well. It was final confirmation that he still did have it. *Once a killer, always a killer.*

"Jake! What the *fuck* are you doing?"

The desperation of Charlie's voice finally registered. Jake slowed down and pulled over to the side of the road.

"You got a license?" Charlie asked.

Jake wasn't sure what was more disturbing: not knowing what the next few minutes held for him or coming to the realization that the awful something he feared still lurked in him. He shook his head no to Charlie's question.

"You don't have a license? How do you not have a license?"

"Never did," Jake answered softly.

"Is this thing registered? Insured?"

Again Jake was silent.

"Is there anything legal about this?"

Looking over at Charlie, he responded, "You."

The cop pulled in behind them but stayed inside his car.

"What's he doing?" Charlie asked.

"Don't know."

"Should we get out?"

"Just be cool and sit tight. Probably running tags."

"Where did you get this truck, Jake?"

"Bought it off a used lot."

"You sure about that?"

"Hold on," Jake said. "He's pulling up."

The unmarked car stopped parallel with the pickup, and the power window came down. A plainclothes cop leaned over the passenger seat.

"Where you two headed?"

California was on the tip of Jake's tongue, but he held it back at the very last moment. What were they going to California for? Buried money, a whole bagful that had a history attached to it.

Surely a cop from Ohio would have no way of knowing any of those things, yet he still felt the need to say otherwise. "Texas," Jake replied.

"Texas? You're a long ways from Texas."

"Yes, we are," Jake agreed.

"What's in Texas?"

"Family...we're going to see family."

The cop leaned farther in across his passenger seat to get a better look at Charlie. "Family, huh?"

Charlie smiled. "That's right."

The cop looked back to Jake. "You were coming out of that tunnel at a good clip. I just got a call, eighteen wheeler jackknifed a mile back, so I don't got time for ya. But consider yourself lucky and keep your speed down."

It was an unexpected but welcome surprise. Jake was obliged. "Will do, Officer."

Both men watched the car pull away, drive across the grass median about twenty yards in front of them, and start heading back from where they came.

Jake grabbed for the gearshift on the column and started off again. After a few moments' silence, Charlie spoke up. "Hey! How 'bout that spell now?"

CHAPTER 47

The sleepless nights, the forgetfulness, the countless unanswered questions, all the madness Charlie had put her through over the years—none of it seemed to matter at this moment. Lisa lay in bed with the covers pulled up to her chin; it was dark outside and had been for hours. Eight thirty felt like midnight. The boys were in bed; a pencil and some want ads were tucked by her side.

The lamp by her bed cast a dim glow, and though she was always aware of the lack of light it gave off, only now did she feel the need to chastise it. Her instinct was to get out of bed, pull its cord from the socket, and throw it out the front door. The lamp, like much of the home's items, had been inherited or taken over, but all of these things—the light, the house, all its belongings—were no more than a purposeful distraction to help occupy her mind. She missed her husband, but more than that, she didn't like the feeling that was seeding in her stomach.

She caught sight of the folded letter Charlie had given her a few days before he left.

She retrieved it from her bureau and read it again. There was heartbreak in its creases; missed holidays and forgotten birthdays were just the start. It dawned on her that Charlie's childhood was all but forgotten. Not a picture to remember it by or a single memento to show he had even lived it; at least she'd never seen or come across any.

He'd shared more in that letter than he had in all their years together. He needed to get this "something" out of his system, and allowing this trip with Jake was going to do just that, but when it was all said and done,

Lisa was sure Charlie still needed help. His letter was proof enough of that.

She'd been full of threats over the years but always knew she could never cash one of them in on him. If they were poor and destitute, she'd still fight to keep her family together. She believed in what they had: love.

She was reminded of a line from that Nat King Cole song. "When I give my heart, it will be completely." Well, years ago she'd given her heart to Charlie, and there'd be no taking it back…ever.

That song—it had been years since she'd heard it. She jumped up out of bed and scoured the depths of her closet for the dusty old shoebox full of her mother-in-law's eight tracks. Charlie had told her on many occasions that his mother had loved to play Nat King Cole, that Nat's voice would "soothe" her.

She picked off the lid, and it was the first one on top. Nat stared back at her with that distinguished smile.

Taking a seat at the foot of the bed, she sank in and listened. Her mother-in-law was right; it was soothing. And then there it was, her favorite line: "When I give my heart, it will be completely, or I'll never give my heart."

She was lost now, lost in the music as she played the song over and over again. The descending violin, the soft piano, the sincerity of Mr. Cole's voice, all of it together made her forget. The bedside lamp she had chastised all of a sudden found purpose. The dim light it cast made for the perfect setting and seemed to go hand in hand with the soft lyrics coming from the speaker. She felt the urge to get up and slow dance with the pockets of shadows that seemed to lurk about the room making her feel she wasn't alone.

And then she actually did feel someone—not to touch, but a presence. Out of the corner of her eye, Lisa swore she saw Mrs. Boone standing in the doorway, her gray, matted hair hanging over her frail face. She quickly turned for a look, but nothing was there, though the door rocked back just enough to suggest someone might have been. A cold chill ran through her. It took several seconds before she could even move, but she finally did.

She looked down the darkened hall toward her mother-in-law's room. She was scared, but why? Her heart was telling her to go check, but her mind was saying *lock the bedroom door, get back into bed, and wait for Charlie's call.* But not without a check on the boys.

She jumped across the hall, peeked into their room, and saw both fast asleep with the night-light on. She closed their bedroom door behind her, did the same with her own door, fell back into bed, and pulled the covers back up to her chin.

CHAPTER 48

They hadn't even touched the outskirts of Indianapolis, and Jake was out cold. Charlie was just happy for them to be on their way again and in some control of the situation.

Indianapolis, then Saint Louis, the Gateway to the West! Oklahoma City, Texas, then off to California. All places he'd never been before. Glancing over at Jake, whose head rested against the window, he was eager and ready to find out why they'd been brought together, and in one of those places the answer surely lay. Hopefully, then, he'd also find a sliver of peace and a trip back home to be with the people he loved.

Traffic got heavier as he approached Indianapolis. A sea of red taillights was coming to a stop about a mile up, and an ambulance passed by on the shoulder as he slowed to a crawl. Now at a standstill, Charlie noticed an exit sign thirty yards ahead of him. It read, "Indianapolis Bypass, I-70 and I-65."

Car after car popped out of the standstill traffic and headed for the bypass exit. He followed suit, and not long after, it proved to be the right move. He was moving again, and at a good clip.

After a few minutes on the bypass, downtown Indianapolis fell from his sights, and his mind returned to home.

Charlie grimaced. He didn't want to wake Jake up, but the big man's body seemed to absorb every bump or pothole that the road had to offer. The most recent jolt slammed the side of Jake's head against the window. He came to with a grunt.

"Sorry about that," Charlie said.

"What the hell was that?"

"It's a tough highway, not a stretch of smooth road on it."

Jake rubbed his neck. "What time is it?"

Charlie looked at his watch. "Ten minutes till eight."

"Well, at least I got some rest. Maybe we'll shove right through Saint Louis. Where do you have us?"

"Couple hours west of Indy," Charlie replied.

The truck's headlights brushed over an interstate sign ahead of them; they passed it as quickly as it appeared.

"I-65!" Jake said. "Did I see that right?"

"See what?"

"That sign said I-65, like we were on it."

"That can't be. We're on 70. I took it right out of Indianapolis."

"Are you sure?" Jake asked.

"Of course I'm sure."

They were approaching another turnpike sign but on the other side of the highway. Jake turned back as soon as they passed it. "Son of a bitch!"

"What?"

"Boy, you're not on seventy! You got us off our road!"

"How could that be?"

"There's no 65 on my route. It was 70 straight to Saint Louis."

"Oh, shit," Charlie whispered.

"Oh shit what? You better start talking."

"There was traffic back in Indianapolis."

Charlie hadn't even finished before the words came from Jake's mouth. "Chicago, Illinois, *sixty miles*? Holy shit!"

"Where?"

"We just passed it, that's where. Maybe if you'd slow the *fuck* down, you'd start seeing some of this shit."

"I'm doing the speed limit."

"I don't give a damn! Now slow the *fuck* down till we figure out what the hell's going on."

Charlie did as he said, crossing over two lanes toward the shoulder.

Jake looked down at his own feet. "Where's that map you got?"

"It's sitting on top of the clothes in my bag."

Jake reached down, pulled the bag onto his lap, opened it up, and pulled the Rand atlas out of it. "If I know anything, we're still in Indiana...I knew I shouldn't have let you drive. One hour from Chicago! What in Sam hell was I thinkin'?"

He put the map up to the window for a better look, taking advantage of any highway light he could. "Just as I thought. I-65, and still in Indiana. One hour outside Chicago…hell, boy, you got us in *Gary, Indiana*! You've been heading north for the last two hours. Now how in the hell did you manage that?"

"Traffic," Charlie said softly.

"Huh?"

"I said traffic! I hit traffic back in Indy. It was at a standstill. So I took an alternate route around the city. The sign said I-65 and I-70. I must have never gotten off the roundabout."

They were approaching a sign: Welcome to Illinois.

"Ahh, hell," Jake yelled. "You've got us so far north we're already out of Indiana. Goddamn it, pull over!" He threw Charlie's duffel bag back at his feet. "I mean, how in the hell? Didn't you know you were heading north?"

"Time got away from me," Charlie said.

"Time? I don't give a damn about time! What about direction?"

"Like I said, the sign said 65 and 70."

"Right, right, right, I know. You told me that already."

"All right, so I made a mistake. It's over. There's nothing we can do about it now. Let's talk about what we're gonna do."

"What we're gonna do is turn around. That's what we're gonna do!"

"Go back to Indy?"

"You're damn right we are!" Jake paused. They were too far north to do so, and he knew it. It didn't make any sense to turn around now. He grabbed for the atlas again. "*Hold On!* We're not gonna head three more hours south just to go back to where we came from. Jumpin' Jeez! I knew I shouldn't have let you drive."

"If we're that close to Chicago, let's just lay there for the night."

That wasn't an option either; he couldn't go back to that town. "We're not going to Chicago. We might pass it, but I'll be damned if we're stopping." He ran his index finger down one of the pages. "Yeah, that's what I thought. We can pick up 55 South outta Chicago. It'll dump us right into Saint Louis. Might be a half day later, but it will do. Now pull over and get your ass out of that seat."

"Why?" Charlie asked.

"Because you're not driving, that's why. Matter of fact, you're not driving the rest of this trip. I'm driving from here on out."

"I think that's a bad idea."

"Oh, you do?"

"You're way too angry to be driving right now. You might do something stupid like you did earlier and get us arrested."

"Son, you got one thing right: I'm angry. I should kick your ass right out the door."

"You got a real anger problem. You know that?"

"Excuse me?"

"I said you got an anger problem."

"Boy, I'll tell you what, I've made some bad decisions in my life, but the last few days? They're on the top of the list."

"Bullshit! You're all talk."

"Don't tell me what I am. That's the second time you've done that, and I don't like it. You got me so riled up I want to run your side of the truck right into that median."

"I made a mistake. Get over it."

"A mistake that took us way out of our way and closer to Chicago than I'd ever like to get."

"What the hell's your problem?"

"I don't got a problem, but I'll be damned if I close my eyes again. And your time's wrong, too. It's seven o'clock, not eight. You're in the Midwest, son. Didn't they teach ya anything?"

"Well, there you go, then. There's a silver lining in everything. We just gained an hour. Now maybe the both of us can stop screaming at each other."

"Ahh, just drive."

Jake sat back and remained silent, still in shock at the pure stupidity of it all. An hour later, still nothing had been said when then the Chicago skyline came into plain view.

"Wow," Charlie said. "Looks like quite a town."

"Yeah, it's quite a town, all right," Jake mumbled.

The very skyline Charlie adored, Jake cursed. It brought back horrid memories for him. How the hell was it that Charlie'd brought him back to this place? What were the chances of this ever happening? He never could have guessed it.

Just four hours earlier, they'd been coasting toward Saint Louis, and now here he was. He felt sweat developing on his forehead. The once-comfortable cab seemed small and condensed to him. For someone used to confined spaces, he was tensing up and getting claustrophobic.

He was so disgusted that he couldn't stand to even look over at Charlie. What he really wanted to do was pull the gun from underneath the seat, tell him to pull over, and leave him by the side of the road. Then off he'd go by himself, as it should have been from the beginning. He was too old for this shit, and he certainly had no business being anywhere near this city.

Why is it Charlie always seems to be reminding me of my past? An image of Thunder popped into his head. Charlie *knew* things. Might Charlie know about Raymond Butler?

"I'm tired, and I gotta call my family," Charlie said. "Why don't we call it a day, get up early in the morning, and pick up this Route 55 you're talking about?"

Jake sat silent.

"Something wrong?" Charlie asked.

"Yeah, something's wrong. I told you I wanted to push on."

"Well, if it's gonna cause you to have a heart attack, then I will."

"Whatta ya mean, heart attack?"

"You're practically on fire over there; you're steaming up the window next to ya."

He shrugged off Charlie's comments. "Eh, it doesn't mean shit. It all means nothing."

"What means nothing?" Charlie asked.

"This. Stopping here for the night in this godforsaken town. You saying one thing and me saying the other. It all means shit!"

"You're not making any sense."

"Do what you want. Do what you have to do, and I'll do what I have to do, and we'll leave it at that. But just stay out of my business."

"Look, if it's gonna eat at you like this, then we don't have to stop."

"Didn't you hear what I said? It means nothing! And I'll be the judge if something's bothering me or not...so now we're stopping. You wanted to stop, so now we're stopping. I'm too fucking tired and confused to do anything else right now."

He sat silent and motionless in the truck. He was aware of Charlie's navigating through the center of town, weaving in and out of traffic, stopping for red lights and pedestrians, but his mind was in an altogether different place.

It was the peripheral, meaningless things that he wished to remember most about that day but couldn't: things like the weather, what he had eaten for dinner the night before, the price of gas. Any one of them would have been a more pleasant thought than the picture he had in his mind.

He had money in his pocket, US dollars issued by the United States Marine Corps for services rendered, money given to him for going somewhere to kill men at will. Did a change of ground constitute a change in action? In those days it didn't.

He had done the drive from Saint Louis in one day. He had been tired and needed to rest his head for a couple of hours before calling on Raymond Butler, but that wasn't how it happened. He slept right through the night at a cheap motel on the outskirts of town, one that rented rooms by the hour. His bill was expensive come the next morning, eighty-seven dollars if he remembered correctly. He gave the scruffy-looking old man behind the counter a fifty-dollar bill and walked out, refusing to pay the rest.

He had his sights set on the man who had cheated him out of twelve thousand dollars from a recent score they'd pulled together.

It had taken him one month and one kill to find his old friend Raymond. Raymond's cousin had given him up for a bottle of gin. Jake remembered that exchange as if it were yesterday, as sad and funny as it was, though these days, nothing seemed very funny about that time in his life.

618 South Jackson Street, Chicago, Illinois. He would never forget it. It wasn't much of a house to look at. It seemed Raymond was living rather modestly on the $25,000 he had neglected to split with Jake, but he was happy to see it.

The plan was simple. Get in, grab his share of the $25,000, and walk.

He arrived at 1:30 that afternoon and sat watch for five hours across the street, but Raymond never showed. Thirsty and hungry, he went to a bar on the corner of Thirty-Third and Jackson...Krazy Kat, as he recalled. He ate a sandwich inside a red booth and then spent the next two hours drinking whiskey and watching a White Sox game on TV. Then it happened.

Raymond walked in and took a seat at the bar. He had a hooker on his arm, and shortly thereafter the two were joined by another man. Jake watched as the three of them drank for an hour. When they got up and left, he followed.

He walked the alleyway behind 618 and entered through the backyard. A rusted-out lawnmower sat idle in some tall grass, and nothing but a ripped-out screen door kept him and Raymond apart. He could hear laughter coming from the front room, and soon thereafter, a radio was turned on.

He pulled a .357 six-inch Smith & Wesson from the back of his jeans and held it in his right hand, then bent over and snatched a .45 Colt from his boot strap. It was a stubby-looking thing with a black face and wooden handle. These were his guns of choice.

He took to the porch steps and quietly stepped into a pantry-looking room. The Rolling Stones' "Nineteenth Nervous Breakdown" blared out of a radio in the next room.

Raymond stood with his back to Jake. He had his pants down to his ankles while the second man, sitting in a chair nearby, looked on. Jake couldn't see the girl, but he knew exactly where she was. There was no need for a formal announcement. He kicked an empty beer bottle as hard as he could across the floor. It slammed into the front door and shattered.

Raymond pulled back, and the girl fell on her ass. The second man jumped to his feet and grabbed for something at his side. There'd be little struggle here. He was taking no chances.

The first bullet went right through the man's kneecap, the second through the man's hand. The hooker screamed at the top of her lungs while Raymond quickly began to reason. Jake had little interest in what he had to say.

It was several seconds of hysteria, back and forth yelling—for the life of him he couldn't remember any of their words. He took Raymond and the girl from room to room at gunpoint, looking for the money. He found a few thousand dollars in an upstairs bedroom under the mattress.

A series of pistol hits to Raymond's face finally brought the truth, but by that time, the whites of the man's eyes were the only trace of a face underneath that pool of red. He dragged Raymond and the hooker down the basement steps and found two wads of cash in a red toolbox, just where Raymond had said it was. Leaving them both where he dropped them, Jake took to the steps, but then Raymond spoke out.

Coughing up some blood, he muttered, "Nigger...you always was one. Nothin' but a nigger."

Jake turned, and from his perch on the steps put one bullet into Raymond's head. The hooker screamed for her life. "Don't kill me, please don't kill me."

He climbed the stairs and locked the basement door behind him, muffling the sound of her cries. He washed the blood from his hands in the kitchen sink and reentered the night through the same door he had come in through.

Charlie tapped on the passenger side window. "How's this?"

Jake jumped in his seat. Dazed, he replied softly, "Doesn't matter."

"You're not sleeping in the car again, are you?"

Jake sat silent, no response. He continued to stare out the windshield, down the small, dark, nondescript street they were parked on. Looking down at his hands, he saw that they were beginning to tremble. He could have cried, but wouldn't. Instead, he used everything he had to keep it in him and wished for a drink. Now more than ever, he needed a drink. *God, I didn't want to ever come back to this town.*

CHAPTER 49

Charlie glanced up at the sign that read Hansjurgen Spotter House. Its faded lettering spoke of its age, much like the building it hung from. The dusty floorboards inside the lobby squeaked as he approached a small, unattended counter. He tapped the bell twice. An old woman, cigarette in hand, shuffled out of a swinging door. "Room?"

"How much?" he asked.

"Twenty-two."

"Yeah, I'll take a room."

"How many nights?"

"Just one."

"Cash only," the old lady said.

He counted out two tens and two singles and placed them on the counter. "Is there a phone in the room?"

The woman laughed aloud, which ended in a smoker's cough. "Nah... no phone. Pay phone in the upstairs hallway. You gotta hold the cord in the receiver; otherwise, it'll fall out. And I *don't* open it up for nobody, so you're not getting your money back if it does."

"How about food?"

"Whatta ya think this is, your momma's house?"

He halfheartedly smiled. "I mean, where can I get some?"

"Bing's Diner. It's around the corner and three blocks south, open all night. Been around as long as me, and they'll tell ya the same: the neighborhood's changed."

Charlie noticed her fingers as she slid over a single room key. They were stained yellow.

"Up the steps, third door on the left. That's the only key, so don't lose it, or else that's three dollars on you." She looked over his shoulder as best she could. "That your truck out there?"

He looked back, wondering if Jake was already asleep. "Yeah, is it OK to park there?"

"Should be fine as long as it's outta there by eight thirty tomorrow mornin'. That's when the delivery trucks start comin' in."

What anyone could possibly be delivering to this place he didn't know, but he was too tired to ask.

The steps to the second floor looked to be one stiff wind away from breaking apart. He gingerly approached his room, counting doors as he did. Much to his surprise and satisfaction, the room was tidier than the rest of the place. What looked to be an army cot lay atop an iron frame, and a quick inspection confirmed what he suspected. It was hard as a rock.

He dropped his bag on the floor and went back into the hallway. The pay phone looked like something out of an artifacts museum, but it would do.

Gripping the receiver with one hand and the cord with the other, he leaned up against the graffiti-ridden wall and waited for Lisa to answer. He smiled when he heard her voice.

"You don't know how good that sounds."

"What?"

"Your voice."

"That's nice to say. You've never said that before."

He could feel her smile through the phone, could picture her in his mind, lying in bed with the covers pulled up tight. "There's a lot of things I haven't said."

"You'll never believe what I did tonight, Charlie."

"What?"

"I pulled your mom's old eight tracks out of the closet."

"Really?"

"I did."

"Let me guess: Nat."

"How did you know?"

"Lucky. What made you do that?"

Lisa paused. "Because I missed you. Where are you?"

"Chicago."

"Chicago? Wow, how is it?"

"We just pulled in, but the skyline was something to see. So many lights, big beautiful buildings, people everywhere. How are the boys?"

"They're good, dreaming of their daddy, I'm sure. Tell me about Jake, Charlie. What's he like?"

"Wow! Where do I start? He's tough to get to know. Keeps to himself mostly. Never had any kids, never been married. Guess it makes 'im a bit of a loner."

"That doesn't sound very good; you never know what people like that are going to do."

"Yeah, but he's fine, babe. He may be those things, but I still like him." He paused, half expecting to hear "Don't lie to me, Charlie," but she said nothing. *Maybe I'm getting better at this.* "Listen, deep down, I think he's a decent man. He's just had a hard life."

"Is he being nice to you?"

He laughed out loud. "What kind of question's that?"

"I wanna make sure he is. Don't take any shit from him. And remember that at any time you can get on a bus and come home. Hell, I'll pack up the kids and come and get you if you want."

Lisa's words of encouragement were fitting for the kind of day he'd had, but going home wasn't an option. At one point earlier in the day, possibly, but from that moment on, he'd made a commitment to himself to see this through till the end. "Don't you worry about me. That old Jake is a good person deep down. I better get something in my belly before it gets too late."

"No, I don't wanna hang up. Tell me what you're gonna do."

"I'm gonna take a look at this city. I've never been to Chicago. Figure I might as well take in some sights before we're off again in the morning."

"OK. You be careful, huh?"

"Always."

"Good night, Charlie."

CHAPTER 50

Charlie threw on an extra sweatshirt and zipped up his coat. He exited the Spotter House and was met by a brisk wind that cut through his skin and chilled his bones. Jake's pickup was nowhere in sight, causing him a moment of pause. It was 9:30 p.m., and with his sights set on the downtown skyline, he began walking the twenty-some-odd blocks toward it.

Minus the occasional hooker or street bum, the streets were empty. Block after block, he cut through the crisp Chicago night sure that the downtown area before him would provide something more to see.

He entered the first bar he came to, Momma's, and one drink later, he moved on. Next was a place called Captain's, followed by the Note.

All kinds of music blared out of the swinging doors he walked by—jazz, blues, rock and roll—but the pulsing sounds did little to help drown out the questions running through his mind. What did the next few days hold for him? When and where would he find the truth? What did this trip mean? He could go on for hours listing the signs in his life that pointed to Jake Mott, but he wouldn't. Fact was, some were too distressing to think about. Hopefully, history wouldn't repeat itself, in the desert or anywhere else. He feared Jake more than he even thought.

"Come on, snap out of it," he said. Maybe it was the booze talking, but by now he had more than a few drinks in him and had forgotten to eat dinner. Thankfully, the liquor in his stomach was keeping him warm.

He came upon a bar and looked up at the sign. It read Kingston Mines. Charlie walked in and took a seat at the bar. A solo blues act was playing on stage.

The inside of Kingston Mines was unlike anything he had seen before. The place was packed as if it were a Friday night at Jerry's, and all kinds were represented. Whites, blacks, suits, working men, even some of Chicago's homeless, and a few ladies of the night as well. People sat family style at tables that stretched the width of the bar while a throng of blues acts came up one after another. He was amazed at how much the city was still alive midweek at one in the morning.

Charlie sipped his beer and studied the patrons who surrounded the little stage. One table in particular had everyone's attention: a long-haired blonde jumped on top of the table and started to dance. He watched her, as did everyone else, but then something caught his eye.

It was dark, and the stage lighting cast a shadow across half the table. He squinted, narrowing his sight for a better look, and at that moment everything around him stopped, including his heart. He slowly put his beer back down on the bar. It was as if a bolt of lightning had just cut through his body. Of all the places he could have been, at that moment, on this night…yet here he was in a bar he'd never heard of, in a city he was unfamiliar with, watching Pop Grey take in the very same scenery he was.

He quickly looked away, shook off some cobwebs, downed his beer, and then went back for a second look. But the result was the same. *My God!* Pop Grey was sitting within twenty feet of him, at the very table the blond girl was dancing on.

His physical body slowly came back to reality, but he wasn't so sure he could feel the tips of his toes or fingers. Was it the cold, the booze, or what he was witnessing? He felt paralyzed, both emotionally and physically. And then it hit him: this was it. He had met Jake Mott, persuaded the stubborn old convict to take him cross-country, and taken a wrong turn two states back only to end up in an unlikely city to run into the man he'd been dreaming of killing since he was thirteen.

He could only see the left side of the bastard's profile; the other side sat in a shadow, but there was no doubting it was him. That eternal look of being fifty-eight, stark white hair, neatly parted, that sarcastic grin.

The bartender tapped his index finger in front of Charlie's empty beer. "Hey buddy, last call."

"Huh?"

"I said last call. You want anything?"

"No, no I don't." Charlie turned back around, but in that instant, the bastard was gone. He did a quick scan of the place and saw him cutting through a maze of occupied seats heading for the front door. He threw a ten atop the bar and jumped off his stool.

He was met by a rush of people outside on the sidewalk. It seemed as if all the bars were emptying out at the same time as a sea of people meandered about. He looked left, then right, but lost him in the crowd. But then he spotted the back of his head, halfway up the block. Charlie fell in line with the crowd, keeping a close eye as best he could. He picked up his pace and closed in on his heels, staying there for another block, wondering what in the hell he would say to him.

He saw his grandfather's right hand go in the air, and a nearby cab pulled over. Charlie paused and watched him lean in for the door's handle.

"Wait! Wait!" He ran up, put his hand on his shoulder, and swung him around.

"Hey! What the hell, buddy?"

Charlie took a step back. While there was some resemblance from afar, up close there was no question—it wasn't him.

"I'm sorry, I—I thought you were somebody else."

"Yeah, who?"

"Forget it. Just forget it."

The man jumped into the cab and slammed the door shut. "Have another drink, asshole!"

He watched the cab pull away, feeling a mix of disappointment and relief. Though he had had a lot to drink, he would have bet his life that Lawrence Gray was sitting at that table inside Kingston Mines. For a brief second, he wondered if it really had been him and that perhaps he'd lost him in the crowd. The night's cold wind was beginning to cut through his two layers of thin clothing. He was drunk and tired.

CHAPTER 51

J ake sat in the pickup truck, every now and again glancing at the clock on the dashboard. Raymond Butler had been on his mind all night, had even called on him in his sleep and asked him some questions not much different than Jake had asked himself over the years. Things like, *Are you ready to kill again? Will you be meeting the devil tonight? When is it your turn to die?*

The occasional police siren would bring him back to the clock. The sun was minutes from lift-off, and he was ready to hit the road. He jumped out of the truck and headed toward the Spotter House. He reached for the door handle and pulled on it, but it was still locked. Leaning back, he pounded on the front door three or four times. More sirens rang out in the distance. He looked in their general direction.

He didn't want this trip to turn into a return down memory lane and swore from here on out it wouldn't. He gave the front door three more pounds of his fist.

A muffled voice from inside responded, "We're closed. Get the hell out, or I'll call the cops."

That was all he needed to hear. He wasn't putting up a fight, at least not for Charlie Boone.

Charlie opened his eyes and for a moment forgot where he was. A moment later, the army surplus cot that held his thin frame had kick-started his memory. He wondered if he'd dreamed the whole thing—the twenty cold blocks, the empty stomach, seeing Pop Grey at the blues bar. But with his head feeling like the thirty-pound weight it did, he figured differently.

He grabbed for his wristwatch; it was 9:15. "Holy shit!"

He jumped out of bed fully clothed and grabbed his bag. The feeling in his gut was that Jake was long gone, and though it hadn't registered with him at the time, he thought he might have even left the night before.

The old lady behind the counter mumbled something as he threw the room key onto the counter and exited the building.

Just as he'd feared, the sun was bright and the street was empty, with no sign of Jake. He looked down the street, but there was nothing but some empty trash cans kicking around in the wind.

"Jake Mott," Charlie said softly. "He'll show me the way."

Jake was moving at a good clip and passing a steady stream of cars as he rode the left-hand lane. Coming back to this city had done some serious damage to his mental state, and he was in a zone, a death zone of sorts. While there had been other victims who'd made their way into his nightmares, this was the first time he had ever dreamed of Raymond Butler.

He slowed down to pay a toll and saw a sign that read "3 miles to Indiana." Handing over his money, he wondered what good, if any, he could do in this world after all the pain he'd inflicted.

True, he'd done thirty years' hard time, but what about the others, the ones they didn't know about? There were five, to be exact, including Raymond, and though not one had been free of sin nor a decent man in Jake's mind, what right did he have to take their lives?

He considered Raymond's question from the night before. Maybe it was his turn to die. But it would have to be by his own doing.

His hands went numb, and his eyes glazed over. He was content to let the truck drive itself and let whatever may be, be. His guilt was winning the battle, and he was ready to give up. He wanted out. He had nothing to live for, a fact that had become grossly evident upon his release from prison. Should he die today, at this very moment, behind the wheel of this shitty truck, there wouldn't be a person in the world it would matter to.

And then he heard a single voice at the forefront of his mind, a request from a stranger who had invited him into her home and fed him his first warm, home-cooked meal in three decades: "You take good care of my husband, now, Mr. Mott. You promise me that."

Jake knew little about women, but he did know people, and he also knew those words had been said for good reason by a woman born of conviction. A vision of Eddie Boone found its way to his windshield, causing him to slow the vehicle to a crawl. He took a deep breath and pulled over to the side of the road.

Sitting up against the Spotter House, Charlie looked at his watch and then tucked his raw, cold hands into his Septa coat. It was twenty past ten.

Still keeping a firm eye on the corner, he saw the nose of an old black pickup appear around a bend. It slowed to a stop alongside him.

Jake looked stoic as ever, staring out the windshield. He didn't roll down the window, nor did he blink an eye. Charlie walked around the front of the vehicle and got in. "Everything OK?"

"I made a promise," Jake replied. "I haven't made many of those in my life, at least not that I've kept, but this one I'm keeping." Jake looked over at Charlie. "If it's the last thing I do on this earth, I'm keeping it."

"And what promise was that?" Charlie asked.

He was just about to say it but held back. Looking over at Charlie, Jake felt something he'd never felt before, and though it was brief, he knew exactly what it was. He felt sorry for the man sitting next to him, for Charlie's life was no better than his own. The realization of what and who Charlie was made him feel compassion not just for Charlie but the man's wife and kids, too. He had figured it out. Charlie was a tortured soul, and that was the only thing the two men would ever have in common.

"It's over," Jake said.

"What's over?"

"This trip. It's time to go back."

Charlie nodded his head in agreement. "OK, it's your trip. I was just along for the ride."

Jake put the truck in drive and began their trip back east.

CHAPTER 52

They had been driving five hours and were well into Ohio. Jake had his sights on being at the trailer by midnight. Their last words to each other had been many hours earlier, and Charlie was just beginning to doze off. A loud bang rang out, and the truck quickly lost speed. Unable to climb above ten miles per hour, Jake pulled over to the shoulder and let out a deep breath. "I think we got a flat."

"That's no flat," Charlie said. "That's the transmission."

"How do ya know?" Jake asked.

"It's happened to me before. No acceleration means the transmission's gone."

He agreed with Charlie's prognosis. "Son of a bitch, what a shitty thing to happen now."

"How far back was that last exit we passed?" Charlie asked.

"About a mile or two. Think it said Strongsville."

Charlie looked out the windshield. "Wonder how close the next one is?"

"Who knows? Could be ten miles or more."

Charlie grabbed his bag. "Well then, Strongsville it is."

Charlie exited the truck and started walking back toward the exit they had just passed. His pace prompted Jake to jump out. "Maybe we should wait for someone to stop."

"Those are your sleeping chambers, not mine."

"Maybe we should hitchhike?"

Charlie called over his shoulder. "Go right ahead. I'll walk it."

Jake grabbed the keys out of the ignition and fell in line behind Charlie's lead. He could just make out the dark silhouette twenty or so yards ahead of him against the backdrop of the night.

Minus the usual big rigs, the highway was relatively empty. The short distance that set the two men apart jogged a memory from Jake's mind. "Creatures of habit, I guess."

"Say again," Charlie called back.

"Habit or instinct? I don't know which, but between the military and prison, I've been walking in lines my whole life. Even these few weeks I've been out, I've found myself following right behind complete strangers. Funny that way."

"Odd for a guy who has a thing with trust."

Jake shook his head in agreement. "Good point. Polar opposites, too. The military teaches you to trust the man next to you at all costs; prison teaches you the exact opposite."

"I wouldn't know."

"Take it from me, only thing in common they have is they'll both chew ya up and spit ya out."

"It's awfully fuckin' dark out here," Charlie said.

"Did a lot of that too," Jake replied.

"A lot of what?"

"Walking in the dark. Only time to march when you're at war. Your eyes get accustomed to it, you might even like it after a while. Hides all the hell around ya. A man can walk in a war zone and dream he's on a stroll through Yellowstone."

"Yellowstone, huh?"

"Well, not me. Some guys would. They'd talk about it, guys who had been there anyway. I'd never been out of Praire till I went to boot camp."

"What's Praire?" Charlie asked.

Jake glanced up at Charlie, debating whether or not to even go there. "It's where I was born, where I grew up. Praire, Texas."

Charlie repeated it aloud. "Praire, Texas. Never heard of it."

"Small, little town."

Charlie laughed. "Well, I'll be damned."

"What?" Jake asked.

"Don't look now, but I just might be getting to know you."

"Not many have done that."

"Oh, I believe it," Charlie replied. "So what did you think about, on your marches? If it wasn't Yellowstone, what was it?"

He pictured that piece of land behind his boyhood home. "Just a little piece of woods. Not much to look at from afar, but up close, it was something else. A stream ran through it, two walls of green hugged its sides. You could throw a branch in it and listen to the water take it away—cool as ice, Uncle Sam always said. I didn't know it then, but it was one hell of a peaceful spot."

"I have to admit, that's not what I expected to hear you say."

"It sits in there somewhere. Pops up from time to time, covered up mostly, by more bad than good."

"You keep thinking that way, and it'll stay covered up."

"How the hell we get talking about this?"

Charlie shook his head. "Something about marching in lines."

"Right. Prison and the military, the two places I never thought I'd get out of."

"And now here you are, on your way to Strongsville by foot a few hours from midnight with a guy you can't seem to get rid of. What more can you ask?"

Jake laughed. "It has been interesting, I'll say that."

Now walking side by side, they shared a casual smile as a blanket of lights, Strongsville, came into view in the distance.

It was half past midnight by the time he and Charlie reached the center of town. There was little to offer in terms of lodging, so they took shelter inside the foyer of a bus station across the street from a place called Tarpy's Auto. Charlie used his duffel bag as a pillow and lay up against a far wall. Jake followed suit, bunching up his jacket in a ball and tucking it underneath his neck.

The foyer floor was cold and damp and reminded Jake of solitary. Though he'd never acknowledge it, Charlie was a welcome presence and made his sleep a bit more peaceful.

A few hours later, a ring of dangling keys bounced off the glass door above their heads. The manager of the bus station opened up the entrance doors. It was 5:00 a.m. He studied both men sprawled out on the floor and then shook his head as if it wasn't the first time and went about his business.

Charlie stood up and stretched. "We forgot to do something."

"What?"

"The truck. We should have left a white T-shirt in the window so at least they'd know you'd be back for it."

Still lying on the ground, Jake nodded toward Tarpy's. "You see any lights on in that shop?"

"Yeah, they're on."

Jake slowly pulled his body off the cold floor. "Cold floors don't do old bones any good."

"I need to call my wife. She's probably worried sick right now."

"How do you know?"

"It's called marriage. Just one of those things. And once she hears everything's OK, then she'll start laying into me."

"Laying into ya?"

Charlie picked up his bag. "Give me a bunch of shit."

"Oh, right. I never did think I was missing anything there…marriage, I mean."

Charlie dug for some change in his pocket. "Yeah, well, it has its good days and bad days. Good luck with the truck."

Surprised at Charlie's abrupt exit, he replied, "Yeah. I'll see ya."

CHAPTER 53

She was in and out of a soft sleep. She jumped up and answered the phone in a panic. "Charlie!"

"It's me."

"Charlie! What happened? Every day, we said, remember? *Every day!*"

"I know, I know, but yesterday was an absolute mess."

"A mess how?"

"Let's say nothing short of bizarre. It was just nuts."

"That's it. I want you home right now."

Silence occupied the phone. She waited for the answer she so hoped to hear.

"Charlie?"

"Yeah, I'm here."

"Tell me what's wrong. Something's wrong; I can tell."

"I don't know what you're talking about."

"Bullshit, you're lying to me, I can tell! You're a horrible liar. You always have been."

Maybe I'm not getting so good at this. "We had some car trouble."

"So where are you?"

"I'm in Ohio."

"You're still in Ohio?" A million different scenarios ran through her mind. She sighed. "Charlie, are you coming home or what?"

"I think so," he replied softly.

"When?"

"I'll probably catch a bus. I need to look at a schedule. I'll call you when I figure it out."

Finally the words she needed to hear. She hung up the phone and took note of the sun beginning to rise outside her bedroom window and declared it to be a great day.

CHAPTER 54

Charlie sat in a booth in the back corner sipping on his third cup of coffee. He was going home and was fine with it. But the scraps of eggs on the plate before him took him back to the woman lying in bed on the second floor. *What am I to do?* Not only for himself, but perhaps it had finally come time to get her the help she needed, if it wasn't too late. They hadn't shared many gentle moments, but the few they did he held close and remembered often.

He'd been away for a while, spending the summer at the beach with Lisa, and hadn't been home in months. The front door had been left open when he got there, leaving just the screen door between his mom and the outside world. That was a good sign. She normally had things locked down tight when she was in a bad way.

She was in the kitchen...he could tell she was losing weight. She was anxious too, going back and forth from table to cupboard without getting anything done.

"How are you?" he asked.

"Good." She stopped what she was doing. "I made egg salad. Is that all right?"

"Yeah, that's fine."

"Good, have a seat. My mother made egg salad for me during the summer. It's a good summer meal."

He looked around the kitchen and the living room. The place was spotless. "It looks good in here."

"I know! The cleaning girl does a great job."

"What cleaning girl?"

"Our cleaning girl."

"We don't have a cleaning girl."

"Of course we do, Charlie." She was mixing the egg salad in a bowl at the sink but stopped what she was doing and looked out the window. "Her name's Beth."

"Where did you find her?" I asked.

"Oh, Charlie, what does it matter? Please, don't give me a hard time."

She dropped two sandwiches on the paper plate in front of him and sat down. "I went out and bought everything fresh today, so eat up. You must be starving."

He took a bite, but it was nothing but shells. He tried for a second bite but got even more. He put it down and didn't go back.

"Did you love him?" he asked.

"Love who?"

"You know who. Did you like going to Trenton all those years?"

She got up from the table and put her plate on the counter. "What kind of question is that? I mean really, Charlie. You haven't seen me in months, and you ask me that?"

"Because I should have asked it a long time ago! Did you love him?"

"Don't you raise your voice to me. Who do you think you are? He was my father. He took care of me. Of course I loved him."

"He wasn't your real father."

"He took care of me…he took care of us."

"Did he? Did he really?"

"You ungrateful…! You're wrong to be asking me these questions. Wrong! What about me? Don't you ever think about me, or is it all about yourself?"

"I am thinking about you, damn it! If you weren't so fucked up in the head, you'd realize that."

She cocked back and slapped him across the face.

He couldn't believe it, nor could he believe he'd finally said it. He sat back in the chair and didn't move. They both sat silent for a long time.

Charlie got up and began to clear the rest of the table. "You look like you're losing weight…you should be eating more. I'm gonna wrap these up and put them in the fridge. You can eat them tomorrow."

She waved her hand at him. "Do what you want with them. I don't even like egg salad. I made it for you."

"I don't like it either."

She gave him her famous grin. "Then why did I make it?"

They both chuckled out loud. He didn't know why she did anything, let alone make him egg salad, which she had never done before. He could count on both hands how many warm, cooked *meals she'd made as he was growing up. Even those weren't very good—either cold by the time they reached the table or just plain awful to taste. But he never complained. He never complained about anything. It would have been nice if just once she was able to understand that.*

He wanted to take back his words, but what was done was done. Maybe he could still change one thing.

"Mom...maybe we could get you back to talking with somebody. What was the name of that guy you liked? Reed? What ever happened to him?"

She shook her head. "Who knows? They're all the same. You look away, and they stick their hand up your dress. They're all the same, Charlie. They creep into your head, and then they try to creep into your pants. That's it—that's all they're worth."

"Mom?"

"They get you asleep in their office, and then the next thing you know, they're rummaging through your purse. You can't trust nobody, Charlie, not ever."

"Mom! I'm sorry...I'm sorry for everything I said."

She smiled at him and then raised her right hand and rubbed his cheek. "You don't have to be sorry for anything. I love you, Charlie. I don't know what I would've done without you."

He started to cry.

"Please promise me one thing."

Anything! Anything for her today. "What?"

"Don't let them take me away. Promise me you'll never let them take me away."

"I won't...I promise, I won't ever."

They hugged and held onto each other as tight as could be. It was a day he'd never forget and a promise he'd keep forever.

Jake walked in, stopped at the register, and looked around the place. The two met eyes and nodded to each other. Jake took a seat at the counter.

Charlie looked at his watch and then downed the rest of his cup.

He stopped next to Jake on his way out. "How'd you make out?"

"Not good," Jake replied.

"What's the damage?"

"A whole lotta money...'bout fifteen hundred worth."

"You could buy a new one for that kind of money," Charlie said. "Transmission?"

Saying it as if it hurt, Jake replied, "You got it. Must've bought a lemon."

"So what're ya gonna do?" Charlie asked.

"Don't know yet, but I know what I ain't. I don't got five hundred to sink into that truck, let alone fifteen." Jake motioned for a server. "Can I get a coffee?"

A waitress dropped a cup of coffee in front of Jake. "What can I get ya?"

"Three eggs over easy, plenty of hash browns, and a side of bacon."

"Plenty of hash browns?" the waitress replied.

"As many as you can get away with."

Jake dumped sugar and cream into his coffee and tasted it. "Seems damn cold in here," he said.

Charlie looked out the window at the gray overcast day, the kind of day that's easy to forget. "Winter's just around the corner," he said.

"It was cold in that foyer last night. I forgot how cold it gets up north. Think the warm weather suits me best."

"Fifteen hundred dollars is a lot of scratch."

"You got that right," Jake replied.

"There's a bus headed east, leaves at three o'clock, scheduled to arrive in Philly tomorrow morning."

"Yeah, I saw that. Not sure what I'm gonna do. Might kick around out here a bit, see what it's got. There's nothing back east for me anyway."

Charlie looked down at his own feet and said, "My mom's crazy. She's a schizophrenic, actually. Undiagnosed, but that's what she is, been catatonic the last few years. Last meaningful words we shared were probably five years ago."

Jake put his coffee down. "How'd all that happen?"

"Not sure. She was abused as a child, probably kick-started things." He looked up at Jake. "I've never told anyone that before."

"Why?" Jake said.

"Why didn't I?" Charlie asked.

"Why to all of it. Why didn't she get help, why you telling me?"

"I don't know the answer to either. Maybe after what you told me last night, I kind of felt the need to share." Charlie straightened up. "Take care of yourself, Jake."

"Hey, Charlie?"

Stopping at the door, Charlie turned around and looked Jake in the eye.

"In another time, maybe, but right now, it just wasn't meant to happen."

He nodded to the plate of food the waitress had just dropped in front of Jake and replied, "Enjoy."

CHAPTER 55

J ake finished his breakfast, bought a paper from a vending machine outside the diner, and walked to the middle of town. Chicago had taken a toll on him. He wanted to sit awhile and be alone.

He found a single bench in the town square. A slight breeze picked up, and a scattering of brown and red leaves skipped over his feet. Strongsville was a far cry from Georgia State.

Georgia State. Would he ever stop thinking about it? Here he was a free man, still struggling with the actions of his youth because the memories were all too fresh in his mind. His former home had a way of blocking bad memories out, but not now. God, he just wanted to be done with it all.

He blamed Charlie for taking him to places he cursed and reminding him of days he wanted to forget. He was glad to be rid of him once and for all. Funny how he had thought taking Charlie across country would provide him the redemption he so sorely needed. He came to the realization that making peace with his past was going to take a hell of a lot more than doing a good deed for some nut job he hardly knew.

"Excuse me?"

Jake looked up. A man in a suit approached him from the direction of the courthouse. The man smiled. "You from around here?"

Guardedly, Jake replied, "No, I'm not."

The suit stopped a few feet in front of him. "I didn't think so. I am—born and raised, actually. Maybe I can help you?"

"How's that?" Jake asked.

"You here visiting someone? Friends, family? Maybe I can help you find your way around town."

"No, no help needed."

The suit laughed. "Listen, I don't want this to come out the wrong way, but this town doesn't have patience for riffraff, and I'm just trying to help ya out, friend."

Jake looked down at the newspaper in his hands. It was shaking ever so slightly, but not from anger. Here he sat with a man half his size before him, a racist fuck who knew nothing of Jake but knew enough that he didn't want the likes of him in his town, and he felt helpless. He had killed men for lesser actions in his past, but today, Jake wore his past on his sleeves. His silence alone spoke of his embarrassment. He was a criminal, a black one at that, in the heart of America. Seemed at least some things still hadn't changed.

Two cops stood on the courthouse steps, keeping a mindful watch. "Just some car trouble," Jake replied softly. "Just biding my time, that's all."

"Car trouble? I'm sorry to hear that. There's a bus station just on the edge of town, about two miles up. Buses leave every hour. Where did you come in from?"

Jake stood up, causing the suit to take a few steps back. "It's not important."

He walked out of the town square and didn't look back. His pride was shot, and more than ever, he felt vulnerable to the outside world. The more days that passed between him and Georgia State, the more his faith seemed to weaken. Perhaps freedom wasn't all it was cracked up to be. At least in the peacefulness and solitude of a man's cell, no one can hurt you. *Ironic.*

It was quarter to three by the time he had the bus station in his sights, and so was Tarpy's Auto. He was surprised by what he saw. Sitting midair on one of the hydraulic lifts was his black pickup. "I'll be damned," he whispered.

He crossed the street and called into the garage. "Thought you said this thing was trash?"

A greasy mechanic looked over at him. "There you are. I just sent one of the kids into town to look for ya."

"For what?"

"Seems you got a friend, mister. A guy stopped in a couple hours ago, bought you a new transmission. Asked me to make it like new, so that's what I'm doin'."

"He did what?"

"Gave me two thousand cash and told me to make it new. I'll have this whole engine rebuilt in another couple of hours for ya. For two thousand dollars, I can promise ya that!"

He looked across the street toward the bus station, but a bus rolled up and blocked his view. Without hesitation, he crossed back over and entered the depot. He expected to see a crowd of people inside, but there were only a few. Charlie was sitting on a wooden bench in a patch of sunlight near a window.

Jake approached him and silently took a seat on the same bench, but a few feet away. "I, ah…" He cleared his throat. "I—"

Charlie cut in. "Don't say anything. There's no need to; I wanted to do it."

"That's a lot of money for someone who drives a bus for a living."

"Yeah, but like I said, I wanted to do it. Seemed like the right thing, anyway. At least you'll be able to get out of town on your own terms. Besides, they *were* your sleeping quarters."

Jake grinned and acknowledged Charlie as being only number two in his life. Charlie and Warden Brendan Frank, the only two men to ever do a kind thing for him. He had never been in a position to return the deed to the warden, but with Charlie, perhaps he was.

After a few moments' struggle, he softly said, "I killed a man in Chicago… many years ago."

The look on Charlie's face said enough.

"Never heard *those* words before, have you?"

"Is that why you went away?" Charlie asked.

Unable to even say the word, Jake shook his head no.

"You think things happen for a reason, Jake?"

"That's a bad question to ask me. I got no one but myself to blame for what I've done. Kid like you, though, it's probably different."

"How?"

"I don't know."

"I've never killed a man," Charlie said. "But God, I've thought about it. In the end, I never had what it took. Even through all the shit, I never had what it took to do it. I thought if I killed him, it would make things right. But something tells me I wouldn't be any better off than I am today. Probably be in jail somewhere, my kids would never know who I was, my wife cursing my name. Life's fragile that way—one decision can change everything."

Jake looked over at Charlie. "Fate?"

"Fate," Charlie replied.

"Who was he?" Jake asked.

"My mother's stepfather." Charlie took in a slow breath and then exhaled. "I don't know how young she was, probably never will. And I'll also never know what she might have been."

Jake rubbed at the cracks in his hands. "It took me a long time to get it, but I realize now you can't take things into your own hands, no matter the crime. Their day will come, but at the hand of someone else." Jake fell silent for a moment. "As will mine. I played judge and jury for too long, and one day it caught up to me. Because of it, I haven't seen my mother for a lifetime. Could probably pass her on the street and not even know it."

Charlie smiled halfheartedly. "Sounds like we're just a couple of orphans."

Jake grinned. "Yeah, oldest ones around, I guess. Ehh! I don't feel sorry for myself, and I don't want pity. It is what it is."

Like a horse in waiting, the bus parked outside the depot belched up some exhaust, as if to say it was time. Charlie looked at his watch and stood up. "Well, I don't wanna miss my ticket back. Like I said, you take care of yourself."

Jake nodded as he let Charlie pass. He had *nothing* to give back. The few dollars in his pocket he'd surely need for food, his heart was still cold from years of solitude, and even a few kind words were hard to put together. He whispered, "Damned if I have anywhere to go."

Looking over toward the exit, he called out, "Charlie!"

It was the first time he'd ever called Charlie by his name. Charlie stopped and looked back.

"You're gonna think I'm nuts, but I'm making a run to California, and who knows, maybe there's something out there for both of us."

"I don't want money, Jake."

"I believe you. But you are looking for me to lead you to something. Well, I don't think I can do that, son, but maybe I am wrong. Maybe we can help each other."

He was hours away from home. "You're going all the way to California?" Charlie asked.

"Money's still money, and if you're in, then you're entitled, and you're all in." Jake grinned. "Where I came from, those were the stakes."

Charlie had a straight shot through the small foyer at the bus driver sitting behind the big steering wheel. The two met eyes. With one hand on the door lever, ready to close it, the driver asked, "You on this bus?"

He had talked about defining moments before, had just had one a few minutes earlier with Jake, and now here he was, right smack back in the middle of another. Should he stay or should he go? Could this be that right turn that would change everything for him? Just twenty minutes earlier, he had been resigned to going home. He was going home to be with his wife and kids and to sit vigil by his mother's side in hopes of one last enlightenment. But now, this.

He looked to Jake. "I'm in."

———

As quickly as they had found themselves, the day before, stranded roadside in the dark of night, they were off again, and this time it was for real. It felt like freedom when Jake hit I-70 and opened up their brand-new truck, courtesy of Charlie.

"Oh, yeah," Jake shouted over the sounds of the open road. "He fixed the radio, too!"

Jake turned it on and stopped the dial at the first melody he heard. Fitting it was Bruce Springsteen's "This Hard Land" belting from the crackling speakers of the old pickup truck. Strings of words such as "back into the dirt of this hard land, been blowing around from town to town and sweeping low across the plains" spoke to both men. There was a different feel in the truck, and whether it be hope or something else, for once in a long time, both men shared a moment of content.

CHAPTER 56

She sat at the kitchen table feeling as if she'd just been given the worst news of her life. "I'm not coming home today. We'll be back as originally planned."

How did this happen? Just that morning, he had been planning to take the next bus home. She gave him hell on the phone and told him there was no room for error from here on out. Two calls home a day, one in the morning and one at night.

There was a loud thump above her. She had a picture in her mind of Eddie, standing atop his dresser and throwing Bear onto Billy's bed. She had caught him doing it yesterday after school and warned him to stop.

She walked to the steps and called up, "Eddie? What was that?"

There was no answer.

Taking to the steps, she continued. "Eddie! If you dropped that dog, I swear, I'll…" Reaching the top, she never finished her sentence. Eddie and Billy stood in the doorway of their grandmother's bedroom. Eddie's mouth was agape, and Billy looked confused.

"Eddie?"

Her son remained frozen in the doorway and didn't answer her.

"Eddie, honey, what is it?"

His mouth began to take shape, but nothing came out of it. She ran down the hall and looked in the room. Mrs. Boone lay face down on the floor.

"Oh, my God!"

She pushed her sons out of the way and lunged for her mother-in-law. As gingerly as she could, she rolled Mrs. Boone's frail body over onto her back and cradled her head in her arms. The sight of her busted lip instantly made Lisa's eyes water. The fact that she was still breathing gave her a brief moment of relief.

She looked toward the bed. "How did this happen? Mom, can you hear me? Are you OK?"

Mrs. Boone let out an uninterpretable gasp. Her mouth was bone dry, and a second look at her lips showed severe cracking. Lisa looked around on the floor and saw her mother-in-law's juice bottle on the floor; it, too, was bone dry. She picked it up and looked over at Eddie.

"I told you to fill this last night! I told you to fill this and come up here and feed your grandmother. I asked you again this morning to do the same thing. Did you do that? Did you do *any of it?*"

His little body started to shake.

"Damn it, Eddie, speak to me! Did you do it?"

He shook his head no.

She looked around the room in a mix of bewilderment, anger, and frustration. The room was getting smaller by the second, and her body felt as if it were spinning; she was getting dizzy. Still holding her mother-in-law in her arms, Lisa felt her own body go limp.

Billy went into a full-throttle cry, and the sound of his frantic tears abruptly snapped her out of it. The first thing she saw was a picture of Charlie on the bureau before her. She threw the water bottle across the room and screamed as she did so. "Fuck!"

She looked back up at her son. "Damn it, Eddie, you said you wanted to help! You remember that? Do you remember saying that?"

Like the rest of his body, his bottom lip was now trembling.

"Don't you even think about crying, you hear me?" She was fighting back her own tears. "Go get that bottle! Go get it and fill it up with water, right now!"

Eddie ran into the bedroom, retrieved the plastic water bottle from the corner, and ran downstairs.

Billy's crying was going to send her over the edge; she couldn't bear it anymore. "Billy! Stop it!"

Her youngest son looked up from the floor.

"Go to your room and shut the door. Do it now. I'll be right in."

Billy disappeared from the doorway, and a moment later, she heard his bedroom door shut. Finally a moment alone to collect her thoughts. "Oh Lord, please don't die."

Her mother-in-law's eyes, though barely open, seemed slightly glazed over, and her breathing was slight. No water for over a day; that was the next thing that came to mind. She needed help. She needed to see a doctor right away, but there was a problem with that.

Any doctor in his right mind would take one look at the situation and have Mrs. Boone admitted within the hour. Looking back over at Charlie's picture, she knew he'd never forgive her. *But how could he fault me?* Surely he'd understand, without being there to help or see the severity of the situation. *Right?* Then again, should anything happen to Mrs. Boone away from their home, it would be on her. Feeling the pressure of the moment made her want to vomit, and then it hit her.

Marny's sister was an ER nurse at Temple. Lisa would have to call in a favor, and she wouldn't take no for an answer.

CHAPTER 57

The last four hours had seemed to go on for days, the only consolation being that her splitting headache had finally subsided. Billy had cried himself to sleep in Eddie's arms on his bed. It was kind of Eddie to take care of his little brother that way. And as for Eddie, she'd have to make things right with him in the morning. No matter what she had said in the heat of the moment, it wasn't his fault…it was no one's fault but hers.

Marny was standing near the kitchen door when her sister Linda appeared from the next room, shooting her a look as if to say, *what in the hell have you gotten me into?*

Lisa noticed.

The no-nonsense-looking nurse breezed by her sister and took a spot up against the kitchen counter. "Well, I don't know what to say."

"What does that mean?" Lisa asked.

"It means I'm not so sure I can keep my bedside manner in check."

Lisa felt herself run cold. "Well, then, just say what's on your mind."

"OK. Do you *realize* what's happening here? Do you have any clue? You don't have the resources or the knowledge to *ever* properly care for this woman." Linda briefly looked over at her sister. "Personally, I'd like to know just how long it's been like this."

Linda's words sank in. "Too long," Lisa whispered.

"I'm sorry?"

"I said too long." She let out a deep breath. "Years, actually."

"Wow! Well, Lisa, your mother-in-law's dying a slow death, and that's the long and short of it."

She knew as much, had known for several weeks but didn't want to admit it to herself, and certainly not to Charlie. Her eyes welled. "I know she is; she has been."

"How long?" Linda asked.

"It's gotten real bad the last couple of months. I was waiting for Charlie to say something, but he hasn't. Either he's in denial, or he's...I don't know what he is, but I've seen a big change in her."

Linda took a seat at the kitchen table and grabbed Lisa's hand. "Lisa, I need you to be honest with me. What's happening in this house?"

She shook her head, as if she wasn't even sure herself. "Charlie...Charlie just refuses to get her help—professional help, you know? He always has."

Linda pulled a tissue from the box on the table and handed it to her.

"She was abused as a child, so he says. It was her stepfather. It started sometime after her mother died. At some point, she got pregnant and was sent away...and then it was just Charlie and her." Lisa was shaking her head. "She was never right, he said, even when he was young."

"Where is Charlie?" Linda asked.

Her heart dropped. She had been waiting for that question all night and was still unsure how to answer it. With both women awaiting an answer with stern looks on their faces, telling the truth didn't seem like an option. "He's on a hunting trip with some buddies from work."

"Since when does Charlie hunt?" Marny asked.

Lisa grinned. "You're right, he doesn't. It was more of a guy thing, you know? Just trying to fit in, I guess. He's never been away ever, so I was fine with it."

Linda cleared her throat. "Well, let's get back to what we know. Her blood pressure is a little low, but her heart rate's normal. She has some bedsores on her backside, but there're no sign of infection in them...yet."

"I treat them," Lisa replied, staring down at her lap. "At least three times a week." Looking up, she went on. "She hasn't left the house in five years. For that matter, she hasn't been down the steps in probably a year. Charlie and I try to walk her around the room at least daily. It's not much, but it's something."

Linda fell still and silent. She looked up to her sister in the doorway and then turned back to Lisa. "I can't do this."

"Do what?" Lisa asked.

"Honey, I know your intentions are good, but you have no business caring for this woman. That woman up there belongs in a psych ward. Besides that, she needs medical attention around the clock. Don't you *see* that? Isn't that painfully obvious to you? I mean, for the life of me, I don't know how she's stayed alive as long as she has."

Lisa's jaw felt suspended in midair, her shoulders shrunk inward, and she slouched in her chair. She felt helpless and guilty, but then something within her snapped. A switch inside clicked on, and pride began to set in. "Wait a minute." Her voice a little louder now, "Wait one minute. Let me tell *you* something about that woman up there. She may not have the benefit of a…"—she searched for the words—"of a hospital bed and all the drugs she could ever need or IVs sticking out of her 24-7 and expert doctors. But what she does have is us! She's got the love of her *son*, the love of her *grandsons*, and the love of her *daughter-in-law*! She awakes every day in the home she made. Her grandchildren spent their infancy at the foot of her bed. She's fed and bathed every day by people who love her. Now you don't think she feels that warmth? Her own son reads to her every night—every…single…night!

"You wanna know what's kept her alive? I'll tell ya. Love! You can't buy it, and it doesn't come in a pill. Now you can sit here and judge me all you want, but I know this much. The day she leaves this house is the day she dies, and there's not a doctor or nurse in the world that can tell me different."

Unable to hold back her tears any longer, she stood up from the table. "I thank you for coming, but you can see yourselves out."

———

Sitting bedside, she held onto her mother-in-law's hand. Linda very discreetly appeared in the doorway. Lisa saw her shadow but said nothing.

"She did have a slight fever," Linda said. "I gave her some Tylenol and left what I had on the nightstand."

Lisa nodded her head.

Linda stopped at the foot of the bed and gently rubbed Mrs. Boone's foot over the bed cover. "You're right."

Lisa turned and looked up at her.

"What you said down there...you were right."

"Thanks," Lisa said.

"You should know that I've heard of cases where patients in catatonic states like this return home, and they have a brief awakening. Before they..." She paused. "Well, you know. Anyway, that's what *might* have caused her to get out of bed. I'd just keep a close eye on her from here on out, and call me if you need anything."

Lisa smiled as best she could. "Thank you...I will."

CHAPTER 58

Jake pulled into a mini-mart. They were approaching Oklahoma City, and he had plans on calling it a day. He put the truck in park and got out.

"What's up?" Charlie asked.

"I'm hungry."

Charlie stepped out of the truck and stretched. With his arms resting atop the hood, he watched Jake walk the aisles inside. Then he glanced over the rest of the place, taking note of a couple more patrons and an attendant behind the counter. He smiled and shook his head. *What is it with him and mini-marts?*

"Gravios Avenue," Jake said, exiting the store. He pulled a can of meat from the brown bag and placed it on the hood.

"What about it?"

"Gravios Avenue. That's what we take into Oklahoma City. Guy inside says there's a couple of motels along the way."

Jake peeled the metal cover off the tin can of meat and dug in with a plastic fork.

"Spam?" Charlie asked.

"Not even. Some kind of substitute. Years of jail food will do this to ya. I crave this stuff. Feel like it's all I can eat anymore. Besides that, the price is right."

"I know it; had my fair share growing up. You could buy a case of it for $3.99 at Leidy's."

"What's Leidy's?"

"Corner store at home." Charlie smiled. "You can do a lot of things with it, too. Mom even made a birthday cake out of it once."

Jake pulled back from his position on the hood.

"No, I'm serious. Candles and all."

Both men laughed

"She was a piece of work."

Jake reached back into the brown bag and pulled out two tall Budweiser cans. He rolled one across the hood to Charlie.

"Looked too good to pass up," he said. "Tall can of cold beer."

Charlie picked it off the hood in midroll and cracked it open. A surge of suds cascaded down the aluminum can while he held it to his open mouth.

"Is this legal?" Charlie asked.

Jake surveyed the empty lot. "Fuck it! Drink fast. There was a guy inside who used to get beers snuck in from Big South," Jake said.

"Big South?"

Jake took a gulp of beer and set it back down on the hood. "Some big-ass redneck with a gun, security guard. He was a real prick; you know the kind— abuse their power, strip every ounce of dignity you got left and enjoy doing it. In my younger days, I would have made him hurt, but not in there. In there, you gotta swallow your pride and keep your mouth shut." Jake chuckled.

"Prison's a fucked-up place. It breaks your spirit, teaches you to conform, you know? Problem is there ain't no two-way street. The institution demands you respect it, but the institution doesn't respect you back." Jake shook his head before he went in for another bite. "Least not where I was."

"What did you do?" Charlie asked.

"Slept, exercised, read."

"No, I mean *what* did you do?"

Jake hesitated at the question and fell silent. He looked up from his can of food, across the hood, and into Charlie's eyes. His words were soft and deliberate. "On the books? Voluntary manslaughter…man's name was John Wall. He was a truck driver. We exchanged words outside a truck stop. Hit 'im a few times, he hit me, we went at it for quite a while. Next thing I knew, I shot 'im."

Taken aback, Charlie asked, "No Raymond Butler?"

Jake slowly shook his head back and forth. It didn't take a clairvoyant to know there were more than just two.

"How did it happen?" Charlie asked.

"I'd rather not get into it."

"Get into what?"

"Any of it."

He respected Jake's wish and fell silent. A few moments later, he spoke.

"You know, Jake, if you got something you wanna get off your chest, you can trust me with it. I mean, I won't judge, and I won't care what it is. I only say it because leaving that kind of shit bottled up inside ya can't be good."

He saw the water filling Jake's eyes. Jake quickly looked away.

"Come on, go ahead and let it out. It'll be good for ya."

Jake took a deep breath and exhaled. "Nah...can't do it."

He was close. He saw the opportunity and took it. "Tell me, Jake. Tell me what happened."

Jake laughed as if it hurt. "He was buying a sandwich. He was buying a *fucking* sandwich and cut in front of me. I told him so, and we had words; words continued out into the parking lot." Jake groaned. "All I saw was fury...pure anger. Uncontrolled, wicked anger. Then...it was all over."

The two men continued to stare at each other for what seemed an eternity. Finally, Jake asked, "Why is it we don't start with the same wisdom we leave with? Why is it life's so damn complicated?"

Jake's question hit a chord with him. "I don't know that answer. I've struggled myself, just in different ways. Struggled with who I am, why I do what I do, see the things I see, the thoughts I have." He stared into the hood of the truck. "Life ain't easy. It's just not meant to be."

"Tragic," Jake said. "Tragic is what it is. I've done plenty of bad in my life, things I can hardly think of, let alone utter, and it's misery to live it. So much misery that most days I wish I was never born."

Charlie'd had the same thoughts and feelings many times. "You know, no matter how useless you may think your life was or is, any minute, all of it can change. I believe that."

"You really think there's still time?" Jake asked.

"I do." Charlie nodded. "For both of us."

CHAPTER 59

Lisa wiped the last piece of trim clean and leaned back on her knees to admire her work. It had taken three hours to scour the wood trim that ran along the whole first floor of the house. Before that, she had scrubbed the kitchen floor by hand, including the refrigerator seal, which was saying something for an appliance that could be called an icebox without irony.

The cleaning binge had begun in her mother-in-law's bedroom. It helped take her mind off things, especially the debate going on inside her head as to how much of the previous night's events she planned on sharing with Charlie.

She dressed Billy for the drop in temperature—it was now in the midforties—while Eddie patiently waited at the door. She'd been so busy cleaning that her weekly trip to Leidy's had slipped her mind. She thought better of leaving her mother-in-law unattended, but with Eddie's help, she'd be done in half the time and wouldn't be gone more than twenty minutes. Besides that, after the previous day's events, she was a little gun shy about asking Eddie to do anything.

It was a cold, clear night with distant smells of burned wood filling the air. Dark smoke rose out of the chimneys of the nicer homes on the block, and occasional leaves fell from the tall oaks they walked under. Pushing Billy in the stroller and holding Eddie by the hand, she looked up at the sky, wondering where Charlie was at that very moment.

"You smell that wood burning, Ma?" Eddie asked.

"Sure I do."

"I like it. Why doesn't our fireplace work anymore?"

"The flue's broke."

"How did it break?"

She had a lot on her mind and didn't feel like twenty questions. She answered as best she could. "I don't know. Smoke came out the last time we used it. Filled the whole house with smoke and ashes. The place was a mess."

"I don't remember that," Eddie replied.

"You weren't born yet; you were still in my belly. I was four months pregnant." Lisa smiled. "Your daddy lit it right before we sat down for dinner." She laughed out loud. "That was one hell of a Christmas."

"Was Grandmom there?"

"She was, actually. I mean as best as she ever was. I cooked a ham while your father was on the roof trying to reattach the antenna that blew off from the wind. I swear, I thought he was gonna fall right through to the kitchen floor. I could hear every move he made up there. Then Grandmom came into the kitchen and said, 'Aliens have landed on the roof.'" It was a warm memory, and one that was turning her mood.

"I remember saying, 'No, Mom, that's just Charlie. He's reattaching the antenna.'

"She said, 'Charlie's on the roof?'

"I said, 'Yeah.'

"She said, 'Well, get 'im down before the aliens take him!'"

Lisa laughed. "Ten minutes later, the cops showed up saying they'd received a call about aliens on the roof. Then, three hours later, a fire truck showed up for a house filled with smoke. Ugh, it's no wonder the neighbors talk."

"How did your ham turn out?" Eddie asked.

"The ham? Turned out to be the highlight of our day."

"Did Dad get the antenna on?"

"He did, but it fell off as soon as he put the ladder away. He said the radio would be our only source of entertainment that Christmas, so we listened to Grandmom's old eight tracks that night."

"Sounds like fun," Eddie said.

While she hadn't considered it fun then, talking about it made her appreciate the moment. "You know what? It was fun. It didn't seem it then, but it was."

"Maybe when Dad gets home, we can get the flue fixed and light a fire this Christmas."

She smiled. "I think that's a great idea. I could even get out Grandmom's old eight tracks."

"Well, if not, I have some money saved up. I'll buy us a new one."

Her son's words brought her to a stop. The kindness and sincerity of his thought, or even wish, hit her in the chest. "You know something, Eddie?"

"What?"

"You're one special kid, and I'm lucky to have you as my son."

Eddie smiled. "You're a pretty good mom yourself."

It was exactly what she needed to hear. She planted a kiss on his cheek and then stood up. Standing there in front of Billy's stroller was a stranger. She jumped back, bringing the stroller with her. "Ahh! Jesus Christ! What are you doing?"

"Excuse me, ma'am."

Catching her breath, she went into defense mode. "What do you want?"

"I'm sorry, ma'am. Didn't mean to startle you. I saw you coming from that home." He pointed over her shoulder.

She briefly looked around for any sign of help. It was dark where they stood and difficult to see the man's face. A hood covered the top of his head, yet she could see that he had blond hair, and his look was odd, almost boyish.

"I used to work at that house, the one you came from. Their name was Boone. A single mother lived there."

"Yes, she still does. When was this?"

"Oh, years ago. I was a handyman for her. There was a little boy there, too." The stranger looked to the ground. "Now let me see—what was his name?"

She was about to say Charlie's name but then thought better. The feeling in her stomach was too weird to compute. "I've never seen you in this neighborhood before."

"Well, I did go away for a little while but just recently came back. I was wondering if there was any work that needed done around the house?"

Absolutely not. Totally freaked out and feeling vulnerable, she again looked up and down the street. "Sorry, there's no work; now if you could step out of the way, I'm headed to Leidy's market." She went out of her way to point out the well-lit corner store just a block up.

"Oh, sure, no problem." He stepped aside and allowed her to pass. "Have a good day, now."

Halfway across the street, Lisa turned. "Excuse me! I didn't catch your name."

He ignored her call and continued to walk away from her. Lisa retraced some of her steps. "Wait, excuse me! Your name, what is it?" She lost sight of him a few seconds later as he fell into darkness. She grabbed the boys and hustled into Leidy's.

The front door swung closed behind her, and with it came the bell's jingle. Leidy stood at the checkout counter with another lady. Lisa quickly turned back around and probed the dark street in front of her.

"Something wrong?" Leidy asked.

Lisa gathered herself. "No, nothing's wrong. Eddie, grab a cart for your mother." Eddie did as she asked while she unbuttoned Billy's coat.

"Is that Lisa Boone?" the woman asked.

It was a poor attempt at a whisper.

Seconds later the woman was next to her, staring into Billy's stroller. "Well, well. He's a real cutie."

With her mind still in the street, Lisa stood up and glanced back out the door.

"You sure nothing's wrong?" Leidy asked again.

"Yes. I mean no, actually. Did either of you see a hooded man walk past the store a few minutes ago?"

"A hooded man?" the woman asked.

"Yes! He had a dark hood, looked to be an older guy. Blond hair, at least from what I could tell, anyway."

"No...no hooded men," Leidy replied.

The woman put her hand on Lisa's elbow. "My goodness, you're shaking like a leaf. What happened out there?"

She looked down at her arm and tucked it into her side, pulling away from the woman. "Nothing. Just really strange, that's all. Some guy said he knew..." She met Leidy's eyes with her own and stopped. "Never mind; it's nothing. I'm sure." She called out, "Eddie!"

He was standing right behind her with the shopping cart. "Oh, there you are. Here, you push Billy while I push the cart."

The woman leaned in to Lisa. "Would you like us to call the police?"

"No, please. It's not necessary."

"Who did he say he knew?" Leidy asked.

"I forget what he said, actually."

Leidy mumbled something under her breath. Lisa ignored her and went about her shopping. Standing just an aisle over from them, she could hear their conversation.

"Don't even bother," Leidy whispered. "I don't even care about it."

"But the neighborhood has a right to know," the woman replied.

"Put yourself in her shoes. Would you tell anybody?" Leidy asked. "Who the hell can feel sorry for her, anyway? She made her own bed with that one. The guy walked around the neighborhood like a zombie for years. Hell, even as a child, he could look right through ya."

"Well, I don't believe it anyway," the woman replied.

"I do, and I bet old lady Boone was sent away with 'im." Leidy continued, "They took 'em both out, in the dead of night. Halloween was the last straw for that family."

"My gosh, can you imagine?"

Lisa hastily threw her items into the cart, making as much noise as possible as she did so. Eddie grabbed a box of Cocoa Puffs off the shelf and held it in the air. "Can we get these?"

The freezer door on the far wall pulled her attention away. Its brass handle rattled back and forth, and then abruptly it swung open. Leidy's son stood in the doorway. His face wore an ugly smile, and his stomach wore a bloodstained apron. He had a butcher's knife in one hand and a slab of meat in the other. The picture before her was soon replaced by something else. The stranger she'd just encountered, the back kitchen door of her home, its dead bolt unlatched, and finally her mother-in-law…alone.

The can of Campbell's soup fell from her hand.

"Eddie, stay with your brother!" Passing Leidy and her friend, she clenched her teeth and gave them an order. "You watch my boys."

She leaped over the store steps and frantically raced down the dark corridor of Nebraska Lane, her fists clenched and her arms swinging up and down at her side like some sort of bionic woman. She could hear her own heavy breathing, her stomach filled with fear.

She said the Hail Mary all the way home, around the side of the house, through the back kitchen door, up the living-room steps, and finally into

Mrs. Boone's bedroom. She flicked on the light switch and took a deep breath. Her mother-in-law sat peacefully in the rocker, just as she'd left her. Lisa fell to her knees and passed out.

———

She lay in the fetal position on the corner of the bed with the same thought running through her mind: crazy. It came in many different images: neighbor's faces, whispers, secrets, adrenaline taking over her body, Charlie, this house, her mother-in-law. The single candle she had lit hours ago was running out of wick and shed little light on the darkened room.

With the telephone receiver to her ear, she stared into the single flame. "I felt it, Charlie; it was like an emptiness in my stomach. I was so sure something had happened." She paused. "Thank God I was wrong. Now the whole neighborhood's going to think I'm crazy, just like—" She caught herself before finishing, though the question begged to be asked. "Oh, Charlie, what's wrong with us?"

"Nothing's wrong with us. Listen to yourself, would you? You were never one to care about what other people thought. Why start now?"

"Because it's coming to a head, that's why. You should hear what they say. They say it at the market, in my own presence. Imagine what they're saying when I'm not there. It's like a never-ending circus. Even the police were asking where you were and why you were away."

"You were harassed by a stranger in the dead of night. That's not something they should take lightly."

"But I wasn't harassed. It was my own head getting the best of me. Who knows who the hell that guy was, but I'm sure it was nothing. He's probably asleep in his own bed right now, harmlessly snoring the night away. It was just strange, how he came out of nowhere."

"What did Eddie think?"

"I never asked him. I ran out so fast that I screamed at Leidy to watch them. The cops brought them down in the patrol car not long after I woke up."

"The patrol car? They must have loved that."

"Billy did. Not so sure about Eddie. Fact is, after the last couple nights, I was too embarrassed to ask what he thought."

"Whatta ya mean the last couple nights? What happened?"

She was in no frame of mind to go there. "Nothing…I'm just tired, Charlie."

"Listen to me: don't beat yourself up about this. You did the right thing. You felt something and you acted on it; if anyone can appreciate that, I can. And fuck everybody else. Tell them what they want to hear and be done with it."

She laughed as best she could. "Tell them you were sent away in the dead of the night?"

"Yeah , straitjacket and all."

It would take years to forget the conversation she had heard in Leidy's. "I want out, Charlie. I want out of this house and out of this neighborhood. Hell, we can jump three states for all I care, but I want out of here."

"You're right," he replied. "It's time."

"How nice would it be to have a fenced-in yard for the boys and Bear? With a big porch out front and a swing set on the lawn."

"It sounds great, all of it."

"Can we do it? Can we really?"

"You bet we can, and we will…I promise."

She smiled. "A promise? I like the sound of that. I like the sound of that a lot."

"Then consider it done. Start looking for homes, and we'll figure it out when I get back."

She closed with the question she usually asked first. "Where are you, baby?"

"Oklahoma City, standing inside a telephone booth."

"Say hello to Oklahoma City for us."

"You bet I will."

She listened to the dial tone while staring at the receiver in her hand. Hanging it up, she leaned in and blew out the candle.

CHAPTER 60

A strip of cheap motels, food chains, topless bars, and seedy watering holes—that was Gravios Ave, just a few miles outside Oklahoma City. The cold weather of Illinois and Ohio had given way to a balmy sixty-five degrees. Jake sat in the truck with the door open, using the light of the parking lot to peruse yesterday's newspaper, which he'd picked from a trash can.

Charlie checked into a room at the roadside motel and found it not much different from any of the other ones he'd slept in: a hard mattress, a few dead bugs, and a TV that advertised cable but only got three static channels. He stood in the doorway and looked out at the lights of Gravios Ave. Cupping his mouth, he called across the parking lot. "Hey, Jake?"

Jake looked up from his paper but didn't say anything.

"I'm thirsty. That cold beer was good."

"Yeah, it was," Jake said, his voice trailing off.

"It's only ten o'clock."

The silence between them was filled by some drunk people stumbling out of a bar across the street. Jake turned to catch a glimpse and then looked back down at his paper.

"Go ahead, I'm staying here. Don't feel like it."

"Don't feel like what?"

"Celebrating," Jake answered.

"Come on, Rip Van Winkle. You've been sleeping for thirty years; let's go tip a few." Charlie made his way toward the truck. "After all, you do drink whiskey, right?"

"Yes, I do."

"Then let's go get you some. I'm sure they got plenty of it over there. What the hell else you gonna do?"

"Place looks like trouble," Jake said softly. He wore a slight grin as he picked his paper back up. "I don't wanna have to bail your sorry ass out of a jam."

Based on the seedy bar's looks alone, Charlie couldn't disagree. "Don't worry about me; I play nice. Besides, I'm not a fighter."

"Sometimes trouble finds you, even if you're not asking for it."

"All right then, suit yourself. You know where I'll be."

Peering through his rearview mirror, Jake watched Charlie cross the street and enter the bar, then he went back to his paper. Every so often he'd look up at the tavern door, only to return his attention to the newspaper. Reluctantly, he finally put the paper down and got out of the truck.

The place was crowded, and Charlie was sitting barside. Jake took a seat next to him.

"Change of heart?" Charlie asked.

"Not really. I just didn't want to see you thrown out on your ass by some biker." Taking up most of the bar were truckers and a few bikers. Women in low-cut tops and tight jeans clamored for the attention of anyone who would give it to them; women who had seen better days, with slicked-back, greasy hair and cigarettes loosely dangling from their mouths.

"No worries in here. Just some lonely truckers and ugly bikers looking to get laid."

Staring at one of the ladies, Jake said, "That's not a bad thought."

"Go for it. I'll even let you use my room."

Jake laughed as he ordered a double Jack Daniels for himself and another tequila for Charlie.

"Freedom's a funny thing. It kind of feels weird sometimes. Sitting over there in the truck, felt odd knowing I could walk over here and have a drink or even turn the ignition and drive off. Go get laid, grab a bite to eat anywhere I'd like."

"It's a feeling you can probably get used to. Might be just the thing to keep you out of trouble."

"Maybe...I'm hoping I don't got any more trouble in me."

"Is it true what they say about old-timers in prison? Kind of becomes home to them? After so long, they don't even wanna come out?"

"Yeah, there're always a couple like that."

"Not you?"

He fell silent for a moment. "I had thoughts about it."

"Thoughts about what?"

He looked at Charlie out of the corner of his eye. "Doing something stupid to stay in, but only because I was more afraid of doing something stupid when I got out."

"Like killing again?" Charlie whispered.

"Yeah, something like that." He downed what was left of his drink and called for another. Jake sipped his whiskey. "The devil comes in many forms."

"Sounds like you knew him personally," Charlie said. "What was his name?"

"Lyle Ginn. I met 'im in Nevada the year I came back from the war." He looked over at Charlie. "Resist the devil and he'll flee from you; let 'im in, and…"

"Life's never the same," Charlie said.

"Not just my own. I blame no one but myself for what I've done, but that man never did help things. Slowly but surely I'm coming to terms with my own offenses, but having sat there idle and watched him do some of his…well, there's only so much evil a man can see until he can't see no more."

Lyle Ginn. That name kept echoing in Charlie's ear while he listened to Jake's story.

"At the start, it was nothing but someone to run with. We'd ride for days, state after state, pull jobs here and there. I'd had my share of run-ins with the law by then, he the same. By the time I met him, he had already served three years in San Quentin." Jake paused for a moment. "That boy just had a taste for crime."

"How did you meet?" Charlie asked.

"Sitting at a bar." Jake looked around. "Not much different than this one. Fight breaks out. Kind of places we sat in, people didn't have any friends…next thing you know, barstools are flying, glass is breaking, it's every man for himself. When things finally cooled down, we were the only two standing—most of the place either took off or fell to the floor. Even the bartender hit the road. Next thing I know, he's over the bar, breaking open the cash drawer. Threw a wad of money atop the bar and told me to divvy it up, so I did." Jake sipped some more whiskey. "And that was it. That started it."

"How bad was it?"

Jake shook his head. "Most of what we did we talked about. Knew beforehand what we were gonna do. Which most of the time meant stealing. I was a thief, among other things. I liked money. It kept clothes on my back, food in my stomach, and women in my bed. *We* robbed, and it didn't matter who or what. Saloons, gas stations, liquor stores, people's homes, people in general. Guys like you see right across this bar."

"How?"

"Shit, easy," Jake said. "Pick a fight with a couple guys, take it outside, and then take them for whatever they had. Back then, I didn't lose, and neither did Ginn. He wasn't that big, maybe five ten and 190 wet, but that son of a bitch could pack a punch and take one, too."

"And if it went bad?" Charlie asked.

Jake put his glass down. "There's nothing right about shooting an unarmed man. First time I saw Ginn do it, it froze me in my tracks and damn near got me killed."

"He killed at will," Charlie said.

"Yes, he did."

"Why did you stick it out with him?"

Jake shook his head. "Probably 'cause I didn't trust 'im a lick. He knew enough about me to have me dead to rights, and I him. Difference was he didn't fear me, but I feared 'im. The only person in my life ever been able to do that."

Charlie looked down at Jake's boots and had that damn dream all over again. The dry mouth, the crawl across the desert floor, the soles of those boots. "You killed him," he whispered. "You killed him in the desert."

He didn't need to see Jake's expression to know he was right.

Jake finished his drink and put it down on the bar. "I'll take another. Of all the bars, over all the years, I can't remember the names of many of 'em, but that one I do: the 1912 Tavern. It sat just a few miles inside the New Mexico border."

The bartender dropped Jake's drink.

"We'd been apart for a little while. I was renting a room in LA for a few months, trying to slow my life down. By this time I was with Wood, at his club, the place where I'd come into that money. Ginn would stop in from time to time and crash at my place, then I wouldn't see him for a few days. Anyway, one day I got wind of a liquor store nearby getting taken down, clerk and customer shot dead, no witnesses…that was always Ginn's MO. Well, I'd heard enough to know it was him, and I didn't see 'im after that."

"I'm not following you."

"The bag of money. By then I'd ran into the foothills and went into hiding for a week. It was too much money, more money than I was accustomed to. It freaked me out, so I buried it. Figured I'd ride to New Mexico and stay down there for a few weeks, wait till things blew over, then come back and pick it up. I wasn't down there a day, and I ran into Ginn. Can't say I was all that surprised—we'd caught up with each other in that neck of the woods a few times before."

"Yeah, so what happened in the tavern?"

"Story around LA was that whoever hit that liquor store walked with fifteen grand." Jake shook his head. "It was bigger than anything he and I had ever done together, and then there I was, sitting there with a smile from ear to ear with $300,000 plus buried in the ground two states away. Well, neither one of us was saying a word to the other. Instead we was just having fun. Drinking and partying like it was our last. Must have been a twelve-hour binge." Jake took a gulp of whiskey.

"At some point, Ginn starts talking to two girls across the way. They come over and start playing ball with 'im. Turns out they were mother and daughter, and they both wanted a piece of 'im. By that time I could barely keep one eye open. I just wanted a place to fall for the night." Jake paused for a long time. "I remember hearing this distant screaming in my sleep. It felt like hours, too… might've been. I finally came to and realized I wasn't dreaming at all."

Jake's bottom lip was quivering ever so slightly.

"The first thing that hit me was the smell of blood." Jake looked at him. "When you can smell blood, there's a lot of it. I felt for my piece and jumped up off the couch. There was this long stretch of hall; I could see a pool of red running out of one of the rooms. The closer I got, the more of her body I saw. Whose it was, the mother or daughter, I didn't know, but she was cut up pretty bad. Then I walked to the end of the hall." He fell silent again.

"Ginn," Charlie said

"He was standing in the center of the room. I couldn't believe what I was seeing. He turned and looked at me." Jake stared into the bar top.

"What did he say?"

"Nothing, but he didn't have to. His eyes said it all. That was the thing about him. He wasn't crazy. Hell, I wish he had been, but he always seemed like he was there…in the moment, like he knew exactly what he was doing."

"What did you do?"

"There was a groan coming from the bed. Ginn looked over at her, then picked up his gun and shot her."

His last shot of Tequila lumped up in his throat. "What the *fuck*?

"I left," Jake said. "As fast as I could, I left. About five miles down the road, the whole thing started collapsing in on me. I'd had it. I had to end it. I pulled over to the side of the road and waited. Sure enough, he wasn't far behind me. He pulled up next to me, and I asked 'im, 'What the hell happened back there?'

"He said, 'Nothing. Just a couple of whores looking to take my money.'

At that moment I knew exactly what I needed to do. He was gonna wish he never ran into to my black ass, ever. I wasn't just gonna kill 'im, I was gonna make him hurt."

Jake looked over at Charlie. "He knew I was hot, so I told 'im about the bag of money, knowing it was the only way he'd follow me into the desert. Plus, it was enough to keep him distracted for the drive. Took us two days to drive up. I told 'im it was buried in the Mojave just outside San Bernardino, even though it wasn't. I knew of a real remote spot out there, where I could take 'im and do what I wanted to him.

"I had him fish for a shovel when we got there. I told 'im it was stashed in some brush on the side of a hill. Then I came up behind 'im and whacked him over the head with my gun. He fell to the ground. I pulled his gun off 'im and didn't wait a second longer. I gave him one shot to his knee, another in his ankle, and then I beat on 'im." He nodded. "I beat on 'im good, until I got tired. Must have been a half hour, and then I shot his other kneecap."

Charlie stared at the lineup of liquor bottles before him and replied, "And from there he crawled."

Jake looked over at Charlie. "Like the snake he was, screaming, cussing, and yelling the whole damn time. I stood around awhile and watched 'im do it, too. He just couldn't believe it; he just couldn't believe I did it."

Charlie got up from his bar stool. He wanted to vomit, not just at the story but at the thought that was tripping around in his head.

"Where you going?" Jake asked.

"Bed," he replied softly. "I think it's time for me to go to bed."

Jake stood up and turned around. "Hey, Charlie, how'd you know?"

"Know what?"

"That I took him to the desert."

He glanced down at Jake's boots and walked out.

———

Charlie sat on the floor of his motel room, motionless, his back against the wall, with Jake's question repeating itself in his head. Dreams and visions—that was exactly how he knew Jake Mott killed Lyle Ginn, leaving him to die on the desert floor thirty years ago. He'd seen it. Hell, he had seen it from Ginn's lowly point of view.

But why? Why had he ever dreamed that, and what bearing did it have on him now?

He had spent the better part of his life searching for something he didn't understand, let alone ever think he'd find, and all the while his mind was nothing more than a jumbled mess. But something was different now. Voices he heard and visions he saw, dreams; they all seemed to have been silenced, stripped away from him the day he met Jake Mott. It was that realization that started the sinking feeling in his stomach.

Springing up from the floor, Charlie collapsed into the tiny bathroom and lunged for the toilet.

CHAPTER 61

Her emotions had been all over the place these last few days: guilt, pity, fear, and selfishness, just to name a few.

It was moments like these when selfishness bore down and took hold. That part of her that wanted Mrs. Boone to peacefully pass away in the night was the same part that wanted a normal life for her family, if such a thing was ever possible.

She couldn't wait to move out of the house and start a new life for all of them: a new school for the boys, new neighbors, new home.

Then there was the other half, the half that cared for her mother-in-law and wished her life because it was her husband's want. But what quality of life could she have in her current state?

It had been years since she'd had an actual conversation with her, and one of the last they'd shared came to mind.

"Where did those flowers come from?" Her mother-in-law stood before the bedroom window, staring out.

"Pretty, aren't they? I planted them myself."

"Where did they come from?"

"From the nursery on the boulevard."

"Did the mailman come yet?" Mrs. Boone asked.

"No, why do you keep asking me that?"

Mrs. Boone shuffled over to the nightstand and opened up the top drawer.

"What are you looking for?"

"My binoculars."

Lisa went to the closet and pulled out a pair that she knew Charlie kept on his shelf and handed them to her.

She played with the scope for several minutes without ever looking in them for clarity, and she then went back to the window. Putting them to her eyes, she pressed the large black metal scope to the glass. "Oh my, they're huge!"

Lisa laughed; she could just picture the image her mother-in-law was seeing.

"They're daisies," Mrs. Boone said.

"No, they're sunflowers," Lisa replied. "There're some red mums in there too."

"We used to have a daisy patch out there years ago. I gardened often when Charlie was a boy. Isn't that right, Charlie?"

"Charlie's not here, Mom. He's at work."

"Work?"

"Yes, he started his new job last week. He's a bus driver now. He had to take a test and everything. Don't you remember him telling you?"

"What bus are you talking about?"

Lisa got busy instead of standing and watching the madness. Pulling dirty clothes from the laundry basket, she replied, "A city bus."

She stopped in the middle of the room and looked back at her mother-in-law. "Mom?"

Mrs. Boone shuddered and then dropped the binoculars to her side. "I don't feel well today. Do we have to go outside?"

"You haven't been out in days. Don't you want to?"

"Maybe later. We'll see how I feel."

Lisa smiled. "OK, we'll see how you feel."

She stood before the very window Mrs. Boone had looked out years earlier. She went to Charlie's closet and pulled the old binoculars off the shelf and returned to the window. There were no more flowers, and there hadn't been in some time. "So much hope," she whispered.

It was depressing to even think about, how *everything* had slowly deteriorated over the years. She focused in on the mailbox, which was slightly bent and rusty. It looked one stiff wind away from falling down. She dropped the binoculars to her side and said, "Change…change everything."

With the floors and baseboards wiped clean from the previous day's chores, she was ready to tackle the outside, and the mailbox was as good a start as any.

CHAPTER 62

S he left Eddie home to watch over his grandmother, along with a set of
should this happen instructions. The man at the hardware store went over
some off-the-cuff directions before sending her on her way.

With orders for Eddie to pull every garden-looking tool out of the basement and for Billy to sit quietly, she went about the job of dismantling the old
mailbox. She grabbed it on one side while she stood on the other and pulled
toward her. Just as quickly she fell on her ass, most of the mailbox coming with
her. She threw it to the side and went about making short work of what was
left of its base, a job done with relative ease as she kicked, poked, and prodded
with a shovel until nothing but a mound of rotted-out wood lay on the ground.

Meanwhile, a collection of garden tools was piling up next to her: a shovel,
hoes, rakes, even a machete, which she saw from the corner of her eye. Just the
sight of the long, curved blade was a bit disturbing.

"What the hell am I going to do with that?"

"Do with what?" Eddie asked.

"That blade."

"I don't know."

One more study of it, and she shouted another order as Eddie made
another trip to the basement. "I think I've got everything I need."

She picked up the closest shovel and shoved it into the ground, but she was
met by unyielding earth. The shovel's handle vibrated in her hands. *Of course.
It's the middle of November.*

Another thrust produced the same result. She carefully centered the point
of the shovel on the ground and jumped on top of the steel pegs.

"Why are we doing this?" Eddie asked.

"Why not?"

"I don't know. It just seems weird."

"Replacing our mailbox is weird? I don't think so." She continued to wrestle with the hard ground. "Weird is the one we have. Look around. You see any mailboxes on this block that look like ours?"

"People are watching," he replied.

She looked up. It was true: onlookers were planted in front of a few kitchen and living-room windows. She shrugged and went back to work, this time with the pickax Eddie had pulled out of the basement. "You know what we say to them by now, right?"

"Fuck 'em?" Eddie replied.

She briefly paused, laughed aloud, and smiled. "That's exactly right. Fuck 'em!" She gave her son a kiss on the head. "Thanks, I needed that."

A slow smile found its way onto Eddie's face, making her feel even better about what she was doing.

She ripped two more swings of the pick into the hard ground and on the last one felt something strange. It was some sort of fabric, jammed into the small, round gully she had just manufactured. She bent down to pull it from its place but came away with nothing but a piece of old tarp. It was light-gray in color, with some faded lettering. Her second pull gave her a bigger swatch of the rough canvas.

Lisa fell to her knees, dug her fingers around the perimeter of the hole, and uncovered more and more of the fabric. A little more digging produced what looked to be a postman's mailbag.

She reached in and pulled out a handful of envelopes, every one of them still sealed, some even in perfect condition. Perched on her knees, she was dumbfounded, and then a slow sickness began to seep in. "Oh, no."

The faded red ink on the corners of the envelopes held dates and years from long ago—December 29, 1978; March 31, 1978; August 16, 1977; July 1, 1981; and one just too close for her own liking: November 25, 1989.

She quickly scanned the senders: Philadelphia Police Department, JC Penney, United Savings Bank, Phoenix Mutual. She looked up at the lone window of the room that housed her mother-in-law and her first instinct was to scream, but she didn't. Keenly aware of the neighborhood eyes upon her, she stood up and attempted to pull the bag from its grave.

She fumbled to get the collection of envelopes piled up at her feet back into the bag. "Eddie, grab your brother and go inside." Not a second later, she said, "Do it now!"

With one last pull of adrenaline, she heaved the mammoth sack out of the hole and threw it to the side. The bag had stood the test of time, and, much to her dismay, was full. She stared at it for several seconds and then looked back down at the hole it had come from. Hell-bent on finishing what she had started, she spent the next hour seeing her production to an end and did so with as much pride as she could muster.

As if it were a monument erected to bury the dead, which in this case was a piece of the past, Lisa stood back and momentarily found solace in her work. Standing erect was one straight, forest-green mailbox atop a wooden four-by-four post with dark, fresh-looking soil at its base, which, in her estimation, was now the nicest-looking mailbox on the block.

CHAPTER 63

Charlie jumped into the truck and shut the door.
"You look like shit," Jake said.

"I didn't sleep much."

"You left in a fire drill last night."

"Yeah, well, like I said, it was time to go to bed."

"And you didn't sleep?" Jake snapped back.

"Right, I know." Charlie looked over at him. "Is there a problem?"

"No, no problem. It's just the fifty questions we played last night left me pouring my soul onto the bar...next thing I know, I'm sittin' there with a bottle of whiskey in front of me with all that shit swimmin' around my head."

"So what's your point?"

"Point is, if you ain't gonna be a good audience, then don't ask! That's my point."

"Ok, got it...I'm sorry"

"I wasn't looking for no apology. If you wanna be sorry for anything, be sorry for the splitting headache I got."

"You're not alone. I got one, too."

They drove in silence for several miles. Staring out the windshield, Charlie asked, "What did he look like, Jake?"

"What did who look like?"

"Ginn."

"Ah, no you don't! I'm not going there again. I don't wanna speak about that anymore. That's over."

"No, really. I need to know."

Jake looked at him hard. "*No*, you don't."

Charlie conceded with silence. A few miles passed and he asked, "Where we headed?"

"Texas," Jake replied.

CHAPTER 64

Droplets of hard dirt sprinkled the kitchen table, scattered through the six piles of letters stacked four and five high. They grew like small buildings in front of her. The canvas mailbag sat up against the kitchen wall. With the tear of each letter, Lisa felt less and less pity for the crazy old lady above her, replaced by a sense of morbid fascination that got stronger with each read.

It was only a matter of time until she found one from Trenton, and she was content to have it come to her as opposed to fishing through the mass of letters like a savage beast hungry for answers. But her patience was never tested; it was the next envelope she picked up.

It was yellow in color with black felt ink. The handwriting on front was calligraphy. "Miss Patricia Boone, 10 Nebraska Lane, Philadelphia, PA." It was dated December 3, 1975.

She carefully opened it, as if something may fall out, and unfolded the thick-stock paper and pressed its sides down on the kitchen table. The handwriting was meticulous and, like the envelope, was done in calligraphy. There was something ritual about its lettering, big wide *R*s and exaggerated *L*s. It felt as if a strange smile was emanating from the letter's creases, as if its sender had sent an expression along with it—but most importantly, as if he'd enjoyed writing every bit of it.

Dear Patricia,

I haven't heard from you in ages. I'll assume all is well and that you are still alive (as the checks continue to cash, ha ha). I do miss you. Things here are good as ever—Raymond has taken over our newest lumber yard outside of Queens—this is a good part of the city for us, as we have no presence west of the island—and Clarke continues to bring in new accounts every day—he really is good with the contractors—the blue-collar type, of which we all have a little bit in us—real people they are, and good to do business with, true to their word—and isn't that what's most important in life, our word? I believe I've always kept mine with you. My heart aches that you haven't always done the same with me. Never mind that today.

Raymond and Barbara just had another baby, a beautiful little boy, healthy and happy, too—they have quite a family brewing over there across town—all the grandkids come on Sundays; Clarke's, too, and Roseanna cooks a small feast for the whole family. Roseanna is another one who's been good to me all these years—more than a housekeeper, she's become family. Without her cooking, I may have grown old and thin.

I do enjoy writing you. I only wish you'd respond or come visit more. I had a dream the other night. You stood in my bedroom doorway with that smile on your face, the one you wore as a little girl—I reached for your hand, and you laughed—we both laughed—I ran my fingers over your beautiful lips and then your skin—how soft it was—I do miss you—your visits are too few these days.

Perhaps you'll dream of me some night, and it will prompt you to make a midnight visit. That would be thrilling, wouldn't it?

I know during your last visit we spoke about sending the boy to camp and you staying with me for the summer—I would pay for it, of course, and camp is what boys his age should be doing. He needs friends, and camp is where he'll find them. I know you have concerns, but I'm not sure I know what they are.

I was wondering recently if you remember the mill on Mercer Avenue; I can't help but think of you whenever I enter that large warehouse. It's often early in the morning, with a chill still in the air and the leftover scent of oak and pine still lingering about, pleasant yet strong. Do you remember our Sunday visits to the mill back then, how much fun we had? Perhaps we'll meet there again some early morning and reminisce.

Life hasn't been fair to us, Patricia, but it's times like these when we have to be our strongest. You have been strong for so long that I worry for you. Please do contact me more often. Maybe I'll even make the trip to Philadelphia during a school day. Well, I guess I shall go, and please do consider my summertime proposal. It's the lumber yard's busiest time of year, so Raymond and Clarke will be busy, busy, and their families will all head to the beach—it would be just the two of us. Anyway, I hope to hear from you soon. All my love, Grey

She read it again and then leaned back in her chair. There wasn't a sound in the house. She wasn't sure what to think.

Like the shotgun start at a race, Lisa ripped into the Trenton letters like the savage beast she had earlier controlled. It was the things she repeatedly encountered that struck her most, the same scrupulous margins on the lineless paper, the same confident strokes of ink, and the same smile emanating from within. The message was always eerily similar, the content always covering the same terrain: his biological children, Raymond and Clarke; grandkids; achy hearts; family feasts; and dreamy nights. And like the tie that binds, each one ended with a remembrance of Mercer Avenue. How sick it all was, and how unfair and absolutely horrifying it must have been to live.

She covered her mouth. She was tired and could feel the beginnings of a splitting headache. Her stomach was turned upside down, she felt that she was going to be sick, but most of all, her heart ached more than ever for the crazy old lady above her.

CHAPTER 65

They sat parked in a sandy gravel pit off Highway 17, a stretch of road that fed directly into Main Street, Praire, Texas—yet it wasn't making his decision any easier. *Is my momma alive?* Surely there was no other family to speak of, so in reality, what was there to go back to? Perhaps he could find some resolution on the very ground he'd played on as a boy. Maybe going back to the place of his birth would provide him a clean start.

With the door swung open and one foot resting on the ground, he chomped on the piece of straw that ran from side to side in his mouth.

"What's the one thing you always wanted to do but never did?" Charlie asked him.

Jake glanced over his shoulder at Charlie and then looked away. "No regrets."

"No regrets, my ass."

"I *said* no regrets."

"I don't believe you. There's something in there you wish you'd done."

"There's plenty I wish I'd done...differently."

"No kidding. That's the obvious, but I'm talking about specific things, things you wished you had done but never had the chance to."

There were plenty of those too; he could list every one of them. Most of them he'd dreamed of while locked up. They were simple things, too, things that wouldn't make most people's lists, but that was fine by him. He considered sharing for a moment, but didn't. "What about you?" he asked.

"I always wanted to play harmonica, something about blowin' sad with just you and a piece of steel. You don't gotta say a word, but you can still get your point across."

"It's tough talking sometimes, isn't it?"

"Is when you don't know what to say," Charlie replied.

Jake paused and then spoke softly. "I had this dream in the can for years. I'm running in the middle of a cornfield, and it's raining out—I mean a downpour—but I just keep running, and I'm happy as a fucking clam doing it, too."

"What the hell does that mean?"

"Not sure, but I think it might have something to do with being free."

"Sounds nice," Charlie said.

"What sounds nice?" Jake asked.

"Running free."

Jake slid all the way into the truck and slammed his door shut. He was feeling a sudden burst of confidence and figured he better take advantage. They pulled out onto Highway 17, headed for Praire.

———

It had been years since he'd felt this many butterflies in his stomach; probably since the first time he put that orange jumpsuit on in Georgia State. Passing the Free Library in the middle of downtown Praire made his stomach weak, and it didn't take long before he started recognizing things.

Ground was being broken on a strip mall to their right, and a Pizza Hut stood to their left. They were new, but he was sure Fred's Hot Dog Stand used stand there. He remembered an old oak tree in town that had a width the size of a small car and thought it would be appearing at any moment. True to his memory, it did.

In search for nothing in particular, he was taking it all in. Structures, people, anything and everything they passed by.

Charlie tapped him on the arm. "Hey, check out that old gas station."

Jake grinned. It was nice to see it hadn't changed since his days in town. It was an old Texaco station that still had the round white *T* sign, complete with two bulky porcelain fuel pumps.

"Matter of fact, I gotta use the head," Charlie said. "You mind stopping?"

Jake pulled in and parked the truck. He recalled many days walking up to this station with his uncle Sam to buy gas for the tractors. Staring into the garage, he saw his uncle Sam now, standing in one of the bays, talking to the attendant.

Charlie jumped out. "I'll be right back."

He entered the small customer service area. A wooden counter stuck out from the wall, and behind it stood a small, slender man with a balding head. Reading some sort of parts manual, he repeated a series of letters into the phone.

Charlie stepped forward. "You have a key for the bathroom?"

The grizzled mechanic pointed to a hook attached to the side wall. There was a key dangling from it.

Charlie grabbed it and headed around the side of the building. Unlike the shop, the bathroom was disgustingly dirty. Pieces of toilet paper lined the floor, various items of garbage spilled out of the trash can, and the mirror had a large crack in it. The old porcelain sink was tarnished yellow and had smudges of grease on its front. Careful not to touch anything, he did his business and then ran some cold water over the six-day scruff that was growing on his face.

Coming back round the front of the building, he immediately noticed Jake was gone.

He walked back into the station. "The pickup that was parked right outside your door. Where'd it go?"

The mechanic looked over his shoulder. "What pickup?"

Charlie glanced at the name patch on his chest. It read Mack. "The one I pulled in with. Didn't you see it out there?"

"Nah, I didn't."

"Son of a bitch!"

"What's the matter? Your truck get stolen?"

Charlie turned back around. "Stolen? It's not my truck. It's his truck."

"Whose truck?"

"The guy I'm riding with."

Mack smiled at him. "Maybe this was your stop and you just didn't know it."

It wasn't funny, but the thought crossed his mind.

The mechanic closed the parts book and threw it under the counter. "Well, I wish I could help ya, but I didn't see it. Maybe he'll come back for ya. You're not from around here, are ya?"

He wasn't interested in small talk. "No."

"Yeah, I could tell. It's that accent of yours; gives you away."

He wanted to turn around and ask him if he was serious, but instead focused his attention on a bearded, heavy-set man entering the shop. He wore a large, surprised grin. "Hey Mack! I'll be a monkey's uncle."

"What? What happened?" Mack asked.

"I think I just saw Jake Mott driving down Main Street."

"Jake Mott?"

"I think so. Got some gray now, but it sure as hell looked like 'im."

Charlie spoke up. "Yeah, that's him. That's who I'm here with."

"Jake Mott! Well I'll be damned. Where was he headed, Hank?" Mack asked.

Hank stared at his own feet. "I think he turned onto Fisher. If I remember right, Fisher's an old back way into Rollins's farm. Probably headed out to his people's old place, out by Miller's creek."

"Now, what the hell would he be doin' out there? Place has been deserted for ten years. Hell, I haven't seen Jake Mott in probably thirty."

"So you guys know 'im," Charlie said.

"Shit yeah, we knew 'im," Mack said. "Small town was even smaller back then. Everyone knew Jake. Kid that size was hard to miss."

Charlie turned to Hank and said, "Take me there."

"Take you where?"

From Charlie's point of view, in the passenger seat of Hank's pickup, Praire, Texas, seemed like a very peaceful town. Cookie-cutter ranch homes sat side by side on tree-lined streets with minivans and sedans parked in their drives while deserted bikes lay adrift in flower beds near the front doors, heedlessly cast aside for a waiting piece of Grandmom's pie. It looked like a nice place to live and a long way away from Nebraska Lane.

Three miles later, however, Fisher Lane turned very different. Nice ranch homes were replaced by large oaks with hanging limbs the size of boulders, which scraped the grass beneath them. Scrolling fields were partitioned by dense woods, and every few hundred feet or so a house would appear; some average looking, but most unkempt and unsightly.

Homemade random signs hung on tree trunks and falling-down fences. They read: No Trespassing, Beware of Dog, and Owner Armed.

The weeds that filled the unfertile fields grew high, and with the wind blowing through them, they seemed to be whispering something.

Hank threw the toothpick in his mouth out the window and said, "That's the old Mott place."

"Where?"

"Down there." He pointed a couple of hundred yards in the distance, across an overgrown field, toward a frail wooden structure. Even from that distance, Charlie could tell it wasn't much bigger than a two-car garage. He studied the dilapidated building until an island of trees temporarily hid it from his sight. He kept his eyes intently focused for its reappearance as they drove around a large bend in the road, past the same family of trees.

Now in plain view, he saw Jake's pickup parked on the side of the road some fifty yards from the home.

Hank came to a stop behind Jake's truck. The two men said nothing as they both stared at the falling structure. The roof was red and had caved into the home in three different spots. Parts of the roof's fall could be seen through the shot-out windows and doorless entrance. The front right corner of the home was sunk into the ground, causing the whole frame to lean to its left. Remains of a small wooden porch sat in half a heap in the front yard, probably broken off by scavengers or kids. In actuality, the place screamed of vandalism. And that was when he noticed the black spray paint: a string of defamations ran under the two window frames: "Dirty Niggers" on one side and "Monkey" on the other.

Glancing over at Hank, Charlie saw him turn away as if he couldn't stand to look at the structure anymore. "I haven't been out here in years," he said softly. "Last I heard, Jake was doing some time. That true?"

He thought better of telling the truth, but what did it matter? "Yeah...it's true."

Hank sighed. "Well, I better get back into town."

Charlie reached for the door handle, wondering if it wouldn't be better if he headed back to town with Hank. He let himself out of the truck anyway and stood at the end of the drive.

Hank called out to him, "Hey, I never caught your name."

"Charlie Boone."

"How long you known Jake?"

He hesitated and then answered exactly what he felt: "My whole life."

Hank cocked his head. "Praire hasn't changed a whole lot since Jake left. For some people that's a good thing, for others not so much. We're a quiet town here…I liked Jake. He and his family was good people, and when I knew 'im, he was a good kid, but this town doesn't need trouble." He paused. "I guess what I'm sayin' is I just don't know that Praire's Jake's home anymore. I'm not saying it's right, but probably how it would be." Hank put the truck in reverse and drove off.

Charlie stood in the entrance of the Mott home, taking it all in. The interior mirrored the same vandalism and destruction that was outside. Weather-beaten drapes as thin as sheets dangled loosely from nails on two of the back windows. A closer study revealed they actually were bedsheets, and very old ones at that. In the far left corner lay a single mattress, pitch black from mildew and years of sitting out in the weather.

In the far right corner stood an oven small enough to fit a loaf of bread and two hot plates on its top. Next to it was some counter space that housed a few beat-up pots and pans. A thick vine growing through a nearby window had tangled itself in and around them.

To his immediate right, the earth had broken through the floorboards, and large weeds now stood erect like indoor plants. And lastly, right before him, not ten feet away, sat a red velvet chair with its insides spewing out all over the floor.

Jake stood silently flipping through a book that sat on a small wooden table next to the chair. Perhaps sensing a presence, he ever so slightly turned, revealing his profile to Charlie.

Charlie could see the tension in the side of Jake's face, along with a tear on his right cheek. Jake closed the book, set it down, and walked out a gaping hole in the home's back wall and into the backyard.

Charlie gingerly approached the small table and reached for the book Jake had been flipping through. It was an old Bible. Its black cover was weather-beaten and fragile. Printed in block print on the inside cover was the name Beatrice Mott.

Like an old lion, years of incarceration had tamed him, and now here he was living the moment he had replayed in his mind so many times before: his return home. He had never expected a party, perhaps not so much as even a smile at the front door, yet nothing he had ever imagined could have prepared him for this.

He considered what his last thoughts on this earth would be. Gazing out into a field of overgrown weeds, he saw himself a young boy, innocent, happy, unfazed by the hardships surrounding him and his family, and certainly unaware of the strife and pain that still awaited him.

He wished little for that child but yearned to stay that age forever, never to grow old and see the pain he'd come to cause so many.

Like a bolt of lightning, a surge of unwanted energy ripped through his body. *Have I done it? Is this what death feels like?*

In a way, yes. It was that one enlightening moment in which he saw himself as a child that made his shame all the more painful. The boy in front of him had dreams, and he had stripped them all away from him. He'd been very few things to many people. A good son, no, and for that he was remorseful. A good nephew, no, and for that he was regretful. A God-fearing good citizen, absolutely not, at least not the better part of his life. These were the things he'd been slowly coming to terms with these last few weeks.

Being on the very ground he had played on as a child made it all too much to bear. The choices he'd made in his life had brought him to this very moment, and there was no one to blame but himself. It was a moment of tragedy, but at least one that had an end.

He'd fired many guns in his day, but none were more warranted than this one. The gripping and regripping of the .45 that dangled from his hand finally came to a stop. He raised the gun to his chest. The glare of the sun hitting the chromed steel shined back into his tear-filled eyes. He took a large breath and exhaled.

Fishing the barrel of the gun through his flannel took just a few tries. The feel of the cold steel against his chest confirmed his misery, and also exactly what he was doing.

It would be one shot to the heart, and after that, all shame would cease, all guilt would rest, and all righteousness would be restored. He would finally serve the penance he truly deserved.

Charlie stood in the gaping hole of the dilapidated home and called out, "Hank from in town drove me out here. I didn't catch his last name." He paused. "I'm sorry for this, Jake. No one deserves this."

"They rotted here," Jake said. "I lived better in prison than she did out here. She refused to leave, and because of it, she died right here—I know she did, I can feel it. She died on this ground, alone, dreaming of the boy she loved. The boy that took her heart and threw it away."

Charlie said the first thing that came to mind. "Hank said your family was good people, Jake. He said you were a good person."

"I was a good kid," Jake replied softly.

Charlie looked toward a brush of woods about twenty yards in front of Jake. "Is that creek back there? The one you were telling me about?"

Jake lifted his head and stared at the woods before him. He marched toward them as if they were calling his name. The gun, once pointed at his chest, fell back to his side.

Charlie saw the gun and realized what he had just walked up on.

Thirty feet into the woods, there it was: the spot Jake had spoken about. Jake stopped short of its edge and looked down into the four-foot drop.

"Looks clean enough to drink," Charlie said.

"Did it every day," Jake muttered. "Was nice to jump in on a hot day, too."

"Probably still is," Charlie replied.

"It feeds into a river about four miles down, all downhill mostly. I used to walk it a lot…it's amazing, actually."

"What?"

"It looks the same, everything about it. It hasn't changed a bit."

"Water can do that. It's timeless."

"Yeah, I guess it is."

They shared a comfortable silence. "There's something out there for each of us, Jake. We just have to find it." Looking down at the gun in Jake's hand, he said, "Why don't you put that away. You've done enough stupid things in your life. I don't think there's much room for any more."

"I just don't see the point to go on."

"I never had anyone to give me advice, and I'm not one to give it out— don't think I'm qualified to—but there's still time for you. What's done in the past is done. People don't have to know what Jake Mott was, and I think if you'd let them, they might like the man he's become."

Jake got down on his knees, leaned into the stream, and splashed cold water on his face. He leaned back on his heels as drops of cold water fell into his lap. "I should have never come back here."

"Sometimes not knowing is worse than knowing," Charlie said.

"Story is, I was baptized in these waters," Jake softly said.

Charlie thought back to his Saturdays in church and recalled something he had read. "You know, Jake, you don't need a priest to confess your sins."

"Who says?"

"Says the church. If it's eating at your heart, then you must confess it. But it has to be an act of perfect contrition—at least, that's what they say."

"And what does that mean?" Jake asked.

"It means that it can only come from inside. It's rooted in your faith in God, and your contrition must be real and sincere, with the true intent of never sinning again, no matter what evil may come. They say if you can do that, you'll be in a state of absolute grace."

"I believe I'm sincere," Jake replied, "but the faith you're talking about...I don't think I have that."

Charlie shook his head and whispered, "Me neither."

Jake looked up at him, a tear running down his cheek, and asked, "What, then?"

CHAPTER 66

They stood on the steps of Holy Angels Catholic Church, somewhere near the Texas state line. Jake looked up at the massive red doors before him and felt awkward entering. He looked back at Charlie, standing a step below him, and then walked in.

The painted glass windows of the church vestibule shot rays of red, blue, and yellow light at his feet. He studied every image on those windows: hearts on fire, saints preaching, animals being sacrificed, angels flying, the Last Supper— Jesus forgiving the sinners at his feet.

Hesitant to go any farther, Jake stared at the altar. "I've never been in a church."

He felt Charlie's hand on his shoulder, followed by a little nudge forward. It was just enough to put him on his way.

He walked the aisle with caution, his focus never wavering from the marble altar before him and the picture of Jesus on the cross in the background.

He stopped at the second pew and rested his hand on the rail. Hearing Charlie take a seat behind him, he sidestepped into the pew and gingerly sat down. The old wooden pew squeaked and squealed under the pressure of his weight. The bench's cry seemed to vibrate throughout the large space, making him even more uncomfortable than he already was.

He was thankful for the silence that once again took hold.

The artwork on the cathedral ceiling was colorful and painfully detailed. An angel's feathered wing hovered over them as if it were standing guard.

"It's amazing," he said.

"What?" Charlie asked.

"That someone's own hands could paint such a thing. How can anyone do something so great?"

"Patience," Charlie said.

"That state of grace you were talkin' about, that person had it."

A statue of Mary stood to the right of the altar. At her feet candles flickered light in the darkened space she occupied. The cast of shadows it produced made it look as if Mary were crying. Jake kept his focus on the statue, eagerly awaiting that illusion each time it presented itself.

"Do you see that?" he asked.

"I do," Charlie replied. "I do."

Jake got up and walked to the altar before her. He knelt down on the cold marble floor, folded his hands, and looked up. "What I've missed all this time. My God, what I've missed."

He looked into Mary's eyes and whispered, "I pray for my mother. Oh, Blessed Mother, please let me pray for my own mother, please bless her soul, and keep her with you; please do that. I know I've sinned and I don't belong on your step, but please allow me this one wish. Bless my mother and tell her…" Jake dropped his head and began to cry a river of tears. Not holding anything back, he stayed there kneeling for one hour, crying all the while, confessing every last one of his sins. His last words were "I'm sorry, I'm sorry…God forgive me for everything I've done, I'm so sorry."

Sitting just three pews behind, Charlie wiped away tears of his own. He'd been touched by more than just Jake's words. The transformation before his very eyes was enlightening. It was as if they were both in a moment of absolute grace and in the presence of greatness.

Grace, patience, inner peace: things he was feeling, things he'd longed for in the past. Hearing Jake confess his sins in the Church of the Holy Angels in front of the Blessed Mother had him wondering if perhaps this was the reason for it all.

Had he come all this way, foreseen the coming of Jake Mott, survived years of mental torment, just to be here and watch another man bare his soul before God and ask for forgiveness? Well, if so, then it was all worth it.

He was born Charles Nathan Boone to Patricia, he was a bastard child who had two boys of his own and a beautiful wife named Lisa, and should he never achieve another thing for the remainder of his life, then so be it. He was fulfilled.

Kneeling in his own pew, Charlie clutched his two hands together, closed his eyes, and prayed to the Blessed Mother that he be given one last chance to tell his own mother how much he loved her and to have her hear his words and know their meaning.

CHAPTER 67

S
he planted Mrs. Boone's two feet firmly on the bedroom floor and then draped her frail right arm over her shoulder. Lisa looked out the top of her eyes at her two sons standing in the doorway. "Well?" she said.

"Well what?" Eddie answered.

"Are you going to help your mother, or are you just going to stand there and stare at me?"

"Why are you doing this?"

"Don't ask questions, Eddie, just help. How would you like being cooped up in the house all day? You couldn't stand it two hours, let alone three years. Now get over here and help me lift your grandmother up."

Eddie wrapped her other arm over his shoulder. "I don't think this is a good idea, that's all. She doesn't seem right, not the way she looks, not the way she is."

"And for a moment I thought you were going to have something compassionate to say. It's gonna be fifty-seven degrees today, and I'll be damned if she's going to miss it. Isn't that right, Mom? I know you can hear me, I know you're in there. It might not be this warm again for months, and we need to take advantage of it." With their arms interlocked across Mrs. Boone's back, they stepped out into the hall.

"It's going to be a different story around here once spring hits. We're gonna get you out every day. That's what's good for you." She and Eddie caught the hang of it after the first couple of stairs and made it down without incident. She took a breather at the bottom of the steps and shouted, "You all right, Mom?"

"She's not that heavy," Eddie said.

Lisa ripped open the closet door and pulled an old coat off a hanger. She put it on her mother-in-law along with a scarf and placed gloves in the coat pockets. They resumed their move onto the porch, where they guided Mrs. Boone onto the wooden bench.

Lisa fell back into a chair next to Mrs. Boone and said, "Not that heavy? I disagree. I'm wiped out."

"Look! I think she just smiled," Eddie said.

Lisa brushed strays of hair away from her face. "Of course she smiled. She's still alive, you know. You should talk to her more than you do."

"I used to talk to her all the time."

"I know you did, but you don't anymore. This is your grandmother, and this is your grandmother's home. The home you were born in. This is the woman who took us in when…" Getting a bit choked up from her own words, she stopped. "I want you to spend more time with her, Eddie; I want you to talk to her. Do it every day from now on. You understand me?"

"Yes," he said. "I think she needs a pillow for her back."

"I think you're right," she replied. "These chairs aren't very comfortable, are they, Mom?"

"I'll get it," Eddie said.

"No, you stay here. I'll get it. Sit and talk with her. I'm sure you have plenty of catching up to do." Lisa got up from the chair and felt a rush of blood go to her head. Her legs felt weak, and without warning, she collapsed to one knee.

Eddie lunged for her. "Mom! You all right?"

She held out her arm. "I'm OK, I'm OK. Just a little dizzy, that's all."

"From what?"

"I don't know. Carrying her, I guess."

"I'm gonna get the pillow. You stay here."

She rose to her feet. "No, really, I'm fine. Just a little out of shape. You sit; I'll get the pillow."

One blanket covered both boys as they cramped together in one chair. Lisa sat with her mother-in-law on the bench. Two large quilts covered Mrs. Boone's legs and chest.

A group of neighborhood kids was gathering on the sidewalk nearby. Eddie looked at her in disgust. "I thought it was going to be fifty-seven degrees today," he said.

"Oh, suck it up. So I was off by a few."

"It feels more like forty."

Lisa laughed. "Forty degrees? Don't be a baby. Plus, it's good for your grandmother. It reminds her that she's still with us. Look at your younger brother with that big smile on his face. He's enjoying himself. Be more like him."

"He's always smiling," Eddie said.

"Yes, he is, isn't he?" Lisa smiled back at her youngest boy. "We should all smile more, like Billy. Isn't that right, Mom?"

"Why do you have to yell like that? Everyone can hear you."

"I don't give a damn if they can hear me. You wanna go play with the peanut gallery? Go ahead. The three of us will stay here and enjoy ourselves without you."

"I don't wanna play with them. I don't like them."

"Then you shouldn't care what they think, Edward. Trust me, honey, you're a Boone, so you better start warming up to it."

Billy laughed out loud as he attempted say their last name. "Boo, Boo, Boo, Boo…"

"Yes, yes, yes," Lisa yelled back. "We're Boones, aren't we, Billy? We're Boones!"

"Holy shit!" Eddie said.

"Watch your tongue, mister! No one likes a sourpuss." She took note of the giggles coming from the corner of the street and looked back at Eddie. "Screw them. Their parents are assholes too. Maybe I'll keep my voice down if you stop being such a party pooper."

"I'm not being a party pooper. We just…" Eddie stopped what he was about to say.

"Just what?"

"We look like idiots! We're sitting on the porch like it's summertime. Why is it always us?"

"Always us what?"

"We look like crazy people! I can see them saying it in school before I even get there. 'Did you see the crazy Boones? They wheeled out the old crazy on Saturday. Did you get a look at the crazy?' Well, I don't wanna be a crazy anymore. I don't wanna be a—"

She lunged across her mother-in-law's lap and grabbed Eddie by his arm. "No! Don't you say it! Don't you ever say it!" Shaking Eddie by his arm, she started to cry. "Don't even think it! This is who we are, and I'm done hiding it. This woman has seen more pain and suffering than any of us combined, and the least we can do is be happy for who we are and what we have. She deserved better than she got, and you have no right to sit here and degrade who she is or who we are just because of those little pricks on the corner!"

Eddie broke free of her hold and ran into the house.

Lisa looked out at the peanut gallery across the street and yelled, "What the fuck are you looking at? Go home! Go home to your…just get out! Get out."

———

She stared at the framed picture of Charlie and Mrs. Boone when he was a young teenager. They were standing side by side in front of a fireplace she didn't recognize. The awkwardness of their smiles and stances showed them to be complete strangers. She wiped specks of dirt off its front and placed it on the hope chest that housed all the scarves and hats, near the front door.

At her feet was a box full of pictures and miscellaneous mementos—the same box she had pulled the picture frame from. The same box that, she'd decided, had been tucked away for far too long. Its sole purpose was to conceal the past, but the past was now being unveiled. They had skeletons—they all did—but it was time to face them, and she looked forward to Charlie's return home to start anew.

Lisa climbed the steps, feeling bad about her earlier actions with Eddie. It seemed she was developing a pattern in that department. It was her own guilt that made her so angry at that moment; she'd been guilty of the same thought many times before.

Still feeling some aftereffects from her fainting spell, she gripped the stair rail tightly and pulled herself up the steps with the wish that she weren't going to bed alone. She poked her face into Eddie's room and saw him reading with a flashlight in his hand.

"What're ya reading?"

He quickly shoved whatever it was under his covers. "Life magazine."

She laughed. "I didn't know you liked that magazine."

"I read all of Dad's old ones."

"You do."

"Yeah, they're real old. He keeps them in the basement."

"You're a reader just like your father...that's good." She entered the room and gave her son a kiss on the forehead. "I'm sorry, Eddie. I know you're hearing that a lot from me lately, but I truly am. You're too young to understand, and I was wrong to lash out at you like that."

"That's OK," he replied. "At least you say it."

"Say what?"

"That you're sorry. Lenny Conway says his mom never says she's sorry, even when she's wrong."

Lisa smiled. "Well, sounds like we're not the only ones with issues."

"I shouldn't have said what I said anyway."

She hugged and kissed him goodnight.

Eddie threw his magazine to the floor and turned out his light, then called out to her in the dark. "Ma?"

"Yeah?"

"When's Dad coming home? I miss him."

"Soon, baby. He'll be home real soon."

CHAPTER 68

With the phone to his ear, he stared at Jake's pickup, envisioning what was happening on the other end of the line. "What the heck is she doing?"

"She's with Grandmom," Eddie said.

"Well, she seems pretty darn excited just for being with Grandmom." He could hear Lisa in the background singing a tune.

"Grandmom was talking last night," Eddie said.

"Whatta ya mean she was talking?"

"Mom said she came into her room, and they talked last night."

Is it possible? By this time he was annoyed and wanted answers. "Eddie, I want you to put your mother on the phone right now!"

"Mom!"

The other receiver picked up. "Charlie!"

"What the hell's going on over there?"

"Charlie, you're not going to believe this."

He could hear the smile in her voice. "What're you about to tell me?"

"Your mom, Charlie. She was awake last night. I mean awake. We talked! We talked for hours, in our room, on our bed!"

"Are you shitting me?"

"Oh, baby, I'm not shitting you, not about this."

"Well what the hell did she say?"

"She said a lot, Charlie. I don't know where to start. I've never heard her this together for as long as I've known her."

"You're killing me. What did she say?"

"She talked about the first year you moved into this house. You were two and a half, and there was a big hole in the dining room floor from some local kids who had broken in while it was for sale and started a fire. And she was right, Charlie! I checked! I pulled back the carpet, and there it was—a cut-out of fresh wood different from the rest of the floor. It was fucking amazing!"

He remained perfectly still. "What else did she say?"

"We talked about you…a lot, you and the kids. She asked where you were, and I said you'd be home soon, that you were away on business. She just smiled. She talked about her own mother, too, Charlie. I never heard her mention her before. She missed her mother, Charlie. She missed her so much."

His body was one big goose bump. His prayer had been answered. Seeing Jake get in the pickup and shut the door brought an urgency to his tone. "I wanna talk to her! Get her up!"

"Charlie, I can't do that."

"Whatta ya mean you can't do it?"

"She's sound asleep, and I don't want to alarm her. Matter of fact, I don't wanna do anything that might set her back."

"Set her back? Are you kidding me? Lisa, I haven't had an audible conversation with my mother in two years. Now, I want you to wake her up right now!"

"No, I won't do it. Listen to me, Charlie. She was up all night, and I think she was really thrown off by things. After a while, we just sat there. She seemed to be trying to make sense of it all. We're gonna do this at her pace. The last week around here has been absolutely nuts. I'm not even going to get into it with you, but I think this has been a gradual process. The other night I had out her old eight tracks, and I was playing Nat King Cole—I told you about it—and I could have sworn someone was watching me. I think it was her now. And yesterday, I had Eddie help me get her out of bed, and we all sat outside on the porch. I think that helped! And I'm talking to her, Charlie. I mean really talking to her about things."

"So what are you saying?"

"What I'm saying is I'm going to continue to play her music, get her fresh air, and talk to her, and I think if I do that, she might get better and better. I think she just might be going through some sort of awakening."

"You think?" he asked. "Do you really think so?"

"I do. And let me tell you something else: things are gonna change when you get back here, and I mean for the better."

"I know they are. I feel that too."

"Oh, Charlie, why don't you just come home right now? Just jump on a bus."

He looked out of the telephone booth at Jake sitting in the truck. "Trust me, I want to, but we're just about a day and a half from where we're going, and then it's straight back to Philly, with no stops. We've already discussed it. He's as eager as I am to get back and start new."

"Sounds like you two are getting along."

Again he looked over at Jake. "Yesterday was one of the most beautiful days of my life, and when I get back, you can bet I'll share it with you." He paused. "He's a good man. Now listen, you keep Mom up tonight so I can talk to her, huh?"

"You bet I will."

CHAPTER 69

The grin on Charlie's face was ear to ear. What were once spastic images and dark visions were now being replaced with visions of what was to be: a new life for them all. Much like the man sitting to his left, he felt as if his soul had been cleansed the day before in the church of the Holy Angels, and his reward for that would be found back in Philadelphia, on the porch of his boyhood home, where Lisa, his two boys, and his mom would be waiting for him. That moment couldn't come fast enough.

"You know, I've been thinking," Jake said.

"About what?" Charlie asked.

"This money."

Oh yeah, the money. It had been days since he had thought about the actual purpose of their trip, and as always, it meant nothing to him other than a bit of intrigue.

"What about it?" he asked.

"I was thinking if it's even there, I'm gonna give some of it away. I mean, I'd pay you back for getting this old hog back on the road, and I'd get myself set up somewhere with a home I can call my own, but then I'll give it away. I'd give it to the poorest church I could find, or maybe an orphanage."

"Nice. I like that. A modern-day Robin Hood."

Taking a deep breath, Jake said, "It's a great day, Charlie, you know that? It's a great day!"

Just then a hard rain started falling. Jake rolled down his window and stuck his head out.

"What the hell you doing?" Charlie asked.

"I feel liberated, Charlie! I feel great; I feel free!"

Charlie had never seen him so animated—Jake was right, it was a great day.

Out his passenger-side window, something came into view as they came around the bend. It was a vast field, five football fields long and wide, with a just a handful of horses grazing in it. "Hey, Jake…what was that dream you had?"

Jake slowed down, pulled over, and stopped.

"It's no corn field," Charlie said, staring out the window, "but I think it would do."

The light bulb went off in Jake's head, and within seconds, the big man was out of the truck, over the makeshift fence, and running as fast as he could, his arms raised high to the sky.

A beautiful, sleek, and dark-haired stallion bolted across Jake's path, then another one, followed by another. It was a majestic scene, and one that prompted Charlie to jump out of the truck and join in. Not a second later, he was through the fence and running as fast he could while raindrops the size of ice cubes pelted him in the face.

Reaching the center of the field, they both collapsed in fits of exhaustion and, while they lay in silence trying to reclaim their breaths, a string of stallions galloped and danced around them.

"You're free, Jake," Charlie said in between breaths. "You're free."

CHAPTER 70

J ake looked over a road map that had been left behind by another patron. By his estimate and the map's confirmation, they'd be in Calimesa by noon tomorrow. Turning around on the counter stool, he looked at the jagged mountainside across the street from the small roadside diner. He wanted to build a fire for the night and camp out; somewhere on that mountain would be a good place to do it.

Charlie stood in a narrow hallway by the bathroom making attempt after attempt to call home, but the pay phone had seen better days. The sporadic dial tone tuned in and out over the crackling sound coming through the line. He slammed the phone down on the receiver, glanced at his watch, and returned to the counter.

"Get through?" Jake asked.

"Phone's fucked up. What are the chances of that?"

"We're sitting pretty tight in a valley. That might be the problem."

"Yeah, I guess. I don't know."

"You seem anxious about it."

"I am. I haven't spoken to my mom in some time. The way Lisa was talking, she was pretty clearheaded." Charlie exhaled. "I just wish I were there to see it."

"Well, the way I see it, we'll be in Calimesa by noon tomorrow. We find that bag of money, and you'll have yourself a first-class ticket back home out of LA, maybe be home by nightfall."

Charlie grinned. "And what about you?"

"I'll make my way back, slowly but surely."

"You think you're gonna plant some seeds in Philly? Call it home?"

Jake paused. "Well, I do know some people there. Might not be a bad place to do it."

"When was the last time you had a home-cooked Thanksgiving dinner?" Charlie asked.

"Shit, not since I was a boy, my momma's."

"Well, if I have any say about it, next Thursday you'll be having Thanksgiving dinner with my family. What do you think about that?"

"That's kind of you, but I don't think I'm quite ready for something like that. Besides, you'll have some catching up to do with the Mrs. when you get back."

"Well, like I said, if I have any say about it."

"We'll see. All I'm thinking about right now is building a nice campfire up in them woods, pulling some old blankets out of the truck, and sitting by it. You in?"

"You go ahead," Charlie said. "I'm gonna stick around here a bit, try to get through on the phone."

Jake stood up. "All right, there's an access road we passed about fifty yards back. I'm figuring it'll take us up the mountain. I won't go up too far." He threw the keys to the truck on the counter. "Look for me about a quarter mile up."

"What are these for?"

"I'll walk it; you take the truck."

CHAPTER 71

"Lisa? Lisa, can you hear me?"

"Charlie, is that you?"

Charlie yelled into the phone. "Yes!" He glanced out at the few patrons left in the diner, who stared back as if he had two heads. He turned his back on them and cupped the phone. "Can you hear me?"

"I thought that was you. The phone's been ringing, but I couldn't hear anyone when I picked up."

"How's Mom?"

"Charlie?"

"Yes! I'm here. How's Mom? Is she up?"

"She is!"

"Well, put her on!"

"Charlie?" Lisa said again.

"Yes, I'm here."

"You're breaking up."

"Put Mom on."

"I can't..." Her voice trailed off.

"What do you mean?"

"I can't hear you!"

Charlie yelled into the phone, "Put Mom on!"

It was several seconds before he heard anything else but the static already coming through. And then, like a break in the clouds, there was a moment of silence—the static was gone. His mother's voice was the next thing he heard. It was weak and rasping, but caring. "Charlie?"

He could barely get the words out over the lump stuck in his throat. He bit down on his bottom lip and blurted out, "Mom?"

"Charlie, is that you?"

He could feel the tears welling in his eyes. "It's me, Mom, it's me."

"Where are you, Charlie?"

Looking at his surroundings, he couldn't begin to answer her question.

"I found your letter," she said. "I read it."

"Mom! You listen to me. Let me get you help, please let me. We both need it; we both do! I know that now. I know it!"

"Charlie? Charlie, are you there?"

"I'm here," he replied, fighting back the tears. "I'm fucking here."

"I need to go." The tone of her voice suggested she meant something other than getting off the phone.

"What do you mean, you have to go?"

"It's time…" Her words trailed off.

"Don't! Don't you do this! I'll be home, I'll be home tomorrow…you hear me?"

"Charlie, I'm sorry."

"For what? What do you have to be sorry about?"

"I love you, Charlie. Tonight I'll sleep with your sweater. Lisa gave it to me."

"No! Please don't! Please don't go! I'll be home tomorrow.…Don't you do this, don't you go!"

Sporadic crackling once again filled the phone line. He repeatedly called out for her but could only hear static and then, finally, dial tone. With the receiver pressed to the side of his head and a vision of his mother in his mind, Charlie hung his head and cried.

CHAPTER 72

J ake sat on a rock by the campfire, poking at the orange coals at the fire's base. Ember tips and sparks rose to the sky.

He could sense the shadow of a man approaching. When he looked up, Charlie was leaning against a tree nearby.

"Hell of a fire," Charlie said softly.

"My uncle Sam taught me how to build a good fire...came in handy on many occasions. Any luck calling home?"

"Yeah," Charlie halfheartedly replied.

"Wasn't what you expected?" he asked.

"Beggars can't be choosers, right?" Charlie replied. "It was great to talk with her. Even if it was..."

"If it was what?"

Charlie ignored his question and stepped closer to the fire. "You got any whiskey?"

He reached down at his feet and picked up a bottle of Jack Daniels. Extending his arm to Charlie, he said, "No glasses."

Charlie took a swig and then took a seat near the fire. "Life's a fucked-up thing, Jake."

"I agree."

"Not in a million years would I ever have put myself here, on a mountainside with you, doing this."

"Sharing a drink...camping out?"

"All of the above."

"You're looking forward to getting home tomorrow," Jake said.

"The mind's a powerful thing. It can really fuck you up at times. I've been ignoring the voices in my head for a lot of years, and the one time I listened, I end up here, with you, three thousand miles from home."

Jake poked at the fire. "I think you called it destiny."

"Yeah, destiny." The embers Jake poked at had Charlie's undivided attention. "I always needed to know; I always needed answers. At the start of this trip, I was looking for truth. But the other day in that church, I said a prayer, and today that prayer was answered, and if I don't do anything else with my life, I'll have that. I may not be going home with the answers I was looking for, but I'll have faith, and with that there's hope…I think."

Newfound compassion for the man sitting across from him blossomed in Jake's heart. His own demons were beginning to heal, and he hoped Charlie's wouldn't take nearly as long. "How did you know what you knew, Charlie?"

Charlie looked up from the fire. "You told me, remember?"

"That was *your* dream, not mine," he replied.

"Yeah, but you were there. As real as you're sitting here now, you were there."

"Real enough to bring you three thousand miles from home with me."

Charlie took a swig of whiskey and sat silent for a moment. "I saw you kill him, Jake. I was there."

"Kill who?"

"Ginn."

Jake felt a glimmer of expectation. "Bullshit."

"No, I wouldn't do that."

"Yeah? Then hand me that whiskey and start talking."

Charlie handed the bottle across the fire. "The boots on your feet—I saw the soles of those boots before I ever met you. I crawled like he crawled, I tasted the sweat mixed with his blood, I felt his thirst."

Jake took two big gulps of liquor. "So let's say you're right. Let's say you was there. Am I supposed to feel bad about it?"

Charlie went on. "The wildfires I followed day and night? They were just my introduction, my intro to the man I'd been searching for, the man I saw coming as a child."

Jake rested the bottle on his knee. "Charlie, what the hell are you tryin' to say?"

"I've always dreamed of a group of faceless people. I step over every one of them to reach the cries of a little boy outside that fucking door. I could never explain that dream, but when you told me about Ginn...hell, I'm sure I know who those people are."

"Who are they?"

"How many people did he kill?" Charlie asked. "How many was it, Jake?"

Jake put his hand in the air. "Hold on a minute. Time out. What the hell are you trying to tell me?"

"You read the Bible. You know what I'm saying."

"Like reincarnation? Like, you was him and I killed him, and he came back as you?"

Charlie remained silent.

Jake took a long swig of whiskey, dropped the bottle to his knee, and laughed. "What's that word you like to use? Fantastic? Well, that's what *that* is. It's a fantastically ridiculous thought. Crazy, too."

He took another swig then extended the bottle to Charlie. "Holy shit! Don't scare me like that. You almost had me there for a second. Why don't you try another theory on me, 'cause I ain't buyin' that one."

Charlie grinned halfheartedly. "The other theory's simple. I'm my mother's son. As crazy as the day's long, as crazy as the woman who brought me into this world."

Jake laughed. "Well, that's just as depressing, but certainly more believable. I'd stick to that one, by the way...I'd bet my sorry-ass life that it's the right one. Hand me that bottle back. The way you're talking, I got some catching up to do."

Jake stood up and downed a couple more swigs, then took a seat on the ground with his back against a rock. He wore a grin. "Lyle Ginn!"

"I'm glad you find it amusing."

"I've heard some crazy-ass stories in my time, but never one like that." Jake's expression turned serious, and he lost his smile. "But let me say this: get it out of your head, 'cause it ain't true. You ain't him, I know that. You weren't ever him. See...the way I got it, Charlie, is you see things. Just like that big Indian in Georgia State, and no different than them old soothsayers in them Texas woods. Generations of people put their faith in those women, year in and year out." Jake shook his head. "Wasn't me, wasn't you, but it was other people, and there's something to be said for that."

Jake leaned into the fire. "You see things, Charlie. You see the lives of those around you, perfect strangers—you see their troubles, the good of their lives, the bad, maybe even the images of their very own thoughts. But it's what you do or don't do once it registers that trips ya up and freaks ya out. Like them wildfires? Maybe it *was* me, or just maybe you were hearing the screams of thousands of people, people who lost their homes and lost their loved ones. And Thunder? Well, I can't say for sure, but maybe you was reading my thoughts and you saw my past, or just perhaps you had my own dreams before I could even lay claim to 'em."

Jake pointed at him. "Now, with all that being said, at the end of the day, this is what I know: you ain't crazy, son. You ain't crazy, and you got *nothin'* to be ashamed of. What you were born with is a gift, and something you should be proud of, because you're a good man. As good a man as I've ever known, and if it weren't for you, I'd be dead on the ground back in Texas. I'd be that lost soul you talked about. You've never broke the law, and from what I can tell, you're not much of a sinner. So keep your head high, boy, be proud of who you are, and be happy for what you got. You're goin' home tomorrow to a family that loves ya. And that's as good as it gets."

Charlie hoped the smoke rising between them camouflaged the tears swelling in his eyes. "That's pretty good advice from a broken-down old man."

"Just one man's opinion. You can take it or leave it."

"Never got advice before, but I think I'll take it."

A comfortable silence was interrupted by the fire's crackling embers and pockets of hissing air.

"You remember asking me about one of those things I always wished I'd done?" Jake asked.

"I do."

"I always wanted to play guitar." Jake laughed. "Must have been the country in me."

"I can see why you laugh. I don't quite picture you with a guitar in your hand."

Jake nodded. "I agree. What was that you said the other day? Blowin' sad with just your mouth and a piece of steel? That's what this fireside needs—a little guitar and harmonica. Now, that's living."

Charlie motioned for the bottle of whiskey. "Blowin' sad," he repeated.

"Besides Willie, I always liked that Glenn Campbell in the clink, but now that I'm out, sky's the limit. Got anything good?"

"'This Hard Land,' Springsteen. Look it up someday. It's the one that was playing in the truck that day outside of Strongsville."

Jake reached for the bottle of whiskey. "Tell me about it."

Charlie shrugged his shoulders. "Seeds of life—some take, some don't. You roll around from town to town, and where you end up is what will be." Staring into the fire, Charlie went on. "You take what you can get. That's life, a ride, sweeping low across the plains…on that Bar-M chopper."

Jake's head lost gravity and then jerked back up again. "Hmm? What'd ya say?"

Charlie smiled. "Nothing."

CHAPTER 73

It wasn't just the wet of the morning dew that woke him from a deep sleep. With his right cheek kissing the hard clay ground, Jake's neck rested against the cold rock he had used to sit on the night before. Now that he had used them as chairs, backstops, and pillows, no rock on this mountain range had ever seen the likes of Jake Mott. At least that was his initial thought upon opening his eyes.

A slight mist filled the air, seen through the rays of sunlight that cut through the tall pines towering over him. He could make out a figure in the distance, some thirty or forty feet away. He sat up for a better view and surmised it was Charlie, who looked to be staring down some sort of drop in the rocky landscape.

He glanced over at the truck and then got up. The closer he got to Charlie, the more evident it became that the drop was more like a cliff's edge, and a sharp one at that.

"What's going on?" he asked.

Charlie glanced over his shoulder and then back down the cliff's edge. "Just thinking."

"Yeah? What the hell you thinking about?"

"My mother passed last night. She passed in her sleep."

Jake looked at their surroundings. "And how do you know that?"

"I dreamed it."

The weight of Charlie's words took hold. The little he had learned of Charlie in just a few weeks' time assured him the man's dreams were not to be dismissed. He took a couple of steps toward him and then spoke in a broken tone. "I'm sorry you're here and not there."

"So was I," he replied, and then turned and faced him. "Then I realized where one life ends another begins."

"For yourself?" Jake asked.

"Maybe, but maybe someone else too, someone we don't know about yet."

Jake nodded. "OK, then, let's get this thing over with."

"Calimesa," Charlie said.

"Calimesa or home?" Jake asked.

Charlie smiled as best he could. "I got one more phone call in me, then Calimesa…then home."

CHAPTER 74

S itting in his truck, Jake watched Charlie bury his face in his hands as he stood in a roadside phone booth. Charlie's demeanor was confirmation enough that his dream had been true.

"Charlie?" Lisa called out as loud as she could, but there was nothing but a painful cry on the other end of the line. "Charlie, say something, please say something. It's killing me, not being able to be with you right now."

Charlie swallowed some tears and did his best to fight off new ones. "Tell me something."

"What?" Lisa asked.

"Anything."

"She asked for your sweater. She held it all night." Lisa let out a series of cries herself. "She loved you, she loved you so much, and she was there at the end. She knew it. She knew everything that was happening."

He hung his head and allowed his tears to flow freely; nothing was said between them for several minutes.

Lisa finally spoke in between some cries. "Come home! Please, Charlie, come home."

"I am. I'm taking a flight out of LA. I'll be home by morning."

He looked up and saw Jake watching him. With a pained look on his face, Jake nodded to him as if to say, I'm with ya.

"I want you to know something," he said. "This man, this man I'm with, is a good man. No matter his past, he's a good man."

"I'm sure he is."

"He has nobody—but not anymore. He's going to eat at our table; he's going to know our children. For once in my life, Lisa, I used the gift I was given and did good with it." He paused. "I think I saved his soul, and in the process found my own."

"If that's what you've done, Charlie," Lisa whispered, "then it's a beautiful thing."

"I'll see you in the morning."

"We'll be waiting," she replied.

CHAPTER 75

I t was a picture-perfect southern California day. There wasn't a cloud in the sky, the temperature was in the midsixties, and Jake and Charlie rode with the windows down. It was half past ten in the morning when Jake turned onto Interstate 215 toward San Bernardino. There was a time, in prison, when a day didn't go by that he didn't dream of driving down this stretch of road. The fact he was actually doing it today was more than surreal.

He thought back to that poor soul who'd sit in his cell for hours thinking about what he'd do with the money when he got it. But today, things were different. There were no thoughts of fast cars or easy women, just uneasiness in his stomach about what the future held. Money just wasn't that important anymore.

Since that day in the church of the Holy Angels, something had changed within him. With a grin on his face and a warm feeling in his heart, Jake acknowledged that this trip had left an indelible mark. It had affected who he was, what he was becoming, and even, perhaps, who he still had a chance to be. He was a better man than the one who had begun this journey, and he couldn't help but feel there was only one person responsible for it all.

Shouting over the wind that cut through the cab of the truck, he turned to Charlie. "By the way...thanks."

"For what?" Charlie called back.

"For coming on this trip with me."

The words weren't fully out of his mouth when he realized what he'd just said.

Charlie smiled and nodded.

A sea of goose bumps bubbled atop his skin. "I'll be damned," he said. "You might have told me, but not in a million years did I ever think I'd say it."

Staring out the windshield, Charlie whispered, "I needed this."

"Me too," Jake replied.

CHAPTER 76

It seemed Calimesa had changed since his last visit. They drove through the main part of town, past city hall, the police station, and a less-than-modest post office. Upscale boutiques lined the street, and Mercedes and Jaguars sat curbside. It looked as if the years had been good to the old town.

"You don't recognize anything, do you?" Charlie asked.

"Not quite how I remember it. Only had a few buildings back then and some modest-looking homes. Looks totally different now."

Charlie laughed. "Maybe they found a big bag of money and started a thriving business with it."

"If that's the case, then they should crown me mayor."

Jake made a sharp left turn, without warning, down a nondescript road.

"See something?"

"Nah, but felt something, though." Another half mile down the road and Jake said, "This is it. This is the road."

"How do you know?"

"'Cause I remember that." Jake pointed out the windshield at the landscape before them. The narrow road, hugged tightly on both sides by dense woods, acted as a tunnel leading toward a range of mountains before them. But it wasn't just the mountain range that made it unique. A single tree with a thick red top stood alone on the mountainside, large enough to be seen two hundred yards away.

"What is that?" Charlie asked.

"Reddest tree I've ever seen. And it hasn't changed in thirty years." Jake looked over to his right. "There should be a small graveyard coming up, just past this thick of woods. That's where it's buried."

"You buried the money in a graveyard?"

"No, I mean not really. Just a real small one, actually. Was a whole family that died in a house fire long before you or I. The town buried them all together on the site of their home; at least that's what the plaque read. I buried the money under a tree nearby."

"Jake." Charlie pointed to a spot of land ahead where a gathering of head-stones jutted up through some tall grass.

Jake set his eyes on the single Joshua tree set a few yards off the head-stones, where the bag of money was buried, and pulled over. "I'll be damned. It looks the same."

Charlie looked over the family of headstones scattered about. "How many did you say?" he whispered.

"How many what?"

Jake's tone seemed distant and somewhat troubled. Charlie turned back toward him. "You OK?"

Whether he chose not to respond or didn't hear him Charlie was unsure, but Jake remained still and silent. "Jake?"

"Just thinking a bit."

"About what?"

"Person I was when I came here thirty years ago. Person I was when I buried that money."

He could appreciate the thought and could imagine the burden Jake still carried. It showed in his voice and in his hardened face. "Don't beat yourself up, Jake. I'd say you're a changed man, remember? A different person."

"I *think* you're right," Jake replied.

He could sense there was something more. "But?"

"I like the feeling I got in my gut right now," Jake said, "the warm in my heart...the calm on my mind. I don't want any of it to go away." He looked over at him. "Not for any amount of money."

Charlie looked back out the window toward the Joshua tree and then back at Jake. With a slight grin, he said, "Did we just drive three thousand miles to get to this spot only to drive away?"

Jake took his eye off the tree and looked at Charlie. "You want it? It's yours if you do. Every last cent of it, and it's not blood money, Charlie. I'll say that again. It never was. Just some gambling money, and that's the truth."

"Are you trying to persuade me to take it?"

"I'm not sure what I'm doing, but I know I don't want it."

Charlie looked at the tree, back toward Jake, and then back at the tree again. "Three hundred?"

"Easy," Jake replied softly. A few seconds of silence passed between them. "There might be a rock. It's an odd-shaped rock with a soft, smooth surface. It'd be sitting right on top of the mark. It's a good size. If it's still there, the money probably is, too."

Charlie put his hand on the door handle and opened it up. He watched his feet land on the tall grass below him. He smiled at the irony of it all: the hardened ex-convict too scared to get out of his own truck then set his sights on the Joshua tree just forty yards away. Admittedly, the prospect of touching that much money was exciting. Maybe he would take some…God knows Lisa deserved that home she always dreamed of.

He entered the small graveyard and took note of the crackling sound underneath his boots; it was the dry plains grass native to the area, still desert land. It was also a sound he recognized…*but from where?* He carefully watched his steps, knowing it was bad luck and disrespectful to walk over a person's grave.

He passed the first headstone and caught just a glimpse of the etched wording on its front. It was a small grave, well worn, probably a child's. He could only make out the first two letters, *H* and *A*.

A second grave was upon him, kind of by itself and a little bigger. This one he saw all of and read its name aloud: "Darrell Raines."

He moved carefully through the maze of headstones, passing two or three more along the way. The next two he saw sat side by side, and he slowed down just enough to read them: Clyde and Beatrice Raines.

He repeated those names in his head: *Clyde and Beatrice.* Suddenly his world was coming to a slow crawl, and his movements weren't the only thing slowing down. Time in general stood still. Standing in the center of the cemetery, he looked around and took note of all the names he could see. Clyde and Beatrice, Darwin, Lula, and Darrell.

He wasn't even sure whether he was there anymore; his body lost all sensation. He took a few more steps and sure enough didn't feel them. *Is it just another awful dream?*

He moved with purpose to the last grave in the yard and read its front: Hanson Raines. Charlie turned, his focus on the very first grave he had passed, and whispered, "Harry."

He stood motionless and considered all the moments of his life up until that very point. In an instant, he was feeling things again, and the weight of the moment brought only one thing to mind: *finally!*

He saw Lisa in his mind's eye; she had put up with so much over the years. And his mother, the person who had suffered the most and the one whom he'd secretly blamed for all his problems. In the end, he'd been right. All these years, he'd been right. He wasn't crazy at all, but gifted. The static rain in Charlie's mind stopped, and the clouds lifted.

"Charlie?" Jake called out from the truck. "What is it? What's wrong?"

Jake stood at the hood of the truck.

"Is it there? You see it?" he asked.

The rock. Charlie turned and faced the overhanging branches of the Joshua tree, which seemed to be standing guard over its base. He was just a few feet away. The grass around him stood knee high, obstructing any clear view of the tree's trunk.

There was one last piece to this whole puzzle that he just couldn't place. The little boy screaming at the top of his lungs, screaming as if he'd just lost his mother. The boy whose face he didn't know but whose frustration and pain he did.

"Charlie?"

Charlie leaned up on the toes of his boots, extended his body for a better view, and caught just a glimpse of something. He quickly rested his heels back on the ground. Whatever he saw looked gray, and though he couldn't be sure, it looked soft in texture.

He headed straight for the truck, now even more mindful of the old friends who lay beneath him.

"What happened? What did you see?" Jake asked.

"I don't know," he replied.

"Well, was it there?"

Looking toward the ground, he replied again, "I don't know."

"Well, didn't you wanna find out?"

Charlie looked up from the ground and slightly smiled. "No. Maybe I'm like you. Maybe I like where I am."

"But you were *right* there."

Charlie glanced at the headstones behind him one last time. "I discovered something else along the way, something more valuable than all the money in the world."

Jake looked over his shoulder at the Joshua tree, studied it for several seconds, and then laughed. "You couldn't even tell the story...no one would believe it, and any who did would say we were nuts."

"Calm on the mind," Charlie whispered. He started toward the cab of the truck. "You just tell them, Jake, there's no amount of money that can buy a little calm on the mind...let's go home."

CHAPTER 77

They sat parked at a strip mall alongside LAX airport, watching planes take off and land just a few hundred feet ahead of them. A large digital clock stood on the strip mall's roof. It was 3:00 p.m.

Charlie stared at his ticket. His plane was due to take off at 7:00 p.m., connect through Charlotte, NC, and land in Philadelphia at 8:30 the following morning. He had already called home. Lisa was excited to be picking him up at the airport. Her last words to him were "I can't wait."

His last words to her: "Thank you."

While the simple pleasantry could have been construed as a response to picking him up in the morning, he was confident she knew what he really meant.

It was a thank-you for sticking by him all those years, for sticking by him these last several weeks. A thanks for allowing him to do something as illogical, irrational, unfounded, and ridiculous as crossing the country with a complete stranger. In his heart he had always known he had to, but now he knew why, and he couldn't wait to return home to tell her all about it.

"There's something I need to get off my chest," Jake said.

Charlie looked over to him.

"I wasn't exactly truthful with you in the beginning."

"How so?"

"Your oldest boy, Eddie. He knew me, and I knew him."

"What are you talking about?"

"I'm ashamed to say it. Even sitting there in the kitchen that day, he knew who I was, but I still couldn't say anything."

"It's OK, Jake…what is it?"

"I almost"—he paused for a moment—"I almost ran them over. I almost killed them. Your boy, he couldn't take his eyes off me. Your wife was so shook up she just hurried off. She was reading her receipt, coming out of the supermarket, and stepped right out in front of me. I thought she was gonna stop, but she didn't. I slammed on the brakes and came within just inches." Jake swallowed the lump in his throat. "She had the little one with her, too."

Jake's show of outward emotion meant a lot. "It's all right, Jake...look how it all turned out."

A few moments passed, and Jake remained silent.

"Hey, what's eating at you?"

"I almost killed them. I almost killed all of them."

"But you didn't, so why are you so upset about it?"

Jake turned to him. "Because I wasn't then. All I cared about was not going back to prison. But to think that I could have done that, to *think* I could have taken your family from you, to know I wouldn't have any of this right now— this trip, last night, the church...I feel all that. It was inches, Charlie, just inches away, and you and I would have known each other, but never in this way."

Charlie nodded. He got it. "I guess that's why they call it fate. It wasn't meant to end that way."

"Wow." Jake chuckled. "What a journey...I think this trip calls for a toast."

"Agreed. How 'bout another tall boy?" Charlie replied.

They both glanced at the small liquor store across the parking lot. "I was thinking the same thing." Jake reached for the door handle, but Charlie spoke up. "No, you wait here. I'll get it...this one's on me, old man."

CHAPTER 78

I once read that life happens to you when you least suspect. Well, so does death. I had come a long way to this point and couldn't help but feel closure. I had answers to all of the questions that had plagued me for so many years. Looking back, had I really thought about it, I'm sure I would have seen it coming, but then I guess that's what happens when you have a little peace in your heart. Your mind eases, you smile more, you're happy.

It wasn't until I was at the back of the store near the cooler, about to open it, that I realized where I was. The cold air filtering through the cracks of the cooler door brought things into check, and I didn't need to hear the sound of a shotgun echoing in my ear to know what was going to happen next.

I saw that little boy's face in my mind's eye long before I heard a single cry. Turning around, I saw his mother lying on the floor next to him, a pool of blood growing at his little feet, and though I had dreamed of this boy's cries all my life, I still wasn't prepared to see or feel his pain.

My mind raced as I grabbed for the gun tucked in my jeans. The gun given to my mother by the man who had caused us so much pain—ironic how its purpose would soon be found.

Life's a heartache. That was exactly what Lisa would say if she were here. It hits you when it's too late. And she was right, because just when I had figured things out in my own life, it was time to leave it. And though I wanted to be angry at the irony of it all, instead I smiled, because in the final moments of my own life, I found the answers, every last one.

Our eyes locked, and for the first time I saw his face. He had the look of death, the kind of look I'm sure Jake had carried years before.

I saw the great moments of my life flash before me; the ones I seemed to have forgotten, like the first time I met Lisa inside Iggie's; the birth of my two boys; the first time Eddie told me he loved me; my mother waking me up on a cold Christmas morning with a smile on her face, a Christmas she remembered.

One shot, I thought. That was all it would take, and a little luck.

He was a madman, but exactly what had driven him to do such a thing I'd never know. Maybe she was his wife and she wanted to leave him, maybe he'd just lost his job or was abused as a child, maybe he was someone like me who never found the answers to the questions in his own head and could no longer take the torment.

Whatever the reasons for his entering that liquor store, on that day, at that moment, there was little he could have ever done to stop it. For I'd seen this day coming for thirty years. It was as much his destiny as it was mine.

I don't remember falling or feeling any pain. What I do remember is coming to in Jake's arms, staring up into the big man's eyes and seeing the faces of two angels staring back at me. There I saw the faces of my boys, Edward Joseph and William James Boone.

———

Jake noticed the small duffel bag in the passenger side wheel well. It was unzipped, and the clothes inside looked tousled, as if someone had rummaged through it in search of something. Peering out of the bag's opening was Charlie's road atlas.

He leaned over and plucked the map from the bag. He hadn't even opened its cover when he heard the first shot ring out, then, seconds later, a muffled scream.

His first and only word, said in a whisper: "Charlie!"

He jumped out of the truck and stopped just short of its front. Jerry's gun. It lay underneath the car seat. He quickly debated whether or not to get it. Then two more shots rang out, and he was off again, unarmed, running into the liquor store.

The scene inside was hysteria. A woman tucked in the corner of the store was crying hysterically, and an older man gripped the screaming child in his arms, holding him away from his mother, whose lifeless body lay in a pool of blood. The gunmen raced past him and took off out of the store. The clerk behind the counter was screaming into the phone for the police as he fumbled with a set of keys. Through it all, the only thing Jake saw was Charlie. He lay face up in the center of the aisle; a single bloodstain on his chest growing larger by the second. Standing high above him, he fell to his knees and gently brought Charlie into his arms.

"What the hell did you do, son?"

Charlie looked up at him, but he was looking right through him, and then a broken laugh came through. "It was *my* breathing," Charlie said.

"Say what?"

"It was always my breathing."

Jake looked up and yelled to the clerk. "Call an ambulance! Call one! Call one now!"

"Jake?" Charlie whispered.

"Now you listen to me, Charlie. You stay here, you stay with me, help's coming. It's on its way!"

"Tell my wife…" He couldn't quite get it out.

"No, Charlie! Don't…don't do this!"

"Jake! Tell her…"

"What? OK, buddy, tell her what?"

"I wasn't crazy. She'll laugh, but tell her I wasn't. Promise me you'll do that."

"OK, Charlie I will. You breathe…just breathe."

"I'll wait," Charlie whispered. "Wherever I am, I'll wait for her."

CHAPTER 79

Charlie Boone died in my arms that day. I served thirty years hard time in a maximum security state prison and did four tours in the killing fields of Vietnam, but neither was more difficult than the phone call I had to make to Lisa Boone that day. It took me three hours just to muster up enough guts to pick up the phone and dial. I felt like calling Georgia State instead and asking for my old cell back, but I knew that wasn't possible. I had enough sense to realize there were now a single mother and two orphaned children who deserved some answers, and as downright crazy, stupid, and tragic as those answers seemed to be, it was up to me to try to provide them.

I flew back with Charlie's body on a commercial airliner two days later. Accompanying me was a federal marshal, Charlie's body in a casket below us.

I had asked the marshal before boarding if I could ride next to Charlie on the way back. He looked at me as if I were half cocked, which at the time I probably was—that, and a little heartbroken.

To say those first days were tough is an understatement. She asked so many questions, and I had so few answers, our conversations always ending with Charlie's last moments, the short exchanges we had back and forth while he lay there. And always his last words to me for her: "I'll wait for her. Wherever I am, I'll wait for her."

Though she always knew where she could find me, I pretty much kept my distance. She finally came into Jerry's one day and pulled up a chair at the small table I was sitting at. She looked as if she hadn't slept in days.

"I can't cry anymore," she said, "at least not today."

"I understand" was all I could come up with.

"No, you don't," she replied. "We've lived in that house for ten years. Charlie his whole life, and not one phone call from a neighbor, not one sympathy card...nothing. It's like he never existed." She covered her mouth in hopes it would stop trembling, but it didn't.

There were no words I could say to take away her pain, and I knew it. She was sitting so close to me, so close that I could smell the salt on her cheeks. I wanted badly to bring her into my arms, to hug her for a day and tell her things were gonna work out, that I was going to see to it, but I didn't. At the time, I just didn't know how. More than anything I was afraid she'd jump back or fight me off, and then I wouldn't know what to do.

To this day, that moment remains my biggest regret—more than any regret I've ever held onto, whether about my own faults or about my mother. Lisa Boone needed someone to hug, and I was the one to give it to her, but instead I said what I was feeling. "Let me do something. Let me help you. What can I do? Tell me what I can do for you."

"Nothing," she replied. "I'm three months' pregnant. I don't know what I'm gonna do, and I don't even know why I'm telling you."

I was instantly taken back to that morning on the mountain and the conversation we had looking over the cliff's edge. I remembered Charlie's words and said them aloud: "Life begins for someone, maybe someone we don't know yet." I told her, "Have that child; you must have that child. He knew you were."

All she did was shake her head and look away. Standing up, she said, "We buried his mother yesterday. There's gonna be a proper ceremony for Charlie at St. Peter's on Monday. You can attend if you'd like."

The day of Charlie's funeral was windy. The sun was shining bright, and there wasn't a cloud in the sky. I bought a suit from a thrift store; it was the first time I'd ever worn one. The only people at the funeral were me, Lisa, and the two boys.

After mass, we drove out to Chelten Hills Cemetery, where Mrs. Boone had been buried just days earlier. There, Charlie was laid next to his mother. I would later come to learn that Mrs. Boone had bought the two plots years earlier from monies given to her by her stepfather.

I stood off to the side just a hair and held Billy by the shoulder while Lisa and Eddie were saying their final good-byes.

I was saying my own good-byes as well, along with a promise that as long as I still walked this earth, his wife and children, including Maggie Charlize Boone, who would be born months later, would be taken care of. I needed him to know that. He needed to know that I would do whatever it took to make sure of it somehow. I asked him to rest in peace for knowing my promise, and just then, coming from a dense tree line in the distance, I thought I could hear the faint sound of an old harmonica, and, watching as they lowered Charlie's casket into the ground, I was sure that somewhere out there, a Bar-M chopper was flying him to heaven.

The days after Charlie's funeral became weeks, the weeks months, and the months years. Though Lisa's heart still ached every day for the only man she had ever loved, she would tell me that each day got a little bit better.

It was an early spring morning in the year following Charlie's death when Lisa went to the curb to get the mail and found a check from the estate of John Grey. It seemed that somewhere along the way, the old bastard had died too. Unaware of what it was, she ripped open the envelope and found herself staring at a check for 2.3 million dollars. It was final validation of just who Charlie's real father had been, and, though it pained her to take it, she knew it would be best for the boys.

Once the initial shock of the money wore off, she quickly went to work looking for that big old home in the country with privacy, a big yard, and the wraparound porch she had always dreamed of. She found it in Chester County—an old farmhouse, where she and the children settled into a very quiet and peaceful existence. She even persuaded me to park my trailer on the 5.5 acres of land that came with the place. If she had had it her way, I would have been living in the house with them, which from time to time I did, with the babysitting I'd do and all. But fact was, I was most comfortable in the trailer, perched at the bottom of the hill near the gate to get in.

There I'd sit and hold watch, Jerry's gun close by, until the last light of the night went out up on the hill, and even then I'd watch a little longer, till my eyes couldn't stay open anymore.

Not long after they moved in, she took a job at the local elementary school teaching second grade. She'd always say to me that she would go crazy if she sat on that porch all day long doing nothing, so I did it for her. I really think she chose to work to be close to the kids, and I couldn't blame her for it. They were all she had.

Her favorite thing to do in the warm months was plant flowers, while mine was sitting in the rocker she had bought me, watching Eddie and Billy play ball in the front yard, which was exactly what I was doing on a midsummer day in June while Lisa was in her bedroom struggling to come to terms with going out on her fist date since Charlie's death.

He was a seemingly nice fella, one she'd met at church, and though it was never my place to give her advice, I approved. He pulled up the drive in a nice SUV, stepped out of the driver's-side door, and waved his hand.

"I guess I gotta do this, then, huh?" she said.

"Go on," I told her. "It's what's best."

With that she stood up, said good-bye to the children, and climbed into her suitor's truck, and down the drive they went.

Just then Billy, holding something in his hand, called out from the center of the yard. "Mr. Mott?"

"Whatta ya got?" I asked.

"A caterpillar."

"OK…and what do they do?"

"They become a butterfly, I think."

"That's right. They turn into a beautiful thing, don't they?"

"When they grow up," Eddie yelled back.

"What do you call it?" Billy asked.

"Call what?"

"What do you call it when a caterpillar turns into a butterfly?"

I sat back and thought about a good-enough answer, and it was at that moment that Ms. Maggie Charlize tapped her little index finger on my knee.

"Yes, child?"

With her dainty hands pressed firmly upon my knee and her little toes stretched to their fullest, she whispered in my ear, "Fantastic."

The hairs on the back of my neck rose, and a chill ran through my body. "Yes, it is, child." I said. "It's fantastic!"

THE END

AUTHOR BIOGRAPHY

Fantastik is C. A. McGroarty's first novel, inspired by a cast of characters his father, a hard working trial attorney, introduced him to at a very young age. Much of the novel was written while living in Chicago and traveling across the Mid-West and Western United States. His short story *A Return to Normalcy* can be found on Amazon Kindle. He lives in New Jersey with his wife, two sons, and their dog, Wrigley. You can find him at www.camcgroarty.com and follow him on twitter @camcgroarty.

48894188R00175

Made in the USA
Middletown, DE
30 September 2017